PRAISE FOR *The Journalist*

"*The Journalist* is both a slightly surreal comedy of manners and a frightening parable on the carnivorous nature of the written word. It's Mathews's most stunning and approachable fiction so far."—John Ashbery

"Harry Mathews's journal-writer is the perfect avatar of civilization and its discontents, a creation both comic and profound, and, perhaps, a new direction for Mathews: it combines his always brilliant social obser- vation with a sustained psychological portrait of great depth and inter- est."—Diane Johnson

"A truly novel and seductive and funny book. Stories, dreams, loves, the elegantly shaped and the humbly unhinged—all we expect from Harry Mathews's fiction comes together as never before. This is his finest work."—Joseph McElroy

"*The Journalist* is an extraordinary feat, combining new extremes of conceptual torture with a credible and all-too-human emotional core—in addition to being quite entertaining and absorbing."—Luc Sante

"The complications offered up by Mr. Mathews are both daunting and funny, in a kind of psychoslapstick way."—*New York Times*

"Harry Mathews invents ingenious formal patterns and combines them with unruly, even crazy, passion. Mad and rational, all head and too much heart, *The Journalist* explores the black, intricately organized inte- rior of paranoia. Somehow the book also manages to portray a utopia of human goodness."—Edmund White

The Journalist
by Harry Mathews

Dalkey Archive Press

A portion of this novel previously appeared in *Conjunctions*.

Library of Congress Cataloging-in-Publication Data
Mathews, Harry, 1930-
The journalist : a novel / by Harry Mathews.; — 1st Dalkey Archive ed.
p.   cm.
ISBN 1-56478-165-8 (pbk. : alk. paper)
1. Diaries—Authorship—Fiction.   I. Title.
PS3563.A8359J68   1997   813'.54—dc21   97-23673

This publication is partially supported by a grant from
the Illinois Arts Council, a state agency.

Dalkey Archive Press
Illinois State University
Campus Box 4241
Normal, IL 61790-4241

*Printed on permanent/durable acid-free paper and bound in the
United States of America*

And the story tells you what you accept
That the missed event is unfulfilled.

Fairfield Porter, "The Reader"

The Journalist

T HE RAIN HAD STOPPED. I could forget about the curve warning signs; the gently winding road, which conformed so gratifyingly to my map, would dry fast. I settled back in the driver's seat and accelerated. The steering wheel came off in my hands.

The possibility had always been real. You never had to remind yourself of it. And it remains real. At such a moment, who are you? Where are you? You cannot dismiss the questions by observing that "you" have become a mere object manipulated by the indifferent laws of physics. One part of you says that; another part listens. Who and where are they? What and where is your identity? What and where is that weaker being that struggles to survive your identity?

Set down such questions here. "Set down" also means "stop lugging around," as with a suitcase full of bricks. Speculation can dissolve ordinary things into purest uncertainty. Of course, uncertainty has a truth of its own — there are moments when I "honestly" can't tell a concert grand from an elephant. But I also like finding ordinary things in their ordinary places.

Ordinary things: the medicine works (chemical name: lorazepam). I slept through; I woke up no drowsier than usual. I can even remember part of one of my dreams: I am reading a book about the history of the pencil, engrossed by a comparison of various qualities of graphite to be found in New England or Siberia. Samples of each are supplied with the book (given the decrepitude of our publishing industry, I should know I'm dreaming). I'm traveling along the coast with a cousin of Daisy's I've never seen. The car (steering wheel firmly in place) proceeds at mule speed down an absolutely straight road, hugging the shoulder even though an oncoming car could be seen a mile away. I start talking about getting into the pencil business. How wonderful to be manufacturing something one really loves! The thought suffuses me with anticipation, a real warmth in my limbs, a pleasure still felt when I woke up.

Perhaps a separate notebook for dreams?

EVENING
Several times during the day, remembering to notice things for these pages made me exceptionally alert. Familiar surroundings looked new – the office, the streets I take every day. I felt independent but by no means separate from my fellows, except in the tiny power I enjoyed in watching them. I played private games, like noticing, for instance, the shoes of all the men in the office: Mr. Valde's oxfords, Stan's Scotch-grain loafers, Fritz's wing tips, Louis's imports. I registered the remarks people made (I can forget a good joke in an hour), such as Naomi's "This is the best possible weather for hairdos" and Cherry's "It's a three-digit spaghetti restaurant." Paying the attention needed to retain the words let me see the speakers in a vividly spatial way. It brought them in from the flat screen of what surrounds me, which usually looks impenetrable no matter how near it is. I felt closer to them.

This clearer view of things lent a gelatinous cast to my morning questions about an "inner life" that I might comfortably do without.

Early on, Mr. Valde called us in to display a new clamp that is coming on the market at a price 18% under ours. It's manufactured in

Romania. Fritz smells an Italian intitiative, because of the mechanical ingenuity and design. We discussed things we might do (although nobody proposed improving our own product or figuring out how to lower its cost). My lot will be "communicating with" (read: pulling and pushing) our distributors. Paul wasn't there – it's quarterly accounting time.

Lunch with Stan. He regaled me with football statistics. My mind wandered into speculations about the Australian Open and what time it would be broadcast. Noticing my distraction, Stan remarked that I'd seemed out of it all day. Was it problems? Drink? Sleeping pills? Instead of defending myself I asked about some player whose name I happen to know; Stan happily went back to talking football. Nodding in apparent attentiveness, I savored this invention of my small, quiet solitude. The solitude was very much my own, with a freshness to it like that of the first sweet air of the day, the air you breathe through a half-open window at dawn.

When I was ten or eleven I used to stand to one side of the bathroom mirror and converse with someone I imagined out of sight around its edge, on the far side of the glass. Often I'm ashamed of such memories, but this one seems a faithful image of how I still am: the flesh-and-bones me sitting at the table and another invisible part of me pursuing its own life. The thought of this "otherness" consoled me. Without it I would never have had my secret childhood raptures, and they, too, have a necessary place in my world: they are what allowed me to sit there happily pretending to listen to Stan. I began listening to Stan. He has a childish vision somewhere. I made a mental note to consult the sports pages for future conversations.

(Went to the park on my way home, to the little clearing, empty as usual, already assembling in the dust its carpet of curled leaves, and so quiet – nothing but toots from buses on the avenue. Speaking in whispers. Walked down to the pond through a break in the dirt ridge that runs along the wood, which was full of a soothing smell of dried summer rot. The pond was quiet, too. Some kids were trying to sail their little boats on the breezeless water.)

.......! This is more conspicuous than the plain name. Why do I suffer from such stupid furtiveness? Daisy wasn't back from the studio when I got home. But as soon as I came in, the familiar objects in the hall came alive with reproach. The good-humored umbrella stand struck its "You old dog!" pose. The little beige-upholstered bench glanced frostily at its brass nails: "She's going to catch you one of these days." I was glad to have time to settle into a domestic mode. I often wonder why, considering the inevitability, the frequency, and the duration of the upsets it brings, I don't end the relationship. But even at thirty yards the sight of C. tells me that giving her up would shut down my life in permanent curfew, and I would then love Daisy and Gert *less* – as things are, I still feel romantic about Daisy. Is this a tale I'm telling myself? Walking into the kitchen, I felt that I exuded a reek of catastrophe. Later, as I lay in the tub, the towels and other bathroom gear started turning into emblems of insanity, insanity not in me but in them: their blind obsession with being themselves, nothing but a bath mat, a washrag, or a shaving brush, when they could so easily become birds or tennis balls. And wasn't I doing the same thing, hanging on tight when I could become (and no doubt am terrified of becoming) hundreds of other men or women, or children or animals, too, or things? And between us and those unpredictable transformations, not so much as a spiderweb to cling to.

Later: shrimplets and sea snails; roast pork (garlic and sage stuffing) with a salad of yellow beans; cheese; fresh fruit; a whiffy chardonnay, a tart gamay.

Better to keep two chronicles? One of definite matters like bean salad, the other of broodings.

Gert preferred to take a tray to his room.

The ten o'clock news.

Gisèle Freund, *Photography and Society.*

This.

Blue, warm as midsummer.

Up 7:45. Breakfast with Gert (apple juice, 2 boiled eggs, tea). He talked, but not about Leonora.

Missing tram, walking two stops for weather (wild duck on Galileo Pond). Office 9:15.

Phone calls: *to* Magix (Donner), Schutte (message with secretary), Cristallo.

   from Blecker (lunch date), Schutte (if we guarantee just-in-time delivery, this will offset 8–10% price margin, maybe more).

Talking tactics with Paul (he can't come to lunch, he's seeing Daisy).

Valde satisfied, "so far" (black buckle shoes today).

Lunch with Blecker (toasted ham and cheese, relabeled *croque-monsieur* – explains 5.50 price? Two beers now 8.50): he knows about Romanians, now deconstructing gambit. Not a problem, he thinks. Suggests calling bluff, whoever's – one way to find out: propose 25% six-week discount; he's willing to go along.

Haba's: volume of early Kertesz photos (on sale), Hegel *Aesthetics* (for Gert) & 2 Handke in paper. Heard pretty saleswoman addressed as Melissa (or was it Melanie?).

Office: 3 out-of-town orders lighten atmosphere (sun helping).

Paperwork with Naomi while waiting for Paul, latish.

Cigars. Paul's newfound verve: Romania an opportunity not an obstacle, new orders to absorb discount, try, push, buy them out, etc. Spine tired.

Around 6 P.M. (exhaust haze, dust, too – presunset orange blur across town): Jago on far side of avenue, joined by Paul, walking off together with hands in pockets.

Phoning C. from pay phone in Discount Pizza (smell suggests investment in oregano farm).

Home: bath, two beers.

Jago for dinner (linguini and chipolatas, salad, cheese, fruit, merlot).

Jago stayed for ten o'clock news.

Freund.

This.

But "this" is incomplete, false, and misleading!

On the day I started keeping this record (yesterday?!), I understandably left things out, some altogether, others in part (like my dream about Daisy's cousins). Since then I've noticed that what I wrote down has been kept vivid for me (I had to see the office shoes to preserve them in writing, and I still see them now). Trying to put in even more led to this list. But the list doesn't give me access to what it contains – its events are as dead as unrecorded ones. Its only benefit has been to show me how much I still leave out, how much more I want to get down, how I want to get *everything* down – impossible, I know, but a man's reach, et cetera.

I remembered a dream this morning and left it out. Gert was wearing jeans of new and brighter blue and a T-shirt with UNION LABEL stamped across the chest; I left that out. While noticing the summery sky from my bed, I was ejaculating against Daisy's hand and belly (she didn't have her diaphragm in and lay in a voluptuous semiwaking sloth that I by no means sought to interrupt, nor she), and I left that out; although this case differs from the others, I deliberately omitted it out of "embarrassment" from not knowing whether I should include such happenings. I forgot to mention taking lorazepam and its effect (good) and, much later, before dinner, a couple of precautionary digestive pills. Before my bath I did twelve push-ups and thirty sit-ups; I left that out. I left out jotting down notes at Haba's from a guidebook to Syria, thus starting to firm up the possibility of a real trip. My jolt of affection for the ducks on the pond, with their more immediate travel plans – left out. For prudence' sake, I left out recognizing the probability that our directors will use the Romanian crunch (and our positive response to it) to postpone any talk of Paul and me getting a raise. I left out my mail, notably a letter from Madre Mia that was waiting for me when I came home. And what about the memories that assaulted me all day long – shouldn't they have a place here? Anyway, I left them out (e.g., an unlighted bus carrying me last year through wet November darkness, past streaky electrical comets, towards Colette). Fritz told me that Stan's daughter, age sixteen, may be having an abortion this week, in which case his sports-fan cheerfulness proves him a cunning dissembler (in fairness to Fritz, he was as much asking as telling me this; the gossip was fifth-hand); I left that out. I learned from the *Morning Post* and made a mental note that the Fink Gallery is planning a show of the French artist Boltanski; I left that out. I left out (twice now) checking, while at Haba's, whether it's *Vaghe stelle dell'orso* or *dell'orsa*. In midmorning, the receiver tucked under her left cheek, Cherry said with quiet delight to her interlocutor, "Now there's sunlight all over my typewriter"; I left it out.

Since rereading the list made me aware of these omissions, it has its use. It's merely incomplete, false, and misleading. Itemizing the events of the day didn't save them for me. Objects and events, once I've *written* about them, emerge from the strangeness of belonging to systems outside my control. They are naturalized. Even their differences, being what they share, make them resemble each other, make them familiar.

Perhaps *all* objects and events, however strange, should be thought of as "perfectly natural." Perhaps they only need to be declared complete in themselves to become so. Justifying them (explaining or adapting) wouldn't be necessary — it'd be done for us. No systems required, human or divine: wouldn't that be a relief?

I was once fascinated by one of Elsheimer's paintings. It depicted the *Flight into Egypt* as if it covered the span of a day: the dawn, emerging from one night on the right-hand side of the picture, was visually balanced by the sunset dissolving into another night on the left. It was hard to say where true daytime began or ended: everything in the emphatic, austere mixture of light and shadow seemed to depend on the darkness preceding or the darkness to come. The painting reverberated with adolescent feelings about my own days, which did not strike me as being days at all, and certainly not my own, but mere transitions between unknown chaoses. I have spent most of my life as though it were dawn and dusk, never broad daylight. Is this why I always make sure I have an order to do everything in — so I'll keep moving on? Have I ever pulled the window wide open in the morning *before* washing my face with cold water?

It's an obscurity of unknown predicaments enshrouding not only present things and events but remembered ones as well. So will writing down memories extend ordinariness to the "dark" past, or merely orderliness? Someday my world will be filled with plain things and people. Not to have everything inspire a wish or a regret — the umbrella I forgot or am sure to lose. And what about the rain? The sky knows what it's doing. I don't need to worry about its reasons.

Transport.	3.00
Rest.	19.50
Books.	38.00

Trying only ½ lorazepam.

Later (officially, next day): in bed I kept thinking about these pages, asking myself what worked and didn't work. I got up to reread them, and rereading reminded me of more things to write (that I'd forgotten to write), but I've restricted myself to one (if Daisy wakes up and finds herself alone she'll think I'm ill). Choosing that one was no choice, because a particular phrase gripped me hard, as though what it alluded to had been not salvaged but threatened by being written down, only two days old and already in the distant past.

"Even at thirty yards the sight of C.": at the sight of her, unimagined projects become possible — not likely, but possible: new meeting places, new travels, "new lives." Not completely new: I want to rediscover with her pleasures I've already had without her (like seeing *North by Northwest*). C.'s secret power is offering me first times again. The implications are saddening. With her, too, the experiences will sooner or later lose their freshness and turn into a battered leather suitcase that keeps falling shut of its own accord. So in theory, beyond C. loom an L. and an E., a row of next ones. Then what's the point? There is no point. When she is close by, I can be unpredictable. That can mean no more than being able to surprise her with what at home would be all too predictable. And I desire her, and when we find each other in a bed or a reasonable facsimile, my desire makes me tremble with pleasure, and with gratitude as well for being given the chance to shake like a dog watching his bowl being filled. And I express desire and gratitude by paying elaborate attention to her, in ways that aren't exactly predictable — at least, they surprise both of us, right up to the moment when we are so surprised we join the legions of everyone and anyone and no one, like angels or squirrels, in the awareness of not being who we are. (Or is it the nonawareness of being who we are? Or neither? This could be the place to work out such questions precisely.) The sweetness lasts after, although not long – we can almost never stay together (sleep together), and the melancholy of withdrawal has to be accepted.

After five hours' sleep, the half pill was enough to make me drowsy. I opened the shutters before washing my face. (The Marcuses have arrayed six pots of Cavendish ivy on their balconies.)

Daisy did wake up while I was writing yesterday. She was not worried, only disappointed: "Even when I'm asleep, having you next to me is my favorite thing in life." She said this as if in some kind of pain. When I asked if she was all right, she said yes, only a little restless.

Since my domestic existence is dedicated to keeping Daisy happy, perhaps I should do this writing elsewhere. That means at the office (I despise the notion of café tables à la Sartre). Setting down my reflections on C. last night was enough to make me nervous, not because Daisy might see them – she barely looks at the pictures on postcards I receive – but because I felt I was smuggling Colette into our household. Why not divide my project by subject: at home record "plain facts" – things I've done or seen as well as neutral matters like memories, dreams, gossip, and so forth – while keeping at the office (in addition to an account of my work) everything concerning C., and also my "speculations," which might worry Daisy, and of course any remarks about Jago or other members of her family that would risk offending her? Such an arrangement could help keep these pages from encroaching on the hours we share.

After taking a phone call during breakfast (apple juice, cereal with grapes, tea), Daisy announced that she would be away overnight. The rug company that's commissioned her wants her to visit the offices she's decorating two towns down the road now that the actual construction is nearly done. I went to work early, hoping to catch C. on the phone after Jago leaves for the day.

Before I forget: I dreamed that I was lying in bed in deep sleep. Daisy is standing by the bed rubbing my chest gently and insistently, telling me to get up, it's late – broad daylight, in fact. At first I can't respond, then I understand her words but am too drugged with sleep to open my eyes. Finally, at the price of immense effort, an effort that takes minutes to bring results, I force myself awake. Pitch blackness, Daisy breathing steadily at my side. Fortunately I have the presence of mind to turn on the light and take notes.

I called too soon. Jago answered, or rather picked up an extension after I had barely told C. that I was free for the whole evening and heard her reply, "No. Just the park." Jago sounded delighted to hear from me. He had intended to call me this morning. Could we dine together? I was baffled. He has never proposed anything like this before. I said I'd love to but wasn't sure I could, I didn't think I could, I'd have to check my appointment book, however I was almost certain I had prior obligations, of course it would be a joy, etc. Silence followed, immediately filling up with the implicit question: why was I calling him? I finally said I wanted his opinion of the carpet manufacturer that had given Daisy her current job. Was the firm reliable? Another pause, as if *he* were baffled, then: "Good question. I'll make inquiries." During this conversation I was distracted by the antics of Fritz, who had also arrived early. He performed an elaborate pantomime in front of me that I could neither understand nor ignore. Once I'd hung up, I learned that he was making himself an espresso and was attempting to find out whether he should make one for me as well. His gesticulations have rather irritatingly stuck in my mind, but they are more than this hurried prose can render.

1:45 P.M.

Jago phoned at around noon to tell me that he has to have dinner with someone from out of town. I called C. We can be together from 6:30 to 10:00 P.M. I felt as though I were a boy and Pater had brought me home a new soccer ball.

In the course of the morning I handled three letters to the company; wrote one letter; took notes on a dozen phone calls (*not* the one to C.!), including a call clearly intended for someone else, about hospital visiting hours. (I posted the information on the bulletin board, but it quickly disappeared. Stan and his daughter?).

I realize there is no need for me to keep a record of my work here. Memos, notes, and letters *are* that record. I'm having Tangerine (alias Naomi) make me photocopies of all such items and have opened a special file for them. This will free up a lot of time.

Lunch with Paul, fast by mutual agreement – he is taking the afternoon off to go to the dentist. A whole afternoon at the dentist's, I asked. Was he going in for major repairs? No, he also hoped to spend time with his old friend Jacob Barrett. Paul and I have been close ever since we took Professor Martinez's course in logic together, and I have never heard him mention Jacob Barrett. I smell romance.

EVENING
I'm too deliciously tired. I'll catch up early in the morning. With Daisy away I can write here and then take the pages to work with me.

THURSDAY
At five sharp I went home to bathe and change, as excited as on a first date and without the worry that on first dates used to make me act – disastrously – like a mortal meeting his god. I did feel some superstitious anxiety about the success of the evening – moods are so precarious, acts so ambiguous. I decided to wear my lucky shirt (soft pale-blue cotton), even if this meant taking time to iron it. The time

didn't seem wasted. I love the laundry room and its comforting offstage look – no decoration except for a photograph of Daisy and Jago at a party, no furniture but the aging chipped-white machines, the sewing table heaped with clothes and cloths, a high stool, a chair, and, sometimes, the ironing board lowered from the back wall. Rest of wardrobe: beige gabardine slacks, white linen jacket, a loosely knotted light-green knit tie.

At 6:40 I rang the bell at C.'s gate; she opened it seconds later. Although the upstairs tenants had considerately shuttered their windows, I accompanied her at a discreet distance until we were out of all possible sight. A first long kiss. She led me to the little pavilion at the bottom of the garden. Originally it was a toolshed. There was only one room, furnished with four armchairs and a sofa where we quickly lay down to make love, in faint light from the blinded window, to the sound of a neighbor diligently rendering a Moskowski étude. In our tender assaults C. and I strain to atone for missed days and weeks; we try to burrow all the way inside each other's bodies. But I did not dare .... her for fear of losing hold. After I had .... several times with mouth and fingers she .... She did this so slowly I writhed with impatience, wishing it would never end.

She lighted three oil-lamps – they had pretty red majolica bases – and fetched our supper: an abundance of smoked trout, with horseradish and cream sauce; bean salad; ewe cheese; flan; a bottle of sauvignon (the first I'd drunk of last year's much-ballyhooed vintage); later, coffee and plum brandy.

Not much time passed before we lay down again and ...... for a long time, in several ways, shifting from one to the next in unhesitating, unspoken agreement (I finally ....). Never forget that happiness (forgetting so easy at home), which could for once subside at agreeable length in caresses and conversation.

I had promised to leave at ten. No taxis, of course. One bus, one tram, home by eleven. I found Gert in the kitchen, drinking beer. He asked me to join him; I did, with a glass of wine. He looked glum. I asked after Leonora. He shook his head. I said I hoped I could meet her someday, just to say hello. Sure. Coming in, I'd noticed the Hegel I'd bought him still wrapped on the hall table. I reminded Gert how, when I was a student, it had put me a jump ahead of the others; I knew it was heavy going. He thanked me once again, told me the course was easier than he'd expected, and with barely a pause said he might have to ask me for a fairly large sum of money. "In a jam?" "I *may* be." "Gambling?" He looked at me with the remembrance of a smile: "Something like that." I know how he feels. At the end of my first night of real poker, I wasn't down that much (fifty? eighty?) but felt the plug had been pulled.

Dream: I'm flirting with an attractive younger friend of D.'s in front of a squat bunker at the bottom of a treeless valley. Figures are standing near me whom I take to be Cherry, Stan, and Fritz, but I can't make sure because I'm dazed by loud sirens rising and falling in alternation on either side of the valley. Mr. Valde and I start singing in thirds along with the swooping tones of the sirens, he with one, I with the other. I experience a shared contentment close to exuberance. Our joint effort produces a decidedly musical effect, something like a conversational exchange in classical opera. We then sing from an actual opera (the sirens have died down), I think Pamina and Papageno's duet from *The Magic Flute*. We sing well together, and for a time we succeed in warding off a new sound, the guttural cries of a gang of horsemen riding down the valley. The leader carries a long hoelike implement whose blade is a smoldering board. He is a "smoker," someone who smokes out animals so they can be caught. From the eaves of the bunker he drives down two pigeons who fly straight as arrows into the net of the rider following. More scared birds are similarly trapped by other horsemen. One hunter in pursuit crashes his horse needlessly into a wall of the bunker. Mr. Valde insists that we keep singing. (He has suggested that I play Monostatos and he Sarastro; I feel it would be tactless to object.) Nevertheless I run towards the hunter to vent my indignation over the felled horse. The rider has disappeared into the bunker; his companions have vanished elsewhere. I shout after him (no answer), then start singing again, thinking he may be German or at least understand German. I change my tune, though, from *The Magic Flute* to the Wanderer's greeting to Mime in *Siegfried*. Mr. Valde taps me on the shoulder, wags his finger, and says, "Mozart, yes; Wagner, no." I wake up in a state of anger and disappointment.

Now I'm late.

MIDDAY

In spite of picking up a rare taxi cruising our street (which was lucky: five hundred yards down the avenue, a tram had run into a cyclist, or vice versa, which meant a long delay), I arrived half an hour late, and Mr. Valde had called a meeting, and the information on our new models was locked in my desk — a mess. Since I'm never late, the expectation that I'd be on time only aggravated my associates' impatience. Whereas when lackadaisical Paul wandered in ten minutes after I had, no one minded. His nonchalance actually soothed our nerves. The work got done. Edith wrote the minutes.

I'm skipping lunch to complete these notes. Paul told me he had an appointment elsewhere. Even though I'd planned to stay in the office, I was depressed when he said this because I'd felt lonely all day. "The world is locking me out." Because of not seeing Daisy this morning? A few minutes ago I spoke to Colette. I'm glad the conversation was brief. We could not find anything to say that didn't remind us how completely our separate lives had reclaimed us. "It was wonderful being with you." Was, was.

The form this account is taking does not satisfy me. After all the time I took this morning, I have again left things out. Only details, but they are the texture of life:

> Weather: by now we take these warm-to-cool sunny days for granted. In a while people will start actively complaining about them.
>
> Expenses: 2 taxis   13.50
> present for C. (Chopin
>   by Rubinstein)   13.00
> lunch   9.50
> sundries (paper)   .75
> _____
> 37.50
> 2 apples (lunch)   .80
> _____
> 38.30
>
> Clothes (office):
> yesterday "suede" jacket, gray shirt, gray check cotton slacks, loafers
> today brown suit, pale-blue shirt, brown shoes
> Medicines: lorazepam (whole), aspirin (2)

As I wrote "aspirin" I was startled by a burst of music inside the office. Live music, a flute playing the opening theme of the B-minor sonata. I'd thought everyone had left. I walked down the corridor and peeked through a half-open door. The noise so close and in so small a space almost hurt — I'd forgotten what trumpetlike force lurks in that little tube. Cherry was practicing, facing the shut window that overlooks the dead yard. I never suspected she'd even heard of Bach.

Lunch: one apple (so far)
Yesterday's lunch: stuffed tomato, cheddar, beer
Mail: postcard from Ivan and Eva (beautiful "painted
Gothic")
Reading: *Post*, too sleepy for G. Freund

What about shoes-type entries? Did I notice *anything*? Writing this is supposed to make me notice everything. Something:

The bicycle by the tram, glimpsed from my taxi through skirts and pants, had a black chassis, rusty handlebars, a wicker basket half torn from the handlebars. Returning from the toilet I heard Naomi (I think) say, "I don't have any idea what kind of pressure he's been getting. At least I know it's not me." (I hadn't thought of this as "noticed" because in my upset state I gullibly took the remark to heart.)

This randomness won't work. Remember Prof. Martinez from our logic course: "Understand, analyze, organize!" Understanding will have to wait. I know Dr. Max (and Daisy) urged me to start this notebook for greater understanding, and my new sense of things suggests his reasoning was sound, despite its being founded on an exaggerated clinical interpretation of what was no more than a prolonged spell of the blues. But understanding's only a result. Analysis and organization are where you start. I ask myself, why am I leaving certain things out? What must be done to get them in?

Questions that must be postponed – Stan and Fritz are back. I shouldn't have succumbed to Cherry's flute. Where organization is concerned, what matters is safe and ample time.

LATE AFTERNOON (OFFICE)

I see time now as relevant to analysis as well as to organization because I have recognized my hindering demon: chronology. How can I expect to include all I want from a day or part of a day I've just lived through if I meekly follow the line that leads from a beginning to an end? That line can only oversimplify. It sticks to the obvious and reasonable, avoiding all that lies outside its "inevitable" progress, avoiding what I *most* hope to record, the *then* and *then* that might not have led here at all and that, even if they did, had anyway their own momentary savor and deserve better than to be flattened into stepping stones on the path to another night's sleep. To follow chronology means fitting things into place, making sure that nothing has happened. How to see things out of place? Analysis will subvert the illusory naturalness of memory left to its slippered self.

To divide my notes into what should or should not be kept at home now seems pointless. I can easily secure what I write, and I cannot afford to lose the time available to me at night or early in the morning, my least harassed moments. The other division I imagined may be useful – that is, distinguishing between "fact" and speculation, between what is external and verifiable and what is subjective. The distinction could supply the rudiments of an antichronological mechanism. We'll see how much more it allows me to garner.

Daisy called: why wasn't I at home when she got back from her trip? Her question sounded more flirtatious than reproachful; I nevertheless decided to forgo my rendezvous in the park with C., whom I then phoned. She said it didn't matter, we'd catch up another day. She asked, "How's Daisy?" I answered that she was fine. "Be sure she has everything she needs. You will be good to her, won't you?" Why did she say this to me? I bit my tongue to silence my irritation. What does C. know about my behavior towards Daisy? Finally, into my silence: "Jago sends his love, too." Was he in the room with her? I did not need to hear these things.

A. tram   3.00
    restaurant   91.00
    movies (for 3)   13.50
    taxis (2)   22.50

Restaurant and movies should have been for four, but Gert didn't join us. On her return Daisy found him pale, tired-looking, and disheveled. She suggested that he shave and wash his hair. He hardly deigned to reply. His sulk led to Daisy's laughingly saying, "Don't be so menstrual!" Gert did not smile but blushed violently and took to his room for the duration.

The big plane tree at the corner of the park was vibrating with dozens, hundreds, tens of thousands of starlings. It's vintage time.

Flower vendors everywhere display thick burdens of white chrysanthemums.

Eve. news: ten whole minutes on "improvements in accommodations" in "detention centers." Getting ready for a fall upswing in the crime rate.

Overheard:

— On the tram, from a handsome blond male in his early forties: "I'd been on the phone half an hour, first with my mother, then with the building. When you finally got through it's a wonder I picked up at all."

— During dinner, presumably through a vent between ladies' and men's rooms, muffled voices: "He told me. But aren't you going to tell him about the colposcopy?" "No, and not about the smear, either." I shut my ears.

Dinner at La Palma: deep-fried small fry, veal cutlet with green beans and pan fries, cheese. The others: roast chicken and flan. Riesling.

Clothes: pinstripe suit, white shirt, navy-blue tie, gray socks, black shoes. I had never seen my sister-in-law dressed as she was tonight, covered from throat to wrist in soft, opaque cloth: an image of chastity. (Daisy: white blouse, black skirt.) Memorial: my grandfather's black homburg, black cashmere coat, silk scarf; custom-tailored shirts of the finest, silkiest cotton, embroidered with his initials in lower case (they are mine as well); double-breasted dark suits of smooth fabric, almost a George Raft look; a collection of bow ties in lively abstract patterns.

Movie: *The Way Home* (De Sica), at the Orpheon.

I began Alpers, *The Art of Seeing*. From Michelangelo: "For the moment I want to note that while reason and art and the difficulty involved with copying the perfections of God are on the side of Italy, only landscape, external exactness, and the attempt to do many things will belong to the north." Will I ever see Florence again?

Exercise: 15 push-ups, 40 sit-ups, all sloppy. My mat was mainly a refuge. A bath helped. But I popped half a tablet of lorazepam before we went out (first daytime use since "the problems").

Daisy said, "I'm *not* tired. I count on you to make a celebration. Take me out for the evening. I asked Colette to come along since she's alone."

B. These events have reminded me how much I am a thing other things happen to. Recognizing this is acceptable provided one relinquishes all claims to running one's own life. (Otherwise the role of unwilling victim beckons irresistibly.) The moments I find difficult, where alertness is both crucial and elusive, are those when surprise blocks out explanations, blocks out the possibility of obvious explanations. Why shouldn't Daisy, in spite of her pallor, feel like celebrating after a successful business trip, instead of sitting in a hot bath with her feet up? What could be more natural than to phone her acute and experienced brother to discuss her latest dealings or, when she learns that Jago was busy for the evening, to invite Colette, whom she regards more as sister than sister-in-law, to join us? Why should Colette refuse? Of course I disliked being irrelevant to what was taking place. The sensation began when Daisy announced "our" plans, leaning against the kitchen counter next to the jar of currants and the scattered cardamom, and prolonged itself through dressing and taxi rides and part of dinner. Colette and Daisy chattered about the new department store, about Gert, about Colette's childlessness, about spots where you could find wild mushrooms, about everything but me, thank God (no, they also discussed folk remedies for thinning hair, each smiling at me with nuanced maternal understanding). I could have gone on feeling excluded, ignored, and exploited, but while waiting for the cheese, I was overtaken by an agreeable languor. I told myself that to be drinking good wine in the company of the two women I loved constituted a rare privilege, one that (in another mode) I'd even daydreamed about. And C.'s being free, which when I learned of it from Daisy had made me wince, could never have led to my seeing her alone, not with Daisy just back. Her coming out with us was the best thing that could have happened. The best thing, circumstances being what they are.

The movie was pure treacle except for the gambling scene.

Why is Jago suddenly so busy (two evenings in a row)?

Gert came in a few minutes ago to apologize and kiss me good night. I said I knew how he felt.

We're deep into the night. Through the window I glimpse the sky, stars, a few dark leaves.

FRIDAY MORNING 6:00 A.M.

A. Lorazepam (½), a little after midnight.

Daisy quietly discouraged my gestures of desire – desire I did not feel (Wednesday had wrung me dry) but thought I might and should feel after Daisy's absence and our evening out. I trust I didn't accept her refusal too readily.

Memorial: as I lay next to C. two nights ago, after shuddering through my second spasm of "pleasure," I saw in front of my closed eyes a night sky thick with stars. A stellar cloud floated from left to right across the still depths. Two ass's ears protruded from the top of the cloud. The cloud stopped, the whole donkey floated into view, in profile, seated on its haunches, bronze-colored, velvety, alert.

B. B should have begun above, between "of desire" and "desire." Perhaps memories also belong in B, since the things they convey, being no longer here, are not verifiable; and perhaps the things I see and hear today? I do the seeing and hearing, and I'd hardly swear to their accuracy in court. Doesn't the act of noticing matter as much as what's noticed?

Looking at myself naked from the side in a full-length mirror: I *am* getting a pot belly, a slump above the pubis. It reminds me of my father's abdominal hernia. (A late dream that woke me up and for once brought relief as I quickly felt for the disheartening, absent bulge.)

I left Daisy in distant sleep. I miss having Paul to talk to. I've been compulsively checking the time on the kitchen clock so that I can call him up. I probably won't – I'm not sure he's alone. Whom can he be seeing these days? I admire his discretion and don't intend to pry. That he can be so discreet with a friend who for years has shared his life week after week only reinforces my trust in him, the knowledge that I can turn to him for advice or reassurance and that he will always provide it. I've seen him so little these past days, because of his work, the dentist, and whatever else is going on. This has made a telling difference.

Opening the window. In the dew and first orange light, our backyards have a rural fragrance, plus two raucously absconding crows. But the crows belong in A.

FRI. 8:45 A.M.

A. Additions to yesterday:

Madre Mia phoned me at the office: the continuing fair weather makes Pater gloomy, but there is *nothing* wrong with him.

Letter from Sukik: he plans to move here, requests help in finding lodging.

(How could I leave *this* out?) Yesterday I went to see Gert in his room, where he'd withdrawn after Daisy's teasing remark. I said to him, "We can't treat her like that. This is a family. If something's wrong, we talk about it." Gert looked at me bitterly, as if to say, "Then why can't I talk to *you*?" I barked, "Too important for the likes of us, I suppose," and walked out. Late at night I knew I had added another stone to my shame load.

Reading: I postponed going on with the Alpers because it is too interesting. Instead I picked up a book I can dip into irregularly, Zara's *Young Days in Bratislava.* An incident in the opening chapter astonished me. Zara reports that one of his aunts, talking to an old friend, told him that not only did she know of his sexual attraction to her brother, but that it was reciprocated, and that she approved and would do everything she could to smooth their way. This in Bratislava, in 1895!

This morning warm as ever (17°C), clear except for the customary blue-gold haze.

Brown linen-wool jacket (note: lowest front button loose – why keep fiddling with it?), medium-gray thin wool slacks, light-gray shirt, brown check tie, loafers.

Daisy is lunching with Paul. I asked if I could join them. Better not – "so long since I've had a talk with him." "You had lunch with

: 25 :

him a couple of days ago!" "True. But it seems long."

Apple juice, 2 buns, tea.

B. Neither yesterday evening nor this morning did Daisy talk about her trip. That's somewhat understandable. A day and a half discussing carpet economics with businessmen who can't tell one design from another would leave anyone sick of the subject. My failure to inquire about what happened may be less understandable. How explain this lapse? Easy. She was back in her comforting role, and everything in between was canceled, as though her nondomestic life didn't count. And this is not so. She has often thanked me for encouraging her professionally. She has said that without me she would never have found the strength to become successful. All the same, she makes an important trip and I forget to ask about it.

Now for "split-ring potential." (And split-ring *power*.) This notion has been gradually forcing itself on me. The "gradually" is more pathetic than ironic: thirty-odd years of private battling with split rings (and keys) should not have been needed to recognize this potential — one encounter ought to have been enough. Exploiting the potential commercially will mean the company has to move out of its prudent routine, into what or how many new products I'm not yet sure. Furniture surely, and other such "passive" constructions, where the built-in strength of the ring will guarantee a durable rigidity tempered with elasticity and (to my mind) no less necessary elegance. The circle has always stood for perfection, and linked circles denote a *ne plus ultra*, as in the Olympics logo. But I'm more interested in actively exploiting the force clamped into the ring's coils. How, I don't know. That's one reason I'm confiding my ruminations here and not to my work file. Naomi's no snitch, but if she noticed what I was after during her photocopying, she might inadvertently spill the beans.

Will production cost be a significant problem? Check this. (Stan?) According to present norms, an increase in the size of a ring by no more than 66% brings an increase in the sales price of well over that – from 8.90 a gross to 15.30. Would the spread grow proportionately to size? But don't forget that the rings would be utilized, and therefore sold and priced, as units. That's where the profits lie.

A. Lunch at office: a yogurt, a pear "popped with juice."

Calls: Pater, at length. I tell him at least once a week not to phone me at work. I know why he persists. He likes to talk without Madre Mia around, and he waits until she's out doing her errands, something that can't happen when I'm at home. (Madre Mia phones me while she's out so *he* can't listen; but not today.) Pater recapitulated his grievances – his "illnesses" and my mother's hearty indifference.

Cherry bashfully invited me to the musical soirée where she will play the Bach sonata. Wondering how to refuse, I realized that the occasion might provide cover for a meeting with C. – the distance to and from Cherry's friends' place could even justify an extra hour. I said I'd come. I can always back out at the last minute.

Mr. Valde discovered Naomi copying my personal papers. He made no comment. Thank God I keep my split-ring notes at home.

B. It's strange that Daisy asked no questions about *my* evening without her. What did she assume? While she was gone, I worried about what I'd tell her and imagined different accounts that would suit her expectations. I decided that an unlikely story would be most convincing. Example: an evening at home with books and records had begun as planned. I listened to the Di Sabata *Ballo* while I frenched my beans. Then Richard called. *Richard* – you remember him. The graduate-school pal I used to play ball with on the way home? He asked me out, we went to the Korean restaurant, and so forth. (But I wouldn't have made the restaurant Korean, because how would I know what I'd eaten?)

I'm glad to have been spared telling this lie, but I ask myself why Daisy wasn't more curious. She is always so anxious about me. Of course, she knows I can look after myself. My Colette, when shall we have another time like that?

FRI. LATE AFTERNOON

A. Eve-of-weekend symptoms:

Mr. Valde makes the rounds every half hour. His expression is meant to discourage imaginary doctors' appointments, illness in the family, sudden indispositions, and other getaways.

Naomi does her nails (mother-of-pearl) out of a kit in the top drawer of her desk, which she slides shut at every faint scrunch of the Valdean soles.

Paul came to my office to scan the heavens for bad-weather omens. Not a real cloud in sight.

As the afternoon passes, watches are checked more and more frequently. Not by me. I enjoy dispatching a week's accumulated chorelets.

By five o'clock most windows are open. It's hot, and the traffic outside is sounding a promise of playtime.

B. When in my office, Paul stopped to chat for a minute. He said he was going sculling with Jago. I felt a twinge of envy for his vigor: I can hardly get through my calisthenics. Going out, he said, "Daisy said yesterday we should get together over the weekend." Fine.

When everybody had gone, I called C. to arrange a meeting in the park. "Didn't Paul tell you I'm meeting him for coffee?" We spoke for a while, C. full of tender attentions and her own eve-of-weekend elation (a sensation no doubt shared by anyone who has ever attended school). I had trouble paying attention. I was obsessed with a grease spot on a file folder stacked on a shelf to the right of my desk. I could not stop staring to see whether it was actually spreading or only seemed to be.

Why did I put the last two paragraphs under B? They're factual enough. (They are *also* factual.) Perhaps because I dozed off at my desk and immediately began dreaming: I enter the office of a foot doctor, on the outskirts of town, in what Americans call a shopping mall. A woman lets me in and tells me I'm wanted on the phone. The caller instructs me to go straight into the back room, no matter what anyone tells me: the doctor knows I'm coming and will join me promptly; I should just make myself comfortable. A large, thuggish man confronts me when I walk to the far end of the front room. His necktie is decorated with burningly bright Masonic eyes. One of them widens into a passage that leads through the door I had been approaching. The large man shuts the door behind me. In the darkened room I'm overwhelmed by a medley of smells, church incense spiked with whiffs of pork and garlic frying. I almost miss noticing the doctor. He barely glances at my toes when I exhibit them but tells me to soak my feet every two hours in a well-shaken mixture of olive oil and gasoline. My shoes have disappeared. I try to hide my feet from the doctor, now looming between me and the curtained window. He says there is absolutely no need to amputate my toes. Their stench makes me retch.

FRIDAY, LATER

I put A items in B because the categories are clumsy and misleading. There's no keeping them out of each other, and rightly so. Never mind:

A. I finished writing the account of my dream, collected the papers I was taking home, and neatened my desk inside and out. I like to find an appearance of order Monday mornings. Through the one western window not darkened by a wall, the sun was pouring streams of orange dye through the drabness of Stan's office into the drabness of my own. Colette phoned back. She was now free. Paul's coffee with her had lasted only a few minutes; he was in a hurry to keep his appointment with Jago. Why had she wanted to see him? She promptly answered, to ask his advice about a present she was buying her husband.

Her answer was too prompt. She'd made it up. I somehow didn't mind. "A birthday present?" I inquired. "A surprise." "Do you often surprise Jago?" "Once in a while." "Why are we talking about this?" "Because you asked me!"

I became foolishly irritated. When Colette came back to her reason for calling – our having a meeting, if it wasn't too late – I declared that it *was* too late. She said she was sorry and wished me, fondly, a pleasant evening.

B. Having been foolish and having realized it, why didn't I call her back? Because I had found myself a reason for refusing her proposal: I "needed to think through" the problem of organizing these pages. I was not entirely making this up. But missing a chance to see her! My self-defeating attitude derailed my ability to think anything through.

If nothing else, this account of myself (whoever he may be) should make me pay attention to priorities. My priorities: Daisy, Colette, Paul, work. And Gert? What position would I in my heart of hearts assign him? Why, in my heart of hearts, perhaps the first. But how much time do and can and should I spend there?

FRIDAY EVENING

A. Waiting for the tram: two birds courting, one walking round the other making soft cries, each fluttering its wings. This in autumn, and both birds male. I pointed this out to a fellow waitress. "Boys will be boys," she said, "*and* girls." (What species? Review birds, shrubs, mushrooms, et al.)

Gert not home.

Daisy's eyes suspiciously pink. "What do you expect, when you're back so late?" Followed at once by a hug meaning, of course it's not that. "I just burned myself" — we were in the kitchen. She added no details. No time for exercises before

Dinner: cold leek and potato soup with dill; salad; cheese; jam pancakes; sauvignon.

I did the washing-up. Daisy then proposed a walk. So late? This has never happened since we moved here. We went as far as Fourier Park, long closed. My easygoing Daisy stamped along at a pace that left me in a sweat.

Cigarette smell meant Gert was back. He said he'd been out looking for Paul and Jago. He had missed them at the boat club and at "their next stop" (?). I pointed out that the weekend would offer time and opportunity to see either or both of them. Why the sudden interest? Gert a little too emphatically explained how much he liked them, how kind they'd always been to him, how he'd always selfishly taken them for granted. I didn't question his reasons. But if he was out with Leonora, natural enough on a Friday night, why not say so?

Gert was wearing jeans, T-shirt, unzippered gabardine jacket, and sneakers that a month ago were white. (I my warm-weather cardigan, office trousers and shirt, and slippers for which as usual I'd changed my moccasins when I came in. Daisy, too, had kept her daytime clothes. I forgot to tell her about the loose button.)

B. Something new and useful for these pages. I've christened it the "incerpt." It comes from realizing that categories like A and B are both accurate and inaccurate; that, besides, there is a *proper* chronology in writing that is worth saving — the chronology of writing itself, the order in which things are set down. Unlike that of events slavishly reconstituted, this chronology leaves room for discoveries and sur-prises. "Incerpt" means letting B material intrude in the A category and vice versa. Thus, if an incident I describe brings up a memory or a possibility, I record it then and there as a B-incerpt. Not only do I salvage what has then occurred to me, I also acknowledge its place in my mental process; and surely the process of thought is more reveal-ing than the alignment of details in correct sequence.

A second innovation: within the categories A (verifiable) and B (subjective), make a further division into what concerns others and what concerns only myself. This would result in four categories: A1 and A2, B1 and B2. Examples: A1 – a phone call; A2 – a book I read; B1 – my love for C.; B2 – my inventing the categories A1 A2 B1 B2.

Incerpts would apply to all four categories. The aim: to make this account as complete as possible.

A1. As I was writing this last paragraph D. appeared and told me to come to bed. She sounded grumpy, as if woken up by a bad dream. It's late enough – past two.

B1. *No* pills tonight. Stopping the lorazepam entirely makes me apprehensive, but I noticed no bad effects from halving the dose. (Two nights ago. Did I mention this?)

SATURDAY, 7 A.M.
B2. I am in a house in the country with my mother. My younger brother and sister are also keeping her company, though neither is pleased to be there or willing to *seem* pleased. My mother believes she is ill and complains about her condition unreasonably. She insists that she's at the end of her rope: "I've had enough, I've had enough, let me die." I'm horrified and indignant. "Madre Mia, there's noth-ing wrong with you." "You can't possibly understand, I've had enough, I want to die." My sister keeps entering the room, looking at her watch, sighing, and going out again. She says she has an appoint-

ment with her astrologer and dreads being late, because "I have to have someone to talk to, and at least he listens." When I ask what she needs to talk about, she giggles, "Why, *us*, darling!" Meanwhile my younger brother has been reading Aristotle's *Ethics* to my mother out loud; whenever she bothers to listen, she nods her head in satisfaction. My brother shuts the book and takes me into the next room. He says he, too, has to leave, in order to call my mother's two doctors. They're the only ones who can say whether or not a lobotomy is advisable. "But Madre Mia doesn't need a lobotomy!" "I'm talking about our sister. Why do you think she's been put on a liquid diet?" When I rejoin my mother, she asks me, "Where have you been? Why aren't you wearing a tie to go with that nice collar? I'm about to send out for something to eat. Care to join me in a liquid dinner?" My sister, who is standing behind me, murmurs, "The only one here who needs worrying about is your little brother."

A1. Around 6:15 I came awake with a jolt, and that was that. I lay in bed for an hour pretending that sleep might return, but for once I enjoyed my insomnia. Shortly after I woke it occurred to me that no matter how worthwhile my incerpt procedure is, it could produce chaos by mixing fragments of all four categories together as inextricably as buttons in a woodpile. At first this worried me. Eventually I saw that the incerpts simply needed to be copied into lists according to their respective categories. So waking early can bring blessings.

A2. I got up and was able to put in a good twenty minutes of recopying in addition to writing my dream.

SAT. 1:45 P.M.
A1. Another cloudless day. This weather is making the world unreal.

In the kitchen Daisy and Gert were eating breakfast. Daisy had been urging Gert not to disturb Paul so early on a weekend morning. Gert, already dressed (same jeans, T-shirt, and sneakers), maintained that Paul didn't act like a late sleeper. Daisy said that anyone on an office schedule deserved the benefit of the doubt. She never for a moment implied that Paul might not be alone. I followed her example. I said to Gert that if he waited to call, we could enjoy his company for more than the usual three minutes. He ignored my remark, which sounded pettier than I'd intended, and replied to Daisy, "Okay, but when you think it's late enough, would you give him a ring and tell him I'd like to see him?" He went out for the paper.

Breakfast: apple juice, cereal with nuts and raisins, tea.

Having fetched the *Post*, Gert pointed to an article on the front page denouncing "radicals who dominate university student unions." What was the point? I asked. "Next week, I guess — what people call trouble. But if *they* don't make a stink, who else will?"

Daisy called Paul at around 9:15; no answer. "Try Uncle Jago." Apparently Colette answered. "This early?" Daisy asked. "No, nothing important ... I'm glad. It's sure to do Paul lots of good." Gert nudged her. "Will they be back for lunch? Gert would like to talk to Paul ... I see." After a longer pause: "That's a wonderful idea. We'll get together soon. Preferably sometime when our men are out of the way."

B1. The thought that C. was alone frustrated and saddened me. A2 Late in the morning, when Daisy finally went out shopping (Gert had disappeared on "student business"), I phoned her. If Jago wasn't back, could I visit her this afternoon? She suggested my calling again after lunch.

A2. Earlier I worked on our car. My task was to rotate the tires (the wheels). At first I resented the whole business. Not the idea of shifting tires around, which is a reasonable way to equalize wear, but having to spend time on the car at all. We drive it so little, barely 5,000 km a year, which might treble if we ever started using it in town, something I'm not as set against as Daisy, though I accept her point that with good public transport, why give yourself parking headaches? (I almost broke the rule when I went to Colette's the other night, but I was sure the car would attract attention in her quiet neighborhood.)

The tires took up most of the morning. If Gert had helped me, as I'd expected, a time-consuming mistake would have been avoided. Tires are normally rotated diagonally, left front with right rear, right front with left rear, and that's what I did. But as I was tightening the nuts on the fourth wheel, I remembered what Gert had pointed out to me weeks earlier: the rear tires had originally been the front ones, and had remained so until the preceding tire shift. They were now too worn to be put back in front and should next time simply be changed left to right and right to left (same with the front ones). So I had to start over. I was anxious not to go wrong this time and spent a few minutes making sure I didn't. I found the obvious solution: switch the tires front and back (left front to left back, left back to left front, similarly on the right). This introduced me to the general question, how many ways can four wheels be positioned? I spent a long time figuring out the answer and enjoyed every second of it.

I reached my conclusion by trial and error. Call the left front tire A, the right front tire B, the left rear tire C, the right rear tire D. With A left unchanged, what possibilities exist? If B also remains unchanged, there are two: C left D right and D left C right:

        A B   A B
        C D   D C

With C taking the place of B, there are two more: B left D right, D left B right:

        A C   A C
        B D   D B

Similarly with D in B's place:

$$
\begin{array}{cc}
\text{A D} & \text{A D} \\
\text{B C} & \text{C B}
\end{array}
$$

Six in all. If A is replaced in turn by B, C, and D and the same shifts are operated, in each case six additional alignments will result. The final number of permutations is thus twenty-four (4×6); arithmetically, the equivalent of $4 \times 3 \times 2 \, (\times 1)$, or more generally, $n \times (n - 1) \times (n - 2) \times (n - 3)$ etc., where n = total number of units. I verified this with groups of five and six, which yield, respectively, 120 and 720 possibilities. Astonished by these high figures, I went inside to tell Daisy about my discovery. Her response was basically so what. Gert, I trust, will be more appreciative.

A2 here would normally have been A1, but because she was feeling nauseated, after preparing lunch Daisy had a lie-down and left me to eat alone: ham, onion pie, salad, a pear, dark beer. B2 I felt insanely lost sitting at the kitchen table half listening to news (U.S. forces back into Latin America – doesn't it ever get boring?), then music (Saturday noontime fare: Lehar overtures), wondering, why am I eating by myself? Getting to my desk was a comfort. I'm beginning to think that these notes, whether or not they're "doing me good," give me a hold on reality that I could never achieve otherwise and so console me for the little losses that punctuate any ordinary day. Where are the people I care about? Gert out of the house, Daisy off in her room, C. out of even telephone reach, Paul and Jago lost to their new athletic mania. Here I can make and keep them present, remembering how they were, envisioning how they are.

A1. I just called Colette. Could I visit? She spoke uneasily. Someone was with her. Jago? Yes . . . no . . . she expected him back any moment . . . I must realize that what I suggested was "too . . . special" (she thus avoided saying "risky" in front of her visitor). She would explain to me when we had time to talk. But I *had* time to talk.

SATURDAY, AFTER MIDNIGHT

B2. Memorial: one August, when Gert was four, we took him to stay with Daisy's parents. They were spending the summer in one half of a capacious farmhouse, specially fitted out for vacation rental. Cousins of Daisy's were living in a cottage at the edge of the nearest village, about two kilometers away. They had a pretty daughter named Louise, about Gert's age. The children liked each other. We arranged for them to visit and play together almost every day. Once, towards the end of our stay, for reasons I forget, Gert was kept home alone. In mid afternoon he asked us if he could join the farmer and his boys in the fields. We were sure they wouldn't mind (he knew enough to stay out of their way) and let him go. After an hour I thought it would be neighborly to make sure he was behaving himself. I found the farmer and his teenage sons on a hillside, spraying the vines. No sign of Gert. I went back to the house to tell Daisy. She deduced that if they hadn't seen him, he must have taken the road to the village. We started off in that direction. At the next house we asked about Gert. A farmhand told us with a laugh, "The beautiful boy taking cornflowers to his bride-to-be? Sure, about an hour ago." Farther on, two men threshing wheat confirmed Gert's passage. "He said he'd like to help, but his girlfriend was waiting. We said he could come back anytime he liked." Three hundred yards farther, an old woman resting at the roadside reported, "An angel from heaven!" And so it went. We found him in Louise's cottage. He was presenting her with the contents of his basket (Daisy's emptied sewing basket): a few pennies, a few gumdrops, an apple, half a chocolate bar, a fragrant pale-pink rose with today's front page round its stem, and the cornflowers he had picked. Louise's smiling mother asked us to stay for tea. On arriving, Gert had offered her another apple diplomatically set aside for her.

A2. During the afternoon I devoted time to my accounts — a longer time than usual because this writing has kept me from adjusting them daily. Even so, what I'd jotted down allowed me to calculate most expenses. For details, see account book. Afterwards, to dissipate a cloud of drowsiness, I went for a walk. Daisy had already left on a walk of her own. Blackbirds and an occasional crow were spotted in vegetable plots behind houses I passed; tomatoes might be the attraction. One yellow-beaked predator was perched on a gaudy scarecrow's head. The starlings must be feasting on unharvested grapes. Dahlias are in full bloom.

A1. I came home intending to get out my encyclopedia, keener than ever to improve my acquaintance with the natural world. Gert had come back from his day in town. I don't know how he spent it, and hardly care. He was in a happier mood than I've seen him in for weeks. He laughed over my mistake with the tires and said that if I'd asked him, he could have done the job before leaving. He let me explain my calculation of the twenty-four permutations with patience and at least a semblance of attention, but without surprise. "The answer is called factorial four," he told me. This is written 4!, which neatly expresses my feelings.

Gert suggested we watch TV together. We endured a melodrama about the effort-laden love life of junior citizens. In one passable scene a young man unburdened his problems to an older woman; I couldn't tell if she was a relative, a friend of the family, or his girlfriend's mother. I put up with the rest for the sake of Gert's company. His comments helped. During this scene, after bringing in beer and pretzels, he said, "Those two are having fun, so I don't see why we shouldn't." By the end of the hour, I have to admit, I was hooked. The style was trivial, not the situation. Of course it became a little too obvious where the relationship between the boy and the older woman was heading.

Daisy at last came back from her walk. I asked how the weather was in the next county. Without answering she set about making dinner. Still so pale.

I said to Gert that I could call Paul and find out what he was doing tomorrow. Gert said all right. Overhearing us, Daisy chimed in, why didn't I let things take care of themselves? I retorted that I was only helping things along. Paul was out. I went upstairs A2 to my room for some fast but not perfunctory sit-ups (35) and push-ups (12) and a shower.

A1. Paul was now home. I told him that Gert was hoping to get together with him. Paul said, fine, but wouldn't he be there for dinner tomorrow? Daisy announced coincidentally from the wings that she'd forgotten to mention it but tomorrow Paul was coming for dinner. Paul then suggested that Gert join him and Jago in the morning for volleyball. I asked Gert, who at first shook his head, then said, "Why not? I'll be there." They would meet between nine and nine-thirty. I felt A2 that I had for once been a useful father.

A1. Dinner – the three of us together! Leeks in vinaigrette, roast chicken, roast potatoes, "garden" peas, cheese, flan, cool pinot noir rosé. Not only was Gert present, he was a consummate presence. He'd changed into "nice" clothes, his beige corduroy suit, a loose-collared off-white shirt that set off his quite wonderful head (he'd washed his hair, too). Daisy asked him whom he was planning to seduce that evening. He said he wasn't going anywhere, but he might as well have answered, "You." He talked with animation through the meal, ostensibly to both of us but in truth for Daisy's sake. He managed to bring some pink back into her cheeks. He chatted about his courses and what his classmates were like. He discussed Hölderlin and Leopardi with her, speculating about why classical syntax and vocabulary were so important to both poets. He didn't bring up politics. He didn't talk about Leonora, either, except to say, when Daisy asked about her, that she was spending the evening with her family (but who are they?). Of course, he did not mention his gambling losses. A2 I was naturally pleased at his cheering Daisy up. I myself was not cheered up. I felt excluded from this family feast. A dumb way to feel, particularly as the "real" reason for it was all my own doing. Since midafternoon I'd been experiencing flashes of dizzying nausea that I was hypochondriacally nagging myself about. My feeling excluded meant only that the others weren't sympathizing with my plight, of which, naturally, I'd given no hint — I knew all too well that if I did, they would immediately ask whether I'd been taking my medicines regularly, which I haven't, but I *know* the nausea has nothing to do with that. Daisy would have scolded me and made me take the pills in her presence (for a day or two, anyway), just as she did when I started them.

I left the two of them to clean up together and withdrew to my desk, ostensibly to read the paper but in fact to organize my incerpts, which are taking up a lot of time, though I remain more than satisfied with them (B2!) as a means of coordinating my material. Having spoken of the newspaper, I realized I wouldn't even have time to scan it. (Glancing at the front page, I did catch a notable headline: New Law to Contain Liquor Abuse.) I'm using three notebooks to do my copying (A1/A2/B1-B2).

A1. (A little later.) I went down for a glass of wine at around ten. According to Gert, Daisy had gone out for yet another airing. This is not like her. She can take walks whenever she wants, B1 but why didn't she let me know instead of disappearing like a thief in the night? Without Gert, I would have been worried sick.

Returning to my task, I could not shake off my anxiety about her — her pallor, her nervousness, and now this quirky behavior. I put on an old recording by Vronsky and Babin of Rachmaninoff's *Fantasy* and played the Barcarolle. As beautiful as the Lermontov poem that inspired it. Where else are such poets and composers bred? They turn us all into Russians.

A1. Gert just came in to say good night. He'd rung up Paul again, but no answer. I remarked that if nine-to-five workers shouldn't be bothered early on weekend mornings, bachelors shouldn't be bothered late on weekend evenings. Gert agreed with a smile. "Who's he seeing, do you know?" he asked, giving the word *seeing* its due weight. Back to incerpting.

1:00 A.M.

Daisy abruptly entered a few minutes ago to insist I come to bed. Why was I up so late when I needed rest? She felt lonely and had worried about me. I told her how worried *I'd* been by her leaving the house without a word. "But didn't Gert tell you?" "Sure, Gert told me." "Then why worry?" "But where *were* you?" She had simply felt like taking a walk. And for how long? "Look, my beloved, it's way after midnight, I'd be so happy to have you in bed with me." I said I would be happy to join her there (I'd done at least three quarters of the copying).

So no pills at all tonight. Not feeling sleepy, I plan to have a glass of gewürztraminer to relax me. I surmise I shall not be permitted to read.

Why didn't Daisy let me know Paul was coming to dinner?

SUN. 5:30 A.M.

B2. Before it fades, a dream: sitting with my parents in their musty dining room, I hear Pater say he's going for a walk. I know he'll head for a bar to meet Mr. Valde and Fritz. I follow him. In this mild weather, the plate-glass windows of the bar's terrace have been replaced by a screen made of wooden cutouts; their patterns are said to illustrate the legend of Phaedra and Hippolytus, with the ending improved (Hippolytus marries his stepmother, Theseus hangs himself). Even if I am unable to see them, I know Mr. Valde and Fritz are sitting behind the screen. Pater walks right by. He proceeds to a parking lot at the back of the bar and there gets into a shiny new car, a foreign make that looks like a cross between a Citroën DS and a Volkswagen. He drives off. I take a bicycle and set out in pursuit. Although his car advances haltingly because of mechanical problems, I have to pedal frantically to keep up. He is following a haphazard (read: evasive) route through a city that I "know" is Barcelona (it looks like my own town, and the street signs are not in Catalan). My father parks in a pretty square filled with a variety of high, leafy trees. He gets out. He looks around him as if for a particular object. He finally spies something in a bank of high bushes. I steal behind these bushes but cannot see anything through their dense, drooping stems, each of which terminates in a purple spike. Daisy has appeared on the sidewalk. My father points to his car; Daisy pays no attention. She takes Pater by the arm and walks away with him down the sidewalk. Trapped in the shrubbery, I have to watch them from an ever-increasing distance. They turn and come back. Daisy walks up to the car and pats its rear left fender, as though the car were a horse. She kicks the tire under the fender. The entire car sinks down on its rims with a terminal wheeze. Daisy squeezes my father's shoulder and shakes her head. Pater in turn kicks the tire disgustedly and shrugs. To me this gesture is one of heartbreaking melancholy.

Waking up almost in tears. It never crossed my mind that he might be short of money.

7:15 A.M.
B1. At seven, restless and nauseated, I woke up for good. I made

myself a cup of tea but could scarcely keep it down. Why? Hardly last night's simple if plentiful dinner. The rosé?

I've come here to finish the copying interrupted last night.

11:00 P.M.

(B1). A long, full day. Why don't I feel sleepy? I had the good sense to take a pocket notebook with me, so that I missed much less of what happened than I would have otherwise. Daisy looked at me pointedly whenever I jotted something down. The practice may be distracting to others, even annoying, but it is of undeniable help in improving this project, which after all everyone originally encouraged.

A1. After preparing breakfast (homemade tomato juice from Madre Mia, sausages and eggs, Edam-style cheese, green grapes, hot rolls with honey and raspberry jelly, also from M.M.), I rousted out Gert at 8:15. He sat up so promptly I was left with a mouthful of unused arguments. Most Sundays, getting him up before eleven is like luring a snail out of its shell. I assumed his date with Jago and Paul explained his docility, but when I mentioned it, he murmured, "Thanks for reminding me." Mystery of late adolescence. A little later I took a tray to Daisy, still in bed. When I opened the shutters, she, too, sat up cheerfully and then announced, "I want to drive out to the country today. Let's go to the lake for lunch." My scheduled self protested, "What about my correspondence?" "Do it later!" (Re my letters: I've always kept a record of them and of course shall continue to do so.)

The day argued in her favor — as still and fair as those preceding it, suffused with veils of late-September haze that make us think that no matter how many balmy days we have had, this can be the last, that tonight wind, rain, or frost may strike all the precarious green into yellow and rust.

Since the least of our departures requires superstitiously elaborate preparations (on this occasion, biscuits and bottles of water for the drive, propitiatory sweaters and umbrellas, reading material, sunglasses, sun lotion, towels, none of which we used), rechecking the car for gas, oil, and tire pressure, and a final forgetting and remembering of keys and the back door and the bedroom window left open, we didn't leave till 10:30. When he went out at nine, Gert showed frank relief at escaping the imminent fuss.

The trip to Lake John XXIII takes an hour and a half. We stopped at the lakeside restaurant to reserve a table, something normally impossible so late on a sunny Sunday, but Daisy's father had been a friend of the former manager, whose successor Daisy adroitly cajoled into maintaining the special treatment accorded her family. We were given one of the rare tables for two at the waterside edge of the terrace; we were introduced to our waiter and heard him instructed to take the best care of us. (He seemed pleased enough with the assignment. He was a thin man of middling height, with recessive bald streaks separating the grizzled hair on his temples from the dark ruin of a widow's peak, and large, brown, friendly eyes. He stood straight and attentive in his black trousers, white shirt, and full-length apron. I was unaccountably glad that he was to wait on us.)

We drove towards the "beach," as the sandless bathing area is called. Daisy announced that she didn't feel like swimming but that, if I did, she would be happy to go for a walk. I replied that in that case I would be happier walking, too. (I avoided saying "walking with you," in case she preferred, as she recently has, a solitary stroll; nor did I point out that we'd left our bathing suits at home.) She didn't argue and suggested that we drive to the lake's less frequented western shore.

There we turned off the road onto a track leading to the water. We parked in a little clearing in the woods that skirt the lake, less systematically tended here than on the other side but easy enough to wander through. Daisy was in no mood for wandering and set off at her brisk pace of two days ago, raising from the forest floor a prodigious racket of snapping twigs and crackling leaves. Autumn is more evident here than in the city: except for the oaks, trees are shedding their leaves. (Light frost at night?) The mushrooms had survived. I used them as an excuse to lag behind. A2 I found the shadowy midday warmth an irresistible invitation to loll, by which I guess I mean to loaf – in such circumstances I always think of the beautiful lines by Whitman, the American poet, "Loafe with me on the grass" and "I loafe and invite my soul, I lean and loafe at my ease observing a spear of summer grass," etc. (B2 In my mind did *loafe* and *soul* fuse into *loll*? How can I ever pretend to be master of my words?) On a log I observed an anonymous orange fungal ear. On the ground I recognized a mushroom or two, at least by family (cantharellus, boletus). I reminded myself, in my pocket notebook, to start acquiring such information systematically. Why haven't I done so already? Do I really have less and less time, as is my impression? At least my wishes in this regard have been recorded. I saw a large, spectacularly grotesque mushroom that I once knew by name. It looks like a reduction of one of Dubuffet's outdoor sculptures. Long ago I took a specimen home for identification. My mushroom guide described it as "edible and recommended." I ate it, but I do not recommend it.

Staring at the dappled and leaf-strewn earth must have queered my vision, because a little later I had an otherwise inexplicable experience. I was gazing across a brook at a stand of young aspens, their thinning leaves quivering and glittering in slightly angled sunlight. While I looked, the leaves became still, and everything else began to quiver – the components of the relation quivering/stillness were inverted, the motion of the leaves was transferred to the aspen trunks, the ground they stood on, the trees around them, the entire world, not excluding my amazed self. Pangs of elation squeezed their way up my spine in the presence of a phenomenon that I knew was both impossible and real. I didn't dare look away for fear of losing touch with it. A1 When Daisy spoke from nearby, I urged her to my side so that she could see what I did. She saw nothing unusual. After a while she murmured, "Time to think about lunch, darling?" I turned to embrace her and answered, "You bet it's time for lunch!" My earlier nausea had disappeared. I was famished.

On our return we found the restaurant crammed with the usual Sunday mix: families and parties of friends from the city, clearly happy to be in the country together on this benign day. As we made our way towards our table we were hailed by familiar voices: Paul and Jago were seated in front of pint glasses of dark beer at the table d'hôte in the middle of the dining hall. Jago and Daisy went off to negotiate with the manager. They succeeded in exchanging our waterside spot for a small table for four right next to it. Sitting down, I was pleased to see that we hadn't lost our waiter.

Ordering the meal was simple. The standard lunch, which at 35.00 cost half what it would have in town, was not only acceptable but inevitable. A half-minute discussion about wines between our waiter and Jago, who loves on these occasions to show his expertise, disposed of that agreeable question. For two hours we applied ourselves to ingesting the following series of dishes, which as I register it may sound copious but left us all feeling light as any weight-watcher. A platter of salami and microscopically sliced sun-dried beef, cured raw ham, garlic sausage, segments of spinach-flavored blood sausage, and the liverwurst that is a house specialty, as good as any pâté (in this country, anyway). A salad of romaine and tomatoes. A pile of deep-fried baby perch fresh from Lake John XXIII. Roast loin of pork with buttered new potatoes and a stew of the same yellow-stemmed, brown-capped cantharellus I saw in the woods, here called September bugle. The celebrated cheese of the region, Summer Orange, a ball made from goat's milk and rolled in onion-flavored toasted bread crumbs. Chocolate nut cake.

Through the fried perch we drank pitchers of an open wine, what in the jargon is termed a "vivacious" sparkling chenin blanc that we couldn't seem to get enough of. It started me down the pleasant slope of abandon at whose mossy foot I eventually came to rest. For the pork we switched to a six-year-old cabernet franc, and at the very end I insisted (Jago had already declared us his guests) on contributing a bottle of Hungarian Tokay, no less powerful than it was ripe. None of these wines can properly be considered local. Barely north of our town, the country around the lake is already too cold for the vine.

As the meal started, I asked the two men why they hadn't brought Gert along. They replied that he'd left the court after an hour's play. "How come?" I asked. "Wasn't he playing well?" "No, he's pretty good." "Except he's in lousy shape," Jago added. Paul went on, "Maybe. He seemed to have his mind on other things. He took off around a quarter of eleven. We kept at it till almost noon."

Daisy was surprised they hadn't let us know they were coming out here. "It was completely spur-of-the-moment," Paul said. "And we did call," Jago insisted, "but you'd already left. Anyway, here we all are." He smiled as he raised his glass: "*Servus.*"

I refrained from asking about the absence of another person. It is my rule never to mention her, and to talk about her as little as possible. No one spoke her blessed name.

We had a jolly lunch. As the only woman present, Daisy was much fussed over. It warmed me to see her abandon her worried look of past days. She told us all about her trip for the rug company, providing an acid description of one nervous, solemn, maladroit businessman that for some reason made Paul and Jago laugh immoderately. I was glad it cheered *her* up. Afterwards Jago turned to me: "I didn't phone you back after you called the other day because there was nothing to worry about. They're a capable outfit." Daisy asked what he was talking about. Jago told her, though I'd rather he hadn't. She gave me a blurred look somewhere between incredulity and exasperation. "My sweet man, I wouldn't have gotten involved if I hadn't been sure of them. You should have asked *me.*" More laughter.

For some time a little girl of four or five had been standing next to our table quietly filching pieces of meat (the first-course medley had been left in front of us during the salad and fish). Busily chattering with her party, her mother noticed her at last and cried out in mock indignation, "Berenice, *what* are you doing?" The little girl put a last slice of blood sausage in her mouth and went back to her table.

The incident led Paul to tell a rare anecdote from his *vie sentimentale*: his final encounter with a young woman named Berenice with whom he'd had a holiday romance one summer on the Romanian coast. (Why does that benighted country keep popping up in my life?) The meeting took place shortly after their return here. Paul had told Berenice, Listen, when we met I warned you not to go to bed with me if you were thinking about falling in love. Our first weeks were wonderful because we didn't worry about consequences. We just enjoyed spending time with each other. Berenice: I still don't worry about consequences. I still love spending time with you. Nothing has changed. That's my point – I don't want anything to change. Paul: It's not so. You want things to turn out a certain way, and you complain when they don't. You complain all the time. Berenice: It's been like that from the start. On our first date you said all the women you'd loved were difficult and demanding. If I'd been easygoing I never would have seen you twice. Paul: But look at us. You're unhappy. I'm unhappy. I can't give you what you give me – I'm not capable of loving you. Berenice: You think I love you? Who ever said I loved you? How could *anyone* love you? With an intuitive speed that astonished him, Paul had got up and left. He had realized that this was an opportunity not to be missed. He did not see her again.

Daisy laughed when he'd finished: "You were right. All the same, the story – *your* story – reeks of sexism. It's the old smear that women are hopelessly illogical and 'impossible.'"

"Women aren't illogical and impossible; humans are. I happened to start the argument, that's all. If she'd started it, I would have reacted the same way. It's a situation where there's no room for anything but self-defense."

I talked less than the others, but before befuddledom set in I managed one cute (if unfair) remark. While the cheese was being served, Paul glanced towards the entrance and asked, "Isn't that Dr. Markevitch?" Jago turned and confirmed the sighting: "The doctor and legal expert." "Let's get him over," Daisy exclaimed, "and make him talk about malpractice suits." "Did you notice," I remarked, "that he's wearing one?"

This was one of my last contributions to the ongoing banter, which I nonetheless continued to enjoy, mostly for the warmth that so manifestly underlay it. I had meanwhile been drawn into another conversation, an intermittent one taking place between our waiter and myself.

His name was Zoltan – he was Hungarian. We felt a marked sympathy from the moment we saw one another. I cannot explain this. I think we guessed at a complicity, at some kind of shared story we might tell. Of his own story, only bits had emerged thus far: he had emigrated five years ago, he'd formerly been a musician. With the Tokay, I asked him to give us a fuller account. Knowing how wine dilutes my memory, I kept my pocket notebook handy.

Zoltan had been born into a working-class family in Erzebet, an industrial suburb of Pest. His musical gifts were recognized in grade school, where the choirmaster noticed not only his fine ear but his uncanny flair for sight-reading. Zoltan also possessed a facility with instruments that enabled him within the space of two years to play middlingly difficult pieces on the clarinet, violin, and piano. His first teachers encouraged him to stick to the violin.

When Zoltan reached the age of fourteen, these early mentors helped him obtain the first of three scholarships that paid for his musical studies through the end of his secondary education. Then and later, his parents' modest resources made it impossible for them to help him, except in one unforeseen way.

Zoltan's mother had relatives in the wine country near Lake Balaton. One autumn, Zoltan and his family went to visit them for the Saturday-night celebration marking the end of the vintage. It was the October of his eighteenth year. Zoltan, who had brought his fiddle, joined the local players in the traditional dances that followed the festive supper. In a class apart from his companions, he began, to the delight of dancers and bystanders, performing dazzling improvisations on the customary folk tunes.

Among those present — vintners, their relatives, a few city visitors — was a middle-aged man who was elegantly dressed and bore himself in a way suited to more cosmopolitan surroundings. This gentleman several times interrupted his conversations to listen to the music, usually when Zoltan was the soloist. The man eventually came forward, asked one of the fiddlers for the loan of his instrument, and joined Zoltan on the podium. Revealing himself to be a violinist of supreme skill, he engaged Zoltan in a series of "answering" improvisations in which each spurred the other to ever greater exploits. The dancing stopped. The company crowded around to listen to this amiable competition between the veteran and the prodigy.

The gentleman afterwards thanked Zoltan for affording him such a satisfying busman's holiday. He introduced himself as Adolph Busch, the first violin of the Busch Quartet, with which he had come to Hungary on tour. He asked about Zoltan's musical background and offered to help him. Zoltan spoke of his material difficulties. Busch promised him his support. He kept his word. In Budapest his recommendation secured Zoltan an audition at the Conservatory. He won a state scholarship that paid for his studies over the next five years.

Because I was busy catching up with my notes, I missed the details of what happened next. In the end, Zoltan became a virtuoso and a knowledgeable interpreter of the classical repertory.

His future was not yet assured, although he now found work easily and supplemented his public stipend by playing in orchestras, in chamber groups, and, most often, in dance bands. The world is full of fiddlers; a soloist's career is launched by winning prizes year after year in international competitions. Zoltan had to find money to feed and clothe himself while paying his way to Bucharest, Genoa, and Paris, and eventually, if all went well, to Moscow and Brussels.

A dance band specializing in the czardas and the verbunkos hired him for a tour through Poland and Czechoslovakia. One of its last stops was Marienbad, a Bohemian spa whose prewar luster still attracted to its casino the hard currency of gamblers from the west. At this casino Zoltan's band played a two-night stand.

On first entering the gaming rooms, Zoltan tried roulette for a while. Out of curiosity he looked into the salon where old-style baccarat was played. He was fascinated by the intensity of the silence and the concentration of the players – "like an orchestra rehearsing with Furtwängler."

For an hour Zoltan observed the activity at one table. Throughout this time only a single person remained seated in the same place: a thin, gray-haired woman wearing silver-rimmed spectacles. She faced a series of gamblers, usually one at a time. She won many of the pots, which ranged from two hundred to two thousand dollars, so that at the end of the hour the gray-haired woman had about thirty thousand dollars stacked in front of her.

This woman sat immediately to the right of the dealer. She was thus automatically the last to be given cards, no matter how many were betting against her. It seemed to Zoltan that against one other player the gray-haired woman always won, whereas with two or more opponents she won only occasionally. Zoltan concluded that the game had been rigged (a notion he later found puerile): the deck was stacked so that with only two players the second cards would make their holder a winner. For twenty minutes Zoltan tried to verify his hypothesis, but his efforts at objectivity were undermined by an intensifying ache in the pit of his stomach. The ache told him that nothing he saw or thought could stop him from betting his hunch. At last, having taken a seat at the gray-haired woman's right to be sure of intercepting "her" cards and having waited for a hand where a single player bet ahead of him, he put down on the table the three thousand dollars that he had carefully saved over the past five years.

His first bets apparently justified his decision. He was dealt a winning deuce, eight, and seven, then an eight, four, and five. When for the third time he found himself with only one bettor to his right, Zoltan sat as if paralyzed, hating to withdraw his stake (now multiplied ninefold), but terrified of losing it. His two antagonists had matched him. Cards were dealt — to him, a nine and a six. Custom, virtually the rule of the game (as the dealer insisted), required him to stay in. Sensing that he was beaten on the board, he decided to draw against the odds and tapped the felt cloth with his forefinger. He was dealt a three. He walked away with over eighty thousand dollars, a sum, he reminded us, worth ten times its current value. His livelihood was assured for years to come.

He wired his small fortune to a bank in Geneva and finished the tour in a state of elation. He often thought of all the advantages he could now provide for his parents, and for himself, too. He imagined a cottage in the country where he could practice day and night; a place no more than half an hour's ride from Budapest, which would be convenient for a companion working there.... And around the cottage an orchard, and a few high trees amid which they might walk, arm in arm, hand in hand.... A hammock for napping together in the hot season..... And for her, a room all her own, out of earshot of his scales and trills. But when the band came back to Budapest, Sophie was not waiting for him.

They had met in a nightclub where he was playing. Whenever he performed popular music, he conspicuously dressed himself in a grotesquely high celluloid collar and old-fashioned string cravat. This attire distinguished him from the other gifted musicians in that most musical of capitals. He soon had a following, and managers regularly assigned him a little highlighted podium apart from the other performers. That was how Sophie noticed him. Before that evening was out she had arranged an introduction. They spent three happy years together.

Sophie worked as confidential secretary to the cabinet director of the minister of trade. The job gave her access to information concerning import-export matters. It was to this that Zoltan, finding himself abandoned, attributed her change of heart. The middle-aged nongentleman from Gyor whom she preferred to him, an enterprising exporter of the country's famous hard salami, hardly surpassed him in personal or social appeal. He surmised that at a time when state control was descending on the economy like mosquito swarms on the shores of Lake Balaton, the man, hoping to exploit her position, had offered her a security that no one in those times could reasonably refuse. Zoltan wondered whether he might not have kept her preference had Sophie known of his triumph at the gaming tables.

I was so anxious not to lose any details that I missed about a minute of Zoltan's story. I then heard him say that he had been brought to trial and immediately asked, "Trial? Trial for what?"

He looked at me, perplexed. Nudging me with sandaled toes, Daisy suggested, "Why don't you put that fucking notebook away and listen?"

He had said "diary," not "trial." Zoltan had started one at the time and kept it diligently ever since. Of course, I began questioning him about his methods. Paul interrupted, "But your music?" Zoltan bent over to lay his left hand palm-upward on the checkered tablecloth. The palm was gnarled; knotted strands of tissue constricted the ring and index fingers, and when he opened up his hand, it was clear that they could not be fully straightened. "The condition is called Dupuytren's contracture." "I know," Paul said, "and it can easily – " "Please. This started decades ago." A pause followed. Jago asked, "What about the money?" "I provided for my family. The rest is still in Switzerland. Close to three million francs, I suppose." "Then what are you doing here?" "Haven't we had a good time together?" We nodded as though we understood.

The afternoon had not ended, the sky was not yet darkening, but the time had come to start home. After Jago paid the bill, he and the others rose from their chairs. I did not mind the glances exchanged over my apparently hopeless immobility. I was too happy. "That Tokay!" I exclaimed to show awareness of my catatonic state. Paul helped me to my feet. Putting one arm around his shoulders and the other around Jago's, I performed a little jig as I stood up to express my good spirits. They all laughed. We proceeded to the cars. It was decreed that Daisy would drive Paul home, and Jago me.

At home I was left to myself. I called C. I confessed my sloshed condition as well as my insane love and indeed lust for her. She replied with determined propriety. I eventually grasped that some-one was with her. (I thought I detected a woman's voice in the background, as if in an adjoining room.)

A2. I went to my desk to clear up the correspondence I would normally have done this morning. I'd barely sat down when I began feeling too drowsy to attend to it. I decided to explore Gert's bathroom drawer. The bennies were there. I popped one and stepped outside for a few breaths of air to get it working. A1 Daisy drove up and I welcomed her home with an outdoor hug.

(A1). Mail log:

Sukik: Places in town scarce and getting scarcer. Do not recommend moving here.

Pater: Do not phone me at office [nth time]. Difficult period for Gert. Regularly seeing girl his own age; in my opinion older woman better for him (happier). [How to find a second Colette?]

Pfeiffer: [answer to unlisted letter: photographer doing series on trades and professions, wants me to model "average manager"]: No thanks.

Somis: Send list of wines currently available.

National Institute of Geography [re walking tours]: Send catalog of maps for (a) Lake John XXIII area (1:25,000) and (b) Syria (smallest scale available).

Hans & Eva: Back in time for opera? (From the *House of the Dead.*)

ASB: Balances confirmed. Transfer 5,000 from savings to checking.

A2. While vigorously executing twenty push-ups and fifty sit-ups I B2 realized that with a free hour ahead of me, I could start implementing my plan to improve my knowledge of the natural world – less a plan than a wish, today boosted by confronting nameless mushrooms. Because it was Sunday and I had only my own books to consult, I considered the possibilities at hand. A2 I went from one room to another, glancing over shelves whose contents were all too familiar: poetry, history, histories of the arts. Would an encyclopedia do the trick? I saw myself taking fragmentary notes as I trudged from WEATHER to ISOBARS to AIR MASSES. I then spied Daisy's row of cookbooks through the kitchen door. They surely contained

a specialized vocabulary worth learning – a full gamut of condi-
ments, utensils, and procedures. B2 And what part of the world, I
asked myself, is more natural to us than the food that we eat so regularly, so unquestioningly, so ignorantly?

A2. As I walked into the kitchen, I understood that I must learn
more than words – more, that is, than their theoretical meanings. I
know how restless I feel whenever I watch Daisy maneuvering her
pots and pans. It is a restlessness compounded of admiration and a
jealous sense of my own inadequacy. Here was exactly what I'd been
looking for.

I knew at once where to begin: by learning how to make a plain
omelet – the kind of omelet that arrives on one's plate in the very
best restaurants, soft, at its center almost runny, as perfectly shaped
as a trimmed fish, with skin smooth and resilient, not browned but
of a yellow at most freckled with tan, and neither dry nor greasy. I
picked out several large cookbooks, all shabby from use, and set out
to discover how this simple, rare delight was achieved.

I discovered one thing immediately: cooks – at least those who
write cookbooks – disagree. In regard to omelets they agree about
nothing except the kind of pan to use (even here one recommends a
"7-inch bottom for 3 eggs, 11-inch for 8 eggs," and another a "10-inch
for 3 or 4 eggs," proportions that are hard to reconcile). For instance,
some say pepper should be used in the seasoning, while others forbid
it. The disagreements that most bothered me were (a) whether, in
preparation, to beat the eggs (with "vigorous strokes") or stir them
("a few gentle turns"); (b) whether to put the pan directly on high
heat or put it on warm heat and turn the flame up at the last moment;
(c) whether to stir the eggs after they are in the pan or let them set
and then jiggle them.

I made a list of possible combinations of these three alternatives.
Ideally I should make eight trial omelets:

beating – high heat – stir in pan
beating – high heat – let set then jiggle
beating – warm heat – stir in pan
beating – warm heat – let set then jiggle
stirring – high heat – stir in pan
stirring – high heat – let set then jiggle
stirring – warm heat – stir in pan
stirring – warm heat – let set then jiggle

It was like the car tires yesterday morning. But yesterday the problem could be solved on paper, and I had plenty of time for it. This evening I wanted to proceed from theory to practice, and my time was limited. My research had taken a good half hour. Daisy was already casting quizzical glances into the kitchen, where she would shortly prepare a real meal for four. I had to take one of my eight options straightaway. I chose beating, high heat, let set then jiggle. The dashing style of one particular recipe no doubt determined my choice, and I reckon it may well be the best, but I was not to find out today.

Because the author insisted that an omelet pan can never be too hot, I turned the oven on full blast and placed an cast-iron skillet in it while I cracked, seasoned, and beat the eggs. I remembered to use a potholder to transfer the skillet to a gas burner. Into it I then poured oil and, after a while, the beaten eggs. A few moments later I suffered a brief and disastrous lapse of attention. The eggs had begun to coalesce; it was time to start jiggling. The sight of the skillet perched familiarly on top of the stove canceled my recollection of its recent sojourn in the oven. I seized the iron handle with my bare left hand. There followed a second of unfeeling shock, after which my hand flew into the air like a startled partridge and I screamed. Daisy, on her way into the kitchen at that moment, opened the icebox door, grasped my left wrist, and thrust the hand, palm up, against the bottom of the freezer compartment. This probably saved at least two layers of skin (it quickly puckered with blisters), but only tomorrow will tell. After half a minute or so Daisy released my hand, turned off the gas, and opened a number of windows to dissipate the smoke and the stench of charred egg.

I consoled myself at the time with the thought that the mishap would give me something interesting to write about.

My cookbook reading added only one new term to my vocabulary: drum sieve.

Gert came home while Daisy was making supper. I was standing in the hall when he walked through the front door. He smiled a smile from his childhood days; my eyes filled with tears. Picking up the still-wrapped Hegel, he undid the package and riffled through the book. "I'll start it tonight. Thanks." He went into the kitchen and spent the next hour discreetly making himself useful. The change in him was unnerving. I didn't dare inquire after its cause.

At three minutes past seven Paul arrived – "almost late, as usual," he said. We were alone. I at once asked him if he'd spoken with Gert. Did he know what was bothering him? Could he explain his sudden weird good-naturedness? Paul looked at me in a way I couldn't define, perhaps impatient, somewhat devious, not antagonistic, concerned (but for whom?). "I've *always* found him good-natured. We did talk a little. Don't worry about him. He'll be all right. He *is* all right." I didn't press the matter. It's fine with me if Gert confides in Paul. A father can't be a good grandfather, too. And I don't mean Pater.

Our big lunch had somehow produced in us a resurgence of hunger and thirst; Daisy, knowing that *l'appétit vient en mangeant*, had cleverly anticipated it. We got through a jar of anchovies and a bottle and a half of riesling before even sitting down at the dining table. There, as if we'd been fasting, we consumed bowls of spiced white-bean soup, a rabbit sautéed in white wine with buttered tagliatelle on the side, lettuce salad, ewe cheese, and raspberries dusted with sugar. Two bottles of last night's rosé were drunk (and Gert drank beer), and we poured slivovitz into our emptied coffee cups. I was astonished at how light and lighthearted this left me.

During the meal Paul was entertaining, Gert attentive, Daisy cheerful (and a little distracted?), and I — who knows? *They* know. B1 I enjoyed them. I was afloat in unconscious happiness — perhaps the only true kind. When C. was mentioned, I reminded myself, The woman you long to be with! and felt only an echo of regret, like a regret out of art, like catching one of Monk's long solos through a window in the summer twilight.

A1. Paul talked at length about our waiter. He had liked Zoltan; he had enjoyed his story; he felt that it was only possibly true. His skepticism had arisen during the Marienbad episode. It sounded too much like a gambler's dream: not one miraculous stroke of luck but a succession of them. There were persuasive details in the story, but Paul wondered if they might not have been added after simpler versions had failed to convince. As Paul listened, it had occurred to him that Zoltan might have reinvented not only the Marienbad episode but *all* the events of his life, as year after year he repeated his story to strangers. Trial and error would have led to modifications that transformed the original anecdote — something like "I went into the casino with my life savings and came out ten times richer" — into one that required the full-scale creation of an imaginary past. The life as told was undeniably interesting; it also carried little risk of exposure: Zoltan's disabled hand, for instance, eliminated the danger that a customer would one day fetch a violin from the cloakroom and ask him to play.

Paul said that in the end he didn't care whether Zoltan had been lying or not. He was plainly a happy man — what difference did it make if his happiness came from his success as a storyteller?

I said flatly that I took Zoltan at his word. Daisy thought that if his tale was false, it made it better. Gert, for whose benefit we summarized what we'd heard, pointed out that in either case Zoltan had shown pluck, since he'd made himself ridiculous by admitting he'd lost Sophie to a hard-salami salesman.

We had scarcely finished our slivovitz when Daisy announced that *Die Meistersinger* was being broadcast at nine-thirty and that she wanted me to listen to it with her. (Gert disappeared into his room; Paul yawned theatrically and went home.) I knew the opera well, and I had my account of the entire day to write, but my protests did me no good. "It's *because* you know it so well that I'd like to watch with you. That way I won't fall asleep."

At least I managed to skip the third act – I loathe it, and not only for Sachs's chauvinistic diatribe – and settled at my desk to compile this report of a busy Sunday.

While writing, I've realized something obvious. My categories (A1 A2 B1 B2) should be split into specific sections. This will be easy to do – e.g., by dividing B (subjective matters concerning what is outside me) into matters involving *people* and those involving *things*, like the overheated frying pan. I'm not sure how to label the sections – I'll straighten that out tomorrow.

It's past 3 A.M. I can't risk sleeping late, especially with this restructuring to do. I'll skip the medicine again (no ill effects so far). I wonder how thick this book will grow before the vase is broken.

B II/a A female figure, forbiddingly helmeted like a horned
Valkyrie, points the way up a muddy trail stamped by
small hooves. I'm sure I know what to expect farther
on but can't remember whatever it obviously is. I slog
along. At the top of the hill I find a chalet apparently
made of writing paper. I approach a window to the
right of the front door. I call out; someone answers. A
conversation begins. "Can you let me in?" "Glue yourself together and follow the ruled lines, here in maxi
format." "Could you please tell me who you are?" "I'm
good-looking, elegant, blue eyes, pink cheeks, yellow
nose hairs." I have my doubts but persist: "Am I doing
something for you or are you doing something for
me?" "It depends. You've got to drill holes for any
kind of archiving, *then* arrange them. Quack, quack!"
"Quack quack who?" "Quack quack estupendous
block block!" I understand I've gotten it all wrong. He
isn't talking to me, he's talking on the phone. But I'm
sure I know him and might be having this same conversation with him. He says, "Stop worrying. You're
stuck halfway up a pine tree and think that's life. Climb
down. Head north." A pause. "Look, it happens to all
of us. Don't let her nail you down." The door is opened
by a handsome, dark-haired young man of medium
height. He looks the way I wanted to when I was
twenty, right down to the off-white linen or flannel
shirt with open collar and full sleeves that I've always
longed for. I write this down. I've been writing things
down on the side of the house ever since I arrived. This
man is not the one I heard on the phone; I tell myself

his voice has less bark and more bite to it. Beyond him, in the household gloom, female sobs can be heard: "Don't leave me." Or that's what I write down.

B II/b   I was confused when I transcribed this. I was under the impression that I was still writing on the side of the house. The writing paper the house was made of A II/b could be torn off in sheets of convenient size. I got up right away, dazed but able to function. Not a cloud.

MONDAY, 9 A.M. (COMPLETED II A.M.)

A I/a+b   Making a breakfast tray for Daisy and taking it to her room: melba toast, honey, tea. She asked, "Is anything wrong?" Gert hadn't left, so we breakfasted together. My usual juice, cereal with fruit, and tea. Gert (he generally eats nothing) methodically swallowed slices of ham on hunks of bread, and a hefty wedge of cheese. A I/a   No less peculiarly, he was wide awake.

    I asked, wouldn't he be late for classes? He was skipping classes. There was a big demo at the university. I suggested that logically that was the business of university students; why get involved? Embarrassed and solemn, he answered, "I know they're older, but they make me feel like a kid again." How so? "They're so *serious* about everything – the way I used to be." I thought of Gert on that summer afternoon when he was four (trailing – to parody Walt Whitman again – clouds of something nice): "You've got plenty of time." "I don't know. When I was little, I had time because it didn't 'have' me. (That's one of their jokes.) I worry about it now. You all expect a lot of me. And people are doing market research now on sixteen-year-olds, right here – on *twelve*-year-olds. We're all going to be scheduled like the rest of the sheep." "Thank you. Is that what the demo is about?" "Basically. Not officially. The pretext is . . . shit, it *is* only a pretext, but I ought to know right off. Let's see – the exam system. No access to professors nominally in charge of courses. Favoritism. Things like that. It's not my business, and I don't much care. But those guys – they know how to *play*." "Higher learning is play?" "Does it have to be misery? Or a bad joke? Playing *isn't* a joke. Come and take a look. They have no age bias, either way." "Gee, that's great! But schools do need rules." "Games have rules, too. The difference is, you don't worry about cheating, it's another way to play, it's playing *with* the rules. And I *don't* mean on exams." "I thought exams –" "More like when Maganoff takes over a political science class, like he did last week." "'The *way* he did last week.'" "The discussion went into outer space. Some guys say they learned more about Spinoza in two hours – " "Spinoza – in political science?" I had no idea what Gert was talking about; and I had never seen him so open. Why was I putting him down? I imagined an outsider watching us: would anyone with a gram of humanity not take Gert's side? Why shouldn't I? "Who's Maganoff?" "He's a hotshot activist. Leonora introduced us. Nobody's ever treated me like that – nobody that age, anyway. He's seven or eight years older than me. He's an academic whiz and a powerhouse in student politics, and he spent two whole hours with me. I started out saying things like you – like 'You have to have rules,' and he'd laugh until

I wondered how I'd ever said it, and then I'd realize I *hadn't* said it, some piece of social machinery had used me to say it." "He sounds clever." "You know Pascal says, 'We try to live in other people's ideas. We neglect what is real in us' – isn't that great?" "What's supposed to be real in us?" "Maganoff says first of all your desires – they're real and they're all yours." "But I can desire anything." "Exactly. *Exactly.*" "That's plain loony." "Listen to him, not to me." "Maybe. Not likely, though." "I'll tell him. Watch out. He may show up."

A I/b   Gert and I left together. Going out, he picked up the canvas gloves, ski goggles, and old silk scarf he'd
B II/b left on the hall table. I would have begged him to stay clear of the rioting if I hadn't wanted to see it myself.
B I/b People on the tram looked no different from other Monday mornings: gloomy and dumb, aside from
A II/b their summery clothes. I wore my beige gabardine slacks, an old medium-blue cotton jacket, white shirt,
B II/b maroon tie, crepe-soled gray-green shoes. "The wind in the silvery wheels of cyclists set obstacles aquiver" –
B II/a the line came back to me from afar. Beyond the dusty tram window unsilvery cyclists were treading their
A II/a way to work. Traffic had been diverted from some midtown streets; clusters of cops here and there. In the paper I found no mention of the students' strike. On the culture page I drifted through an article about a show in the capital, of Coptic nocturnal landscapes; by the end I knew less than ever about a subject of
A II/b which I was totally ignorant. The paper cost .75, and it's not fit for the outhouse.
A I/a   I was hurrying down the office corridor to begin

these notes when I noticed a puppet on Fritz's desk. It had a wooden head and neck (grainy wood surrounding the mat-painted neck veins, hair, mouth, and eyes) and solid hands inside Mickey Mouse gloves; the trunk and arms were of cloth whose Prussian-blue ground was embroidered with ivy-leaf designs in scarlet thread. Asking Fritz about it, I learned he was a puppeteer. He had been invited to perform at some event

A I/b later in the day. He was more sportily dressed than is his wont, in unfitted, or more accurately, loose-fitting gray cotton-flannel slacks and a black sweatshirt above which a redemptive brown necktie peeped. (A collar-

A II/b less undyed linen jacket was hanging on the back of his chair.) I myself was wearing a white shirt, maroon tie, beige gabardine slacks, worn blue cotton jacket. Cheered by this discovery, I settled into my office to record recent events.

MONDAY, 2–6 P.M.

A I/a As Brünnhilde to Siegmund, so did Mr. Valde appear to me after I had written all but the last twenty lines of the preceding pages. As he stood in the door to my office, his posture expressed relentless calm. When I at last noticed him, he was staring at my hands – at my right hand, holding this pencil against this pad. He glanced round my tiny office, and business-oriented as it is, its aspect may have mollified him, because nothing worse than gravity lightly salted with impatience sounded in his question: "What in the name of the dead gods are you doing?" I spread my arms in rhetorical perplexity. "You are not unaware that six salaried human beings are attendant on your benevolent decision to join them?" I rapped both kneecaps as I stood up in a lurch of shame: I'd forgotten the Monday-morning conference. I'd even forgotten to write it down.

The meeting went well enough. I entered in Mr. Valde's wake to a hushed medley of averted eyes, *in petto* smiles, straightened chairs, rustled files. Only Cherry winged me a friendly look. In a short opening statement, Mr. Valde disposed of routine matters and set the stage for Paul, who had good news to report: he has meticulously established the resemblance of a spring used in our competitor's "Romanian" clamp to one he designed for a clamp of our own a year and a half ago. Mr. Valde drove the point home: Paul's spring was patented. "We can tell them to get their junk off the market or get sued. If we have to sue, we can get a restraining order that will sure as hell keep them out of the stores." Some questions about details then followed. In a speaking-of-springs mode, I offered to present my split-ring ideas, but I didn't insist. In the collective euphoria at being let off the hook, no one wanted to talk about something else. I don't blame them. And then Paul was busy conversing on the side with Mr. Valde.

A I/a

When I returned to my neat office, it looked to me like a prison cell. Why do I so hate this furniture? The wood gets scraped, the plastic cracks and chips, the chrome retains thumbprints with high-tech precision. And yet every item goes on filling its own bill. The strict tubes of the armchair, the pointedly rectangular filing cabinets, the five-inches-too-short and too-nar-

A I/b

row desk, the ill-joined shelves, the scarred ashtray, the bruised wastebasket – nothing, whether scarred or bruised, exudes anything but minimonumental smugness at being made to last, although often it hasn't. I wished I'd worn clodhoppers so I could give them a good battering, or had a maul handy (no survivors!), or, best of all, had tools to take apart these solid yet vulnerable "sleeping partners" of my days. I'd reshape and reassemble them into novel units where functions would be where *I* wanted them: the files suspended handily in midair, the in/out trays at tooth level, who knows. I could sit on the desk in semi-lotus position with a pad in my lap, or paper the walls with the company's pathetic secrets. I remembered that on New Year's Eve Romans drop discount chests of drawers out their windows into the street (while the local traffic cop is penned in with cakes and flagons). And then, and then.... Pity for these bits of junk crept into me, and with it a kind of respect. They were only doing what had been asked of them – doing it, according to their means, to perfection. In this, I had to admit, they showed not smugness but decorous (if hardly decorative) modesty.

BI/a

BI/b   I calmed down. I asked myself: So what's the point – the point for *you*? This: your dismaying earlier mistake – forgetting the meeting – is no reason for fruitless self-recrimination. It will be redeemed not by some anguish-ridden atonement but simply by being recorded here. (If I have time, I must reconstruct exactly the sensations that bustled around me while Mr. Valde stood in the door.)

A II/b   At this point I furtively completed the earlier entry begun on my arrival at the office. Before proceeding any further, I waited for lunchtime. People wandered out, and after a while I checked Mr. Valde's office and made sure that he too had left. I then started bringing my account of the day up to the minute. As I reflected

A I/b on the past morning, I happened to look up briefly

A I/a and again saw a figure framed in the doorway – not Mr. Valde but an unfamiliar young man. "Gert said I could visit. I need a break, okay? I'm Maganoff." I think I blushed, like a schoolboy meeting his teacher out of school. "Of course. Would you like something to eat?" "Why not?" He was wearing standard, some-what smudgy post-sixties casuals: sneakers, jeans, T-shirt, belt-length denim jacket.

A I/b   I hurried off to the deli. Luxemburg Boulevard smelled faintly of tear gas. No cars except parked ones. Some pedestrians appeared from side streets with

A I/a handkerchiefs pressed to their faces. In the deli I pointed to a robust sandwich of hard sausage, cheddar, and lettuce, was told its name – "'Swain in Shade,' one

A I/b of our specials" – and bought two, plus a bottle of merlot (total: 14.50). I had started back to the office when the approaching sound of muffled outdoor com-motion made me stop. A minute later an irregular cortege of onlookers and demonstrators edged onto the boulevard, accompanied by a clumping noise I did not understand.

     At the center of the group a flat, low wagon mount-ed on six squat tires was being slowly drawn by a gang of eight unstalwart youths, who leaned their shoulders into two draw-ropes. A grand piano took up most of the space on the wagon platform. A young woman sat at its keyboard. Her steady, indeed furious playing produced only occasional notes from under the raised lid, beneath which dozens of books were heaped. (Many more books were stacked under the instrument itself.) A male student standing at the piano's concave side was reducing the pile of books by busily handing them out to bystanders. The music emerging thus gradually gained in frequency and coherence as additional strings were freed.

A I/a   I walked over for a closer look. The book distributor was smiling at me: Rudkin's son, Alex! He knelt down to pass me a small volume – *The Kreutzer Sonata*. While I stood there rather foolishly staring at the spine of the book, which I held at arm's length, several notes were struck in unexpected succession, fast, melancholy, and familiar, like a bewitching fragment that flits irretrievably out of a radio as you inattentively spin the dial. This music then changed into a

A I/b   brief, Sonny Rollins-like riff and after that into our national anthem, played straight. I reentered our office building.

A I/a   On my return we fell to our Swains and merlot, Maganoff with gusto. I described the piano scene. He nodded. "The lits did it with the music school." "I knew the boy handing out books. Dr. Rudkin's a friend of ours." "Alex is a cultural-demolition specialist. How was he doing?" "Enjoying himself." "What did he tell you?" "We didn't talk. I didn't know what to say. I wasn't getting the point." "It's called deviation. You eliminate the obvious significance of something, like a piano, then invent a context where it can mean something new." "Oh. I'm afraid my reaction basically was that they were putting something over on me – trying to make *me* do something." "That's how I feel most of the time. How about you?" I thought of myself at this morning's meeting, unable to make myself heard. "Maybe." I remembered feeling "excluded" at last Saturday's dinner with Daisy and Gert. "I feel like that at home sometimes. But not most of the time." "Most of the time I feel every step has been planned for me. But being offered a book is a little different, isn't it – more like an invitation?" "I don't know. I don't know enough about it to say." "Sure you do. You do or nobody does. No wonder you feel exploited." I was getting irritated. "What's that supposed to mean?" "Let's say we all play roles. Feeling imposed on and thinking you can't understand what's going on sound like the same role." "Well, it's not a role I want." "Me neither. It's what we've been stuck with. It's a disguise the world doles out to get us through the day." "Your meaning eludes me." "Look at Alex's father. You know him, and I don't, but from what I hear he's now busy playing the aging role." This was conceivably true. With no visible cause, Robert Rudkin at sixty had changed from an energetic practitioner and slightly rambunctious acquaintance into a model of polite resignation. Maganoff went on, "My own assignment is the promising-youth role, also a big waste of time. I didn't choose it. I *don't* choose it." "Alex and your friends downstairs are playing roles, too, and you don't object. That's pure theater." "But that kind of theater is something *we* make up." "And why theater?" "What else is there? I'm doing my tell-it-like-it-is act for you right now." "I see your point. But we can't spend all our time performing happenings." "I don't know of anything better to do. Think of making love, of how great it is when we 'stage' it." I thought of that and sighed. "But the whole place would fall apart. In two weeks we'd all be poor, sick, and bored. You know we've got to make *some* sacrifices." "Uh-uh. You never have to betray your desires. They're you." "Look, what about my job? I *want* to look after my family. And myself, too. If I lived your way I'd already be dead of cirrhosis." "So what's better, dying whenever after a life you've been happy with, or chugging on and on on two cylinders, having things done to you? When I forget my desires, I turn into a kind of zombie waiting for the world to tell me what to do. You know what that's called? Common sense. Don't eat too much sugar, easy on the booze, don't fall in love too often, exercise regularly, get to work on time. Go on living, but be sure it's in slow motion, or you'll have a nervous relapse." (What did he mean by "relapse"?) "That's where the sacrifices start. And when I make sacrifices, I become exploitable. If I do the exploiting myself, I end up getting paid for it." "It's not *all* sacrifices. You're not sorry you had an education, are you?" "I'm not sorry. And what's it for? *That's* what I'm sorry about. For most people, having a good education is like having a good car. It's a way of letting people know how to think about you." "That's unfair. I honestly judge people – not even judge, I'm drawn to people – regardless of their education, or anything they may own." "Not even their books?" A palpable hit. "All right. But granting the possibility, why go to all that trouble to avoid getting what we like?" "Because we're trained to accept our roles as natural, and we end up valuing them *over* our lives. Why? Because they protect us from seeing how miserable our real lives have become. We call our roles reality and dream of better times." "There have already *been* better times – in my life, anyway." "Exactly. Lots of better times in the past, and lots more in the future. 'Memories of liberty and dreams of escape save the jailbird from suicide' – who said that? What about right now? – I'm due back."

He had stayed for three quarters of an hour. Often I had asked him to repeat what he'd said. He was so convincing in his intensity that I had found myself

B I/b nodding agreement to words I hadn't understood. By the time he left, I was at a pitch of tonic confusion.

B II/b Memorial: five years ago, after I had put aside enough money, we realized an old desire and took a vacation at the seashore. We shared a roomy house with Jago and Colette; Paul, then involved with a woman called Susanna, rented a bungalow two hundred yards away. On our second morning, the first time we went swimming, I stepped on a broken shell and gashed my right sole. The doctor who dressed the wound advised me to keep my foot up for a week. I was condemned to the house and its garden. Since Daisy had spent the past months working hard, Colette, with only her household to attend to, volunteered to look after me when the others went sightseeing, as they did most days in that benign climate. We had heretofore not known each other well; I had never had more than an incidental moment alone with her. We now passed hours in each other's company. I learned all she could tell of her earlier life, and she no less of mine. We spent the early afternoon in the shady garden behind the house, reading out loud to one another amid blossoming buddleias and impatiens. As our first book we chose Jane Austen's *Emma*. On the third afternoon we started an eighteenth-century German novel, once considered scandalous but tame by modern standards. During one of Colette's turns she read:

> I wish you could see her! A magnificent creature. She has at her disposition manners that both provoke desire and wreathe it in cold disdain. The sensual pleasure in her face takes on a guise at once lively and noble. Her eyes pierce your yearning like a hawk's, while her ravishing mouth refuses every sign of encouragement. In the daring thrust of its erectness her body swells under her clothes so winningly you cannot help longing to tear it free – her breasts as fervent as twin suns rising in June mist, and their terrestrial echoes, the globes of her loins, as luscious as grape clusters in autumn. The promise of love shines from the oval of her cheeks and chin like light from a lamp. And the way her dark locks dangle when she runs along the strand! And when she dances, the way her glance blurs in a languor

of movement and music, her legs disappearing and reappearing like cloudy lightning! No god could be happier than the man she encloses in her arms. But no doubt we should heed Socrates: it is best not to have been born or, if it is too late for that, to return at once to the place whence we came.

I was gazing at Colette as she read, thinking of death and of the one time I had seen her in a bathing suit, a few days before. She raised her eyes from the page: they were moist and remote. My own eyes filled with tears. I struggled to my feet, to my one and a half feet, and bent over to kiss her. Our reading hours had ended.

B II/a   A little stone gets into your shoe. You ignore the intermittent twinge, though your big toe tells you not to. Finally you remove your shoe and shake out the

B I/b   pebble. Gert's remark when I woke him up yesterday stuck in my shoe: he thanked me for reminding him about meeting Paul and Jago after he had repeatedly told us how anxious he was to see them. Why does this make a pebble? Because of further oddnesses: the improbable account of his Friday evening spent looking for the two men; the lack of *any* account of his Saturday. When I organized my speculations, four possibilities emerged:

1. Leonora: his relationship with her has changed. He used to speak of her often, less to me than to Daisy, but never bothering to conceal his rather turbulent interest in her. Have things gotten more "serious"?

Taken a turn for the worse? But he's been so good-humored recently. Why not confide?

2. Gambling: did Gert really lose enough to be in trouble? What has he done about it? He only *implied* that he'd been gambling. Since he knows I understand the problem, why not tell me about it?

3. The student movement: Gert may have wanted to conceal involvements that could get him hurt or arrested. My encounter with Maganoff should help here. But he was *already* perfectly open on the subject this morning.

4. Something else – but what, or who? Where did he go yesterday after leaving the volleyball game? "Something else" means he's hiding a matter of importance from us.

Note that all these incidents came after my fiasco with him on Thursday evening. After Daisy's teasing had made him flee, I addressed him as a "stern father" when what he needed was brotherly counsel. My stupid incapacity may supply the likeliest explanation of all.

A II/b   Little of this got written during the afternoon.
A I/b   Whenever I felt absolutely safe I jotted down more notes on Maganoff. Several times Mr. Valde on his big cat feet walked slowly past my door, gazing pointedly at the papers on my desk. His third appearance left me
A I/a   so unnerved that I went to talk to Fritz. Was Mr. V. still angry with me? Fritz said that his behavior signified no more than normal "Monday causticity" – I shouldn't take it personally.

Cherry dropped by on her way out to ask if I was

coming to hear her play. "If I'd thought you were in the office that day I'd never have started practicing. But since you were – " She told me I was the only one here who knew she played the flute. Why the secret? Because it was the greatest joy in her life, "and I like it that way." Only the musicians she worked with knew about it. What about her friends? Her boyfriend? "Don't talk about men. I like *you*. It's not the only reason, but you never came on to me." I did not comment. "Want to know what I did Saturday night?" After taking a bus out of town, she had walked into the vineyards and in their midst sat down and played for two hours, "alone, just me and the moon." The moon? "A brand-new one." She described watching, through vines still laden with fruit, lighted trains passing half a mile away against a backdrop of fields and woods. She had felt like the queen of her world. I asked her if she knew that Fritz was a puppeteer.

I at last called C. to say that I was too busy to meet her (but not that "business" meant catching up with the day's events). We had a long talk. She told me how pleased she was about Paul and Jago's new enthusiasm for athletics. "Today I suggested water polo. That should be a sight. We'll have to go watch." She mentioned that Jago had lunched with Gert. "Are you sure?" I asked. "I thought Gert was fighting the good fight." "I suppose he took time out. Jago loved talking to him, although he couldn't figure out why he'd made the date. By the way, did you see any of the action?" I spoke of the piano. She said, "A little while ago I walked past the political science building. No demo, no cops, only students sailing paper planes out the windows. Each had a kind of maxim written inside the center fold – they were like aerial fortune cookies. Two I picked up read, 'Playtime is eternity' and 'Orgasm is the exemplar of communication.'" Our talk left me content, as if we had taken our walk in the park together.

I phoned Daisy to say she shouldn't expect me before eight.

MONDAY, 8:30–9:30 P.M.

A I/b With so many pages to write, I started home late – not until 7:30 did I reenter the "voluptuous and godless world." It had never looked so good. The Maganoff effect? On *them!* Many people about, much livelier than usual. The tram was abnormally crowded; it moved sluggishly through belated traffic. It was as if the population were filling the earlier midtown void. To pass the slow ride home, I set myself a mental task: exactly how many passengers were riding on the tram? I needed to count the heads of those already on board, then add and subtract those getting on and off. By the first stop I had only reached nineteen. Eight passengers climbed on, one got out: twenty-six. I added fifteen to my tally before the next stop, where three people eventually struggled to the exit door, diverting my attention from those entering – ten, I'm almost sure (one a rather aged "student" accoutered with the demonstrator's scarf and gloves). Forty-eight, plus nine arrivals at the next exchange and two departures, to which I added a mere five stable passengers (the crush made counting difficult). I worried about having to trust my visual memory to tell newcomers from the rest, but later it occurred to me that the distinction was superfluous: I was counting methodically from front to rear, which meant (as long as I noted ons and offs) that identities didn't matter. Fourth stop: three on, ten off, with eleven more stables. Then eight got off and only one got on, and I finished with another batch of eleven, imagining I had reached the end; but I'd missed two riders exiting by the front – I spotted them only on the sidewalk. Finally, as I prepared to get off, having settled on sixty-six as a last count and pushing my way towards the central platform, I realized that I had left one traveler out from the start: myself. Typical!

B I/a   Throughout my calculations, words spoken by certain passengers had infiltrated some independently attentive layer of hearing (was this because my attention was newly directed outward and not dispersed, as usual, into fantasy?). Two samples: From a pretty middle-aged blonde: "It's not a place you go to for the food, and that's the best thing about it." From a crescent-nosed young man: "This weather makes my hair so dry."

A I/b   Daisy was waiting, dinner was waiting, not a word
B I/b said, but I dropped my hopes of sit-ups, bath, and pre-meal slug of vino and sat myself humbly down at my place at table. My urge to act apologetic (I was as late as if I'd had a dishonest-to-God tryst with C.) soon yielded to Daisy's ways. She behaved as though, late or not, my simply being there made her happy. She had

changed into a wraparound housedress of pleated gray and blue striped cotton, at once sober and alluring. If only she were less haggard — a strong word that expresses what I feel. What a blessing of a woman!

A II/b After her day's work she had produced a perfect, simple repast: anchovies (yesterday she had desalted and then marinated them in layers of coriander); pork cutlets with fresh apples and *rösti* on the side; field salad to which a few slices of raw mushroom were added; fresh snow-white goat cheese; and pears so ripe they must have been stolen from a neighbor's tree — all with a slightly tart young pinot noir, exactly right, exactly what I would have picked and, likewise, slightly chilled, if only I'd come home at a decent hour.

A I/b Fetching the cheese, Daisy stopped to look at herself in the little kitchen mirror, fluffing her hair with one hand. As she sat down she announced, "I'm having my hair dyed." I said, "Great — me, too." "I mean it." I did not approve. Through her natural dark blond run streaks that suggest the humane triumph of a brilliant hairdresser. They give her a look both endearing and "aristocratic." "I'll make it all a nice palish copper and forget about it...." The prospect dismayed me. "You're beautiful the way you are." Tears came to her eyes. I felt I'd best not ask why. I kissed her hands across the table: "You'll be beautiful whatever."

A II/b After the meal I hurried off to the bathroom (the normal proportion between what I drink and what I excrete has yielded to a magic process that produces a liter of piss from a glass of anything, and vice versa); once alone I remembered these pages waiting to be

filled. Not only filled but provided for. A full account
AII/a   of my life requires a full life. Example: I can't report
what I read unless I read. Having scribbled these paragraphs, I'm going to do precisely that. *Young Days in*
BII/b   *Bratislava* – not comparable to Goethe or Henri Beyle,
but good enough to make me want to write memoirs
of some sort. I'm no writer, but if I ever became one,
what greater gift to readers (at least I'm a reader!) than
that of past times judiciously salvaged in the written
word?

11:30 P.M.
AII/b   1. Things not done:
        – exercise (see above)
        – account of daily expenses (something I can do
            anytime by collating particular outlays, noted
            scrupulously as they occur). (Most of the time.)
        2. Mail: a letter from Nina. How am I, what am I doing.
        Our unforgotten youthful months together. Her
        career is flourishing (I suspect her domestic life is not).
        "Our months together": as students we dated; but
        were we ever "together"? I did think I loved her, and
        she willingly agreed. Daisy scotched those illusions
        with a few kindnesses: thick ankles were not a serious
        flaw; there was no need for a wife to share my passion
        for Italian opera; in time I would learn to love moun-
        tain climbing; while not very sexy, Nina was certainly
        sweet. Daisy's mouth and body did the rest.
AI/b   I'd read only two pages when Daisy interrupted and
        gently chided, "How about spending a little time with
        me? I don't mind, but it *is* your shirts I'm ironing." I
        followed her and sat down at the kitchen table, a few

A II/a feet from the door of the laundry room where dearest Daisy was plying her steam iron. A delightful coincidence then occurred. I had turned on the classical music station; it was playing a pretty, early romantic work for piano, which the announcer identified as a sonata by Clara Schumann. Now, the very last sentences I had read in *Young Days in Bratislava* quoted the author's mother praising Clara Schumann's composi-

B II/b tions and bewailing the neglect into which they had fallen. I felt blessed. If I had not undertaken to keep these daily pages and make them as complete as I could, tonight I would not have – almost reluctantly – opened that book. The music was not only a reward: it was a proof of my undertaking. Of course it demands time; does that matter if it makes the world one?

A II/a A news program followed. The report of the student movement was loaded with clichés like "rioting" and "destruction of property."

A I/b Gert came home at 10:30, exhausted and exultant. He hugged me right off the floor. "How *about* him?" "He was interesting. I hear you had lunch with Uncle Jago." "I'm not sure *he's* ready for the revolution, but you never know. Who told you?" "A friend." "You mean Colette?" "It's not *Aunt* Colette anymore?" "I guess not." "Did you see her, too?" "Why, did she tell you that?" A perverse hunch made me say, "Yes – wasn't she supposed to?" "I really love her." I could not tell what he meant by this. I asked, a little stiffly, "How is Leonora?" Gert laughed. "Come *on!*" He gave me another hug.

A II/b The system of incerpt classifications I began using today works as follows: A = what is verifiable and objective; B = what is subjective. The previous secondary divisions represented the same subcategory in both A and B: 1 = what involves others; 2 = what concerns only myself. These numbers have been replaced by the Roman numerals I and II and subdivided thus:

$$
A \begin{cases}
I \begin{cases}
a = \text{communication of some kind} \\
b = \text{other actions and events}
\end{cases} \\[2em]
II \begin{cases}
a = \text{cultural events (all entertainments)} \\
b = \text{other matters}
\end{cases}
\end{cases}
$$

$$
B \begin{cases}
I \begin{cases}
a = \text{things observed} \\
b = \text{other people} \\
\quad \text{(ideas, feelings about)}
\end{cases} \\[2em]
II \begin{cases}
a = \text{dreams} \\
b = \text{"thoughts about"} \\
\quad \text{(e.g., planning future)}
\end{cases}
\end{cases}
$$

B II/b   While these subdivisions increase thoroughness and accuracy, they should themselves be broken down more precisely. (For example, A II/a should be separated into "reading" and "other.") When I've finished cataloging the day's incerpts, I shall move to this next level of classification.

There's no denying that rearranging the incerpts is laborious, and each ramification will make it worse. Would indexing be more efficient? I must look into the possibility.

A I/a   When Gert came in to say good night, he was holding a book, his index finger marking a page. It was

: 84 :

Plutarch's life of Pericles. A sentence had been under-
lined and my name penciled in the margin. It read:
"These things coming into my memory as I am writing this, it would be unnatural for me to omit them."
Gert said, "It reminded me of your project." I was
touched by Plutarch's words, if not in a way that Gert
could guess. My Memorials had, as it were, been
authorized, and literature had provided me with a distinguished colleague. Like Clara Schumann's music,
the coincidence of Plutarch's opinion with my own
confirmed me as a journalist – not yet a master, but no
longer the beginner I so recently was.

TUESDAY, 6:30 A.M.

A II/b   With notes on this morning's dream in hand, I first
must write down the improvements in classification
that I imagined last night. While getting ready for
bed, I mentally extended the example of dividing A
II/a into "reading" and "other." The results are provi-
sional, but I shall nevertheless start using them today.

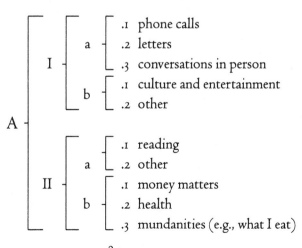

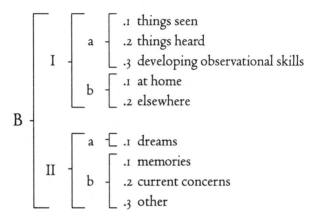

B
- I
  - a
    - .1 things seen
    - .2 things heard
    - .3 developing observational skills
  - b
    - .1 at home
    - .2 elsewhere
- II
  - a
    - .1 dreams
  - b
    - .1 memories
    - .2 current concerns
    - .3 other

(Those "other's" already look foolishly vague. For instance, in A II/a.2, "other" means and should be replaced by "TV," "opera," and so forth.)

B II/a.1 Torrential rain is falling out of an iron-gray sky. I'm running down a not-too-soggy forest path; or I glimpse myself running, as if taken by a movie camera trucking parallel to the path, through thrashing leafless boughs and moss-mottled tree trunks (oaks?). At the same time I'm drenched and winded, and my hands and bare legs are chilled by early March wind. I wear black shorts and an orange sweatshirt with Corpus Christi Tech printed across the chest. Coming to a clearing, I reenter my body.

Dressed in a long brown wool skirt, a steely-eyed woman is mounted bareback on a gray horse. The horse stands still near the edge of the clearing. A man facing the horse is trying to adjust its bit. The bit keeps slipping out of the horse's mouth. I offer to hold the bridle, and the man hands me the wet black reins. As he uses both hands to set the bit firmly between the horse's teeth, I skid on the grassless earth, pulling the bit loose again. Glancing at the soaked ground, the man shakes his head understandingly. I notice that the mud is so soft the horse's legs are sinking into it, and not only because of its weight: the woman is rocking her pelvis back and forth on the animal's back. I realize at once that she's wearing nothing under her long skirt and that she is rubbing her pubis against the bony gray crest.

The man takes a trowel from his back pocket and starts gouging runnels that lead from each of the horse's legs to lower ground. Pools form at a distance from the horse, which now stands on a low but firm mound. Strung beneath her jacket collar, a wafer-size medallion stamped with the astrological symbol of Aries hangs on the woman's breast. Her eyes close, her lips part; she raises the medallion she has been fingering to her mouth and bites it rapturously. The man, who I sense is German, takes out his penis and begins masturbating. He gestures to me with his free hand to follow his example. I try to comply, but though I am intensely aroused I cannot achieve an erection, and my member flaps woefully in the rain. I wake up crying.

I quickly fall asleep again, someplace in the American Far West, à la Delmer Daves. An old wooden ranch house overlooks prairies and woodland. In a rocking-chair on the porch of the house, a middle-aged woman dressed in black sits with a shotgun on her lap, gazing into the distance. She says I'm a fool not to go on subdividing the sections of my classification system. As I start telling her that I have already

done so, I wake up, abruptly aware that this is what I
A II/b.3   should be doing right now, even with so little sleep.
(No medicines since last Friday, three days in all. No
problems, either.)

Some time left for incept disposal.

TUESDAY, 8:30 A.M.

A I/b.2   Breakfast with Gert: ham, cheese, bread and butter
(more for me than for him). We ate early. He was eager
for the start of the day's action; I wanted to get to the
office and write. I took Daisy's standard tea and melba
A I/a.3   toast to her room. Today she expressed no surprise but
thanked me warmly enough – in fact, she embraced me
at such length my impatience must have shown. She
laughed at that. "Don't jump on any moving trams!
But you've got a spot on your knee – no, the other
A II/b.3   one." How did I get mud on my pants in this weather?
I brushed most of it off (wetting would have spoiled
the crease). Today's outfit: old blue cotton jacket, white
shirt, no tie (for a change), beige slacks, and sneakers,
A I/b.3   since I might get into a demo. Gert was waiting in battle array. We sallied out into the warm, sunny day.

I was not the only one to arrive early. Mr. Valde just
stopped by to ask if I would "mind summarizing an
up-to-date report" on the problematical clamp. Mind!
He knew I'd have to say yes. I almost refused, then
took the papers with a cursory nod that I trust decently
B II/b.2   expressed my mind. My plans are ruined. I couldn't
care less about these shitty clamps, at least not now.
People like Mr. Valde turn work into degradation. I
hope I see Maganoff again someday. He'll respect my
feelings on this score.

A II/b.2   I took my revenge; although "took" suggests a deliberateness I can't claim. "It" took me, "it" being the need to expand my classification procedure as I'd foreseen. My "insight" – that the culture subdivision (A I/b) should "obviously" include two sections – seemed

B II/b.2   pathetic. Why two, when five was an obvious minimum? But this specific point was the least of my worries; I was more concerned about my other activities. I scarcely have time for culture now, whatever I mean by the word (something to investigate under B II/b.2, or possibly .3?): so many other concerns are practically forced on me, and one of my goals in perfecting my

B I/a.3   recording technique is to accept them without resentment. I do need time, more and more of it, not simply

B I/a.1   to record but to see and notice. This morning (I put on my reading glasses for the occasion) I had a more than cursory glance at my stool, partly because it had an element of *diaré* (I know my French spelling is wretched, but I hate our word for it), and saw that it was laced with blood. If I can attend to my shit, I can attend to the world's shit, too. My closer look was more affectionate than clinical (is this possible?) – it wasn't clinical at all. Here's what I require from an efficient method of notation: more time for seeing, more time for others. And more time for my work: the half hour (maybe more) that I devoted to this problem will benefit Mr. Valde as much as me, and he'd know that if he had a particle of imagination. But there's not

A I/a.3   one chance in $2^2 \times 5^2$ of that. Fritz warned me twice to watch out. I told him I *had* been watching out; Mr. Valde has not been spotted in our neighborhood.

"Anyway, what am I doing that's so reprehensible?" "I don't know, but obviously it's more interesting than your job. It's not just him. He has eyes."

B I/b.2 (Review of possibilities: he didn't mean Paul or himself, unless he has acutely divided loyalties. That leaves:

Louis, who inhabits another part of the floor; I never see him

Stan: possibly; if so, his public absorption in football standings and his daughter's abortion or whatever it is that's making him look so revolting suggests that he missed a great acting career

Edith: does see Mr. V. a lot, us not much

Tangerine: conceivable, but not by me. [But that's me. It has to be one of the women]

Cherry: impossible, in spite of being my most frequent visitor)

A I/a.3 Around this time – I had returned to my own work – Paul came in for a copy of the clamp report. Spurred
A I/b.2 by remorse at disserving my best friend, I promised to bring it to him in twenty minutes, and did so. (Mr.
A I/a.3 Valde should have seen what I'm capable of.) He asked me to stay while he looked it over. He said, all too casually, that he might not be working here much longer. Jago was looking into a position in his company that was more interesting and better-paid. Why not? Paul is talented enough to call his shots. I congratulated him, but I wanted to cry. He added that he was discussing the details at dinner with Jago this

evening. "Give Colette my love." "I won't be seeing Colette. It's the two of us." My withheld tears evaporated. I took my leave.

B II/b.1   Memorial: before returning home from the seaside, Colette and I decided we must renounce being lovers – or *she* decided. On our last afternoon together, she spoke to me with a determination that made my wishfulness clumsy, brandishing ready-mades such as "Obviously we can't go on like this!" (In difficult moments why does everybody fall back on the dialogue of '30s movies? Are they in fact the supreme authority for our sentiments?) I acquiesced. I had no ground to stand on but my pleasure, my eternal-holiday rapture in fucking and being fucked by this woman whom I hardly knew outside the inexhaustible rehearsals of her own rapture. I also knew that our affair was in some way complete, and that C. was wise in getting us to move on; but where could we go? One slack day at the office, I invited her out to lunch – "a quiet lunch, someplace you like." She accepted, on other terms. (As the poet says, "Women are wiser than words," and she heard right through mine.) For an improvised, plausible reason, she claimed that she could not leave home. I must come there for lunch, and early, too; so I did, and we thus had time to discuss our way out of abstinence and back into bed. We knew at once that this "lapse" would be our rule: we could not give up such enchanted opportunities of joy, certainly not I, older and all too sure that this revelation might be the last. We both knew what our choice meant and had sense enough to talk about it. We belonged to a compact, happy group – Daisy and I, Jago and she, and Paul, who was chronically unattached to anyone but us. C. and I were setting up an asymmetrical pairing that if revealed would bring misery to the others, and to us the double misery of losing two irreplaceable sources of happiness. We swore not only everlasting passion but everlasting prudence.

Back in my office I immediately phoned Daisy to tell her I'd be home very late in the evening. By now it was well past noon; I wasn't hungry but thought I'd better eat something. I hadn't brought so much as a Mars bar, the thought of which supplied the appetite I needed. I was preparing to go out for a snack when a familiar silhouette loomed in my door: Maganoff, dressed in the same clothes as yesterday, yet somehow *cleaner*. I didn't mind the interruption. I was glad to see him, and not only for what he held in his big hands: a bottle of red wine and two bulging baguette sandwiches (I wondered: unwrapped, therefore stolen?). I stood up: "What a nice surprise!" "Not really. No cop is going to look for me in your office." He put the provisions on my desk. I fetched glasses and paper towels. When I came back he'd begun eating. Each sandwich contained a layer of cured beef on a bed of mixed salad – lettuce, celery, carrots, radishes, fennel. Maganoff said the deli's title for this was "Bismarck in his garden." "They even call the wine something exotic – *refosco*, I think. What's wrong with the local name?" He filled our glasses. I bit into my Bismarck – not bad, except too much bread.

Maganoff was not in a talking mood. I asked him

why. "Sometimes I listen to myself, and it sounds as though what I think about Ivan Lendl matters." "You watch tennis?" "I love it. That doesn't make me a tennis player. But it reminds me I exist. Like driving from midtown out to the thruway: I know a back route one and a half minutes faster than anybody else's, except for the four hundred and twenty-one other drivers who know the same back route, and if I'm so clever, I must be alive." He was making me uneasy. It wasn't like yesterday.

Maganoff emptied his glass. I knew there wouldn't be enough wine. He abruptly said, "Yesterday was a party; today's a lot more righteous. Serious types are starting to run things, and others will buy in. It's not easy being your own lively self. It's easier to hook up to a reasonable leader. Or be a good father. Or identify mushrooms." I winced.

I asked what he'd done since yesterday. He only said that he'd been to see Alex Rudkin at Lincoln Hospital. "Burn from a tear-gas canister, nothing much. He could leave now, except his father, who got him into the place, is pulling rank to keep him there unless he promises to stay home for the duration. It evidently doesn't matter that Alex is a consenting adult. Dr. Rudkin's back in business using his prestige for the 'good' of his son. And I'll bet you a Bismarck to a Swain he doesn't enjoy it."

I offered to intervene. "Can you set fire to his car and dacha? That might do it. Talking won't. He's already had all his answers carved for eternity. In soap." "Why don't you have a few sexy students gang up on him?" Maganoff took me seriously: "That *would* work. He has erotic fantasies, at least. You have more than fantasies, don't you? And if you also love your wife, I'll believe that, too." I was so taken aback I whispered, in a spasm of fright, "Does Gert know?" Maganoff guffawed. "*I* didn't. I meant you don't look like someone settled into domestic routine." I was dizzy with shame. "I'd be sick if Gert found out." "Don't you know him better than that? What are you scared of? Not Gert." (Not Gert; but I *am* afraid. I haven't yet had time to find out of what.) I said, "I'm not sure what kind of new world you're planning, but I don't think I could take it." "No plans. Except to get rid of planners — hierarchy is what survives every struggle. It's what has to go." (I can't wait to tell Mr. Valde.) "Everything else we need is already here. Sex should saturate life, the way it does. My cock is longing to find a universe it can love the way it loves itself." "That's why you've been tying up traffic for two days?" He laughed. "Dynamite works faster, I know. But real freedom can blow away all the shit in the world. You know, when Pavlov's lab was flooded, some dogs drowned, but the ones that didn't forgot to salivate when the next bell rang." He stood up. "Gert tells me you've had troubles. Come on down and you'll see what I mean." "I wish I could." "Don't get stuck in it." I said that keeping this record of my life was helping. "Great. I write a lot myself. Never a dull moment." We said good-bye, and I started taking notes.

Other notes: back to the pebble in yesterday's shoe. After what Gert told me last night, possibility #4

BI/b.2

AI/b.2

BI/b.1

: 94 :

("Something else") clearly applies, without precluding the possible relevance of the other three. Simply put, Gert went to see Colette. But that raises a new question: why did neither Gert nor Colette tell me spontaneously about their meeting? On reflection I once again came up with four rational hypotheses:

1. Family affection. Gert may have become aware (as he did last week with Paul and Jago) how much he'd been taking Colette for granted. This version appeals to me, not because I ever take Colette for granted but because nothing could surprise me less than that anyone, and especially my dear and complicated son, should find Colette likable and indeed lovable and worth an impulsive visit at any time of the day or month. If only I could call on her so nonchalantly! This does not, however, explain why I wasn't told about it.

2. An accidental meeting. I can imagine Colette out shopping and running into Gert between demos. He stops, surprised and pleased but knowing he mustn't tarry. Colette fusses over him with almost maternal concern, making sure he's not hurt and hasn't forgotten to eat. Such a meeting is more likely to have gone unmentioned because it was brief and happened in the midst of other preoccupations.

3. Gert consulted C. about his problem (whatever it may be, and if it exists). It's conceivable that neither would then volunteer a report to me (to "spare" me?), though this is improbable in C.'s case. Loyal discretion about Gert's secret would not take precedence over loyal indiscretion to me – she may be fond of him, but

not to the extent of risking my confidence in her.

4. Something else. What else could there be?

One guess: yesterday's meeting was not the first but one of several. This would of course eliminate hypotheses 1 and 2; in the case of 3 it would exacerbate the mystery of why C. kept me so thoroughly in the dark. On the other hand, if the explanation was simply a desire not to upset me, another irritation regarding C. would also be removed. On recent occasions she has spoken to me less than frankly. Her account last Friday of her "coffee with Paul" had the ring of fabrication. Did she have coffee with Gert instead? When I called her next day, she put off my proposed visit, and that afternoon she would not tell me who was with her, or that anyone was with her. How did she spend her time Sunday while the rest of us were at the lake? Later on it was a woman's voice I heard in the background, not Gert's, and nothing proves he was there earlier – it's only a possibility, and I prefer it to the possibility that she was with someone else and didn't tell me about *him.* Nothing proves that Gert has turned to her with his insufferably, ridiculously secret albeit hypothetical problem; but it *would* have given him a reason for seeing her confidentially. During all the time we spent on the phone yesterday, I can't fathom how C. could give no hint of this.

A I/a.3   After Maganoff left, Stan came in and asked who he was. "That's what I thought – no mistaking that red mustache. What are you doing with a guy like that? People say he's a new Hitler type." I laughed. "I'm not kidding. He hangs out with bums. He's tough, too – a friend of mine goes to a gym where he works out, weights mostly, he's built like an ox. They say he stays out late and picks fights with drunks for the fun of beating up on them. And look what that bunch are doing to the university, wrecking the place, anything to get in the limelight." I said I'd found him interesting. "Don't believe a word of it! Was he armed? Not a gun, more like a knife in his right boot. Why doesn't somebody stick him in the clink and teach him an honest trade? Not that I'd want him cutting my hair. They should never have let him get into school here. When a creep like that starts getting ideas, it's murder."

B I/b.2   Can Stan possibly be right? I have a gullible side. Maybe Maganoff *is* a new Hitler.

A I/a.1   I finally remembered to call C. about meeting her this evening. While the number was ringing, a steely feeling came over me so that when she answered, the first words out of my mouth were, "Why didn't you say you'd seen Gert?" After a least pause, no doubt due to my bluffness, she laughed and answered, "But I see Gert all the time! Not *all* the time, but from time to time. The more the better. I adore him. He's your son, remember?" C. knows how to charm me. I informed her that I'd learned Jago was going out and I'd told Daisy I had a business engagement, but the only business I had in mind was her. Where could we meet — possibly at her place? C.: "If only you'd called me earlier! Now I've been asked out to dinner, and I accepted because I never dreamed you'd be free." "So call back and say you can't come. Tell them your mother was murdered." Colette smiled audibly as she replied,

"Darling, with this hostess it won't work. It's Daisy." I longed to inflict real pain on myself. I'd pissed the day away. If I'd called her this morning after I spoke to Daisy, I could have had what I wanted. I said something like, "I see, that's funny, I'll talk to you later," managing to end our exchange as curtly as I'd begun it: I needed to salvage something of my hopes. I phoned Daisy to explain that my business dinner had fallen through and that I would be home early. I had a story ready to make this plausible, but Daisy showed no surprise (does she take me for some kind of flibbertigibbet?). She expressed no pleasure, either. I was unprepared for that. I said I thought she liked me to come home for dinner. Naturally, she replied, but this evening she and Colette had counted on having a long conversation about Paul — she'd invited her only after I'd told her I would be out. I said, "That's preposterous. I know Paul much better than Colette does. If you have to discuss him, why not with me? And what am I supposed to do now — take my 'Bismarck in the Shade' and go sit in the park?" A pause. "Are you okay, darling? Of course you should come home. You *must.* We won't only talk about Paul. It doesn't matter. It can wait."

B II/b.1   Memorial (emerging as I wondered, after hanging up, What's she after?): Paul, Daisy, and I met at the start of our first year at university. In a neighborhood traditionally frequented by students, we had all taken rooms in the same small house. This made our meeting inevitable, but not the immediate complicity that sprang up between us — an undeclared allegiance that became central to our lives. Hardly a day passed without our sharing a meal, and we took every opportunity available to discuss our particular concerns – our courses, politics, choice of music, books, and movies, our private anxieties and desires.

Across the street lived a woman student whose path often crossed ours and whom we came to know slightly. Paul found her attractive; the attraction increased when he learned that she had a steady boyfriend to whom she claimed to be devoted. This woman's name was Märtchen, baptismally Margarete, which her German parents had oddly shortened otherwise than to the usual Gretchen. Her boyfriend was one of several Harrys I remember from those years.

For a week or two Paul persevered in his courtship without success. Kept informed, Daisy and I were convinced that his charm and dauntless enthusiasm for womankind would triumph. But he finally turned to us for help. I felt too inexperienced to be of use, but Daisy responded to his appeal promptly and almost aggressively.

Paul had reported that according to Märtchen, Harry was "hard as nails" and would never tolerate her seeing anyone else. Daisy had her doubts about this. She asked Paul for a free hand.

We knew the café where Märtchen and Harry went for coffee or beer in the late afternoon and evening. With me in attendance, Daisy became a regular customer. On our fourth visit we joined the couple at their table. "Hard" or not, Harry was impressively tall and muscular and moved like someone sure of his strength. Afterward Daisy confided, "He's a baby. It's the Kraut who's tough."

During the next days a few casual questions gave Daisy the information she needed: the times when Märtchen was busy at school and Harry came to the café alone. We scheduled our visits accordingly and found him on our third try, early on a midweek afternoon.

We sat down at his corner table, with Daisy between us. She turned the conversation to the subject of his physique. She admitted it frightened her. She hoped Märtchen was stalwart, because she herself could not imagine making love to such a colossus (she looked tiny enough at his side). Harry protested. He was anything but a brute; anyway, he wasn't as big as all that. "No?" said Daisy. "Look at your wrists. I'll bet they're twice as thick as mine." She raised her left forearm and with her right thumb and middle finger encircled her own slim wrist. "I'd need both hands to get around yours." Harry obligingly extended a bared and hairy arm. Daisy took it into her small hands, and I cannot say exactly what she then did (I would one day learn what miracles she could effect with mere fingertips), but Harry blushed, his mouth fell open, and his body stiffened, then slumped in pleasure. "You see?" Daisy innocently continued. "You are big. Strong, too, I bet. If you are, I've got ten cartons of books waiting to be carried up to my room." Harry dazedly nodded. Daisy glanced at me: "That's good news for you, at least." I said I'd take care of the check. Not letting go of Harry's arm, Daisy led him away.

Her success brought unexpected results. From the start Daisy had instinctively disliked Märtchen. What Harry told her confirmed her suspicions: Märtchen was domineering, unimaginative, cold. Daisy found Harry himself appealing and fearfully naive. Märtchen was his first lover, he felt deeply obliged to her, and she encouraged his illusion that she had sacrificed herself on his behalf. Daisy had no desire to take Märtchen's place, but she liked Harry enough to help him out of his entanglement. Since she now saw no point in abetting Paul's courtship, she resolved the issue by bringing Paul and Harry together and making friends of them. They shared a passion for postwar black jazz, so she invited them together to listen to Cecil Taylor records bought for the occasion. She introduced both to younger women whom she went out of her way to recruit. She told Paul fearsome lies about Märtchen — she was a neo-Nazi, she was addicted to raw onions, she enjoyed making love only at the peak of her menstrual flux. Paul never learned that she had seduced Harry. In these circumstances Harry somewhat neglected Märtchen, who obligingly made a scene during which she declared he must behave or get out, which he promptly did. At Daisy's urging, Paul took Harry's side in the dispute — a move that ruined his chances with Märtchen and in fact his interest in her. I don't know how Daisy disengaged herself from Harry. I still find it incredible that anyone benefiting from her attentions should not fall in love with her. That was what I did as a result of these events: the despair I felt that afternoon when she left the café on Harry's arm was too horrible to contemplate enduring again.

A I/a.3 After I'd spoken to Daisy, Cherry came in, with "something on her mind." I waited; at last, forcing a smile, she said, "It doesn't bother *me*, but when you make private calls, maybe you should keep it down." I was dumbfounded. I managed to thank her.

B II/b.2 Having no urge to think about what she meant, I distracted myself with my split-ring notes. I always carry them in one of my pockets these days. Of late I've consulted them all too rarely; I've hardly developed my first ideas at all. If only Paul hadn't become so busy with this and that, I could have confided in him. With his engineering know-how and my ideas, we would have quickly found concrete propositions to present to Mr. Valde and our colleagues. So I'll do it on my own. Maganoff is right about some things – "The future started this morning. If I'm waiting for it now, I've died in the meantime." Go split rings! There'll be a chance to promote them in a day or two. Why hesitate? I'm not asking Mr. Valde for anything, I'm giving him something.

B I/b.3 (Another venture occurred to me last night. Nothing to do with the split ring or the company. Nonreflecting glass for eyeglasses: there would be millions in it. The glint is what makes glasses noticeable. Customers would be lining up around the block. Is this worth exploring?)

A II/b.3 Getting on the tram to go home, I found I'd left my
A I/a.3 monthly pass at the office. To my relief, the driver recognized me. I explained what had happened. He shook

his head: rules were rules. I had to pay. He didn't even apologize when he said this. As I started to protest, he broke in with a loud "Next!" I stepped back onto the sidewalk, awash in rage. I shouted (screamed, really), "I've been riding with you every week for years! You son of a bitch! You asshole!" I turned away with a vision of yanking him out of his seat onto the pavement and poking holes with my fountain pen into his self-righteous face.

B I/b.2

I noticed a buzzard staring down at me from its perch on the crown of a plane tree. I shuddered with humiliation — not only public shame but disgust with myself. How could I surrender to such repulsive feelings? I began walking up and down the sidewalk while I waited for the next tram.

B II/b.3

A I/b.2

As I did so, I enjoyed an "encounter." Not a true hallucination, alas, but a rapid mental elaboration of an object in my field of vision: one of the old-fashioned wooden barrels our municipality uses as trash baskets. Out of it, in my mortified solitude, I concocted a strange companion: a creature about forty centimeters in diameter, spherical except for a slight flattening at the apex, and mobile. I could not decide whether it should move on feet, wheels, or casters. The shell that englobed it was made of overlapping gray-brown shingles, each at least six centimeters across. In the midst of this rough surface two upper shingles popped open to reveal pink, almost red eyes that peered up at me with a sheepish mixture of discretion, reproach, and understanding. The appearance of this companion — it at once began following me as I paced

B II/b.2

to and fro – soothed my agitation. I was especially fascinated by the location of the eyes: they occasionally snapped shut and stayed shut for nearly a minute, until I forgot exactly where I had last seen them. I decided that they remained in one place, but of this I was never entirely sure. Why, after all, must two special shingles correspond to points that could perfectly well revolve underneath the shell according to changing need? But my conviction that the eyes did not shift invisibly but stayed in place behind particular shingles gave me real satisfaction. Not so great perhaps as that derived by Lichtenberg when he observed that a cat's eyes are so precisely placed behind the slits in its face. The present correspondence hardly suggested the unquestionable existence of God. It did, however, suggest the unquestionable existence of me.

A II/b.3   The shingle ball coasted at my side as I once again approached the oncoming tram. Bunches of tall blue asters were being sold by an Asian on the corner. The world's sounds crept back into my hearing: traffic starting and stopping at the streetlight, chatter among those in line for the tram, percussive sizzle issuing from button-size earphones on the head of the youth

A I/a.3   in front of me. I paid the normal fare. From the win-
A II/b.3   dow I noticed the wealth of vegetation this city offers – at a fruit stand, piles of grapes, peaches, apricots, plums, and pears; the massed varied flowers of a florist's sidewalk display; planes and linden trees along an

B II/b.3   avenue; periwinkles and salvia at the center of a traffic circle. I consoled myself by thinking that my outburst with the tram driver would have its use: it will break the routine of events I record.

A I/a.3   Needless to say, on arriving home, after a quick hug,
A II/b.3?   I went straight to my desk to start writing. I haven't
B II/b.1   written so much since my finals at the university. I
remember the topic: "Gargani has said, 'Explanation
intervenes where understanding is absent, that is, when
all hope of understanding has been lost.' What concept of knowledge does this statement imply?" For
four hours I filled page after page. What has become
of all those ideas?

A II/b.3   No time for calisthenics, but I stole five minutes for
a hot bath. My knees emerged from the foam like primordial islands.

TUESDAY, 11 P.M.

A II/b.3   At the risk of betraying my goal of including everything, I must concentrate my descriptions of events.
It's their rhythm that's hard to catch. Externals can
A I/b.2   readily be noted – e.g., this evening Daisy wore vel-
vet slippers, a loose ankle-length skirt of light flannel
(I think) and the darkest of blues, a white blouse with
long sleeves and high neck (meaning it came right up
to the throat), and two bracelets. Colette had on the
same lovely dress she wore out to dinner with us last
week, with a new scarf of gauzy patterned green that
made her eyes yet more beautiful. I didn't dress up
(trusting to my maroon polka-dot neckerchief for
panache): gray slacks, brown linen jacket, pale-blue
shirt, house shoes. Before dinner we opened some fizzy
chardonnay that Jago had asked Colette to bring for
my opinion.

A I/a.3   Whatever the three of us expected didn't happen.
Fragments of our expectations appeared during the

meal. Colette at one point suggested that Daisy follow an iron-rich diet she'd heard of (Daisy had mentioned how tired she'd been feeling). Later Daisy ventured to ask Colette about our ailing plum tree, since Colette has all those trees in back of her place (I instantly smelled them, with retroactive, slightly embittered delectation). I fished for hints of exactly what it was about Paul that the women would have discussed if I hadn't come home (only one thing could have kept me away, and she was here). None of us got far.

Gert had also come home. His intentions squashed ours with a force fueled by two days of activism. He arrived four minutes before we sat down to eat, unkempt, unclean, and frazzled. In four minutes, to the astonishment of everyone except perhaps Colette, he went to his room, into the bathroom (roaring waters), and back to his room, to reappear scrubbed and impeccable. No need to scratch one's cranium for an explanation of this untypical feat. Gert beamed at Colette, begged to sit next to her, from the beginning to the end of dinner talked to her (or at least *at* her), and sometimes made her talk to him. Colette obliged him, politely doing her best to include us in the conversation, whereupon Gert always found a way to return to center stage – at one point, to my amazement, because I'd said Maganoff viewed our society the way the Greeks viewed the end of the world, he made a brilliant distinction between the Hallstatt and La Tène periods (brilliant but irrelevant: the Greek Iron Age was *not* historical). I didn't feel offended by what happened. I finally learned what Gert had been up to during the past two days, not to mention other things he would never have confided to me. Only one moment distressed me: today he had again met Colette, and no one had told me. He didn't tell me now: after letting slip his "like what you said this afternoon," he blushed and clasped his head in his hands like a silent-movie comic, adding unconvincingly, "I'm crazy – whenever it was, yesterday, I guess."

Do such things matter? I'll have to think more about that. At the time I looked away from Colette, I looked away from everyone, I studiously dropped my napkin and retrieved it with second-counting awkwardness. My sadness didn't last. I soon realized that I was anything but sad. A sense of blessing filled me. I was sitting with the three people I most care about and sharing a meal with them, even if "sharing" doesn't strike the right note – it felt as though each of us were making a gift of the food to the others. And what food! First a kind of pie with olives and onions that Daisy proclaimed a *pissaladière*, which in the wake of Bismarcks and Swains suggests "Pisser in the salad" – delicious. Roast chicken stuffed with a cloud of parsley, garnished with horns-of-plenty and sautéed string beans. A "plain" green salad. Hard cheese. Raspberries in lemon juice, sugar optional. A solid if youngish cabernet franc. If only I could have simply watched and listened and tasted – but –

Odds and ends:

A II/b.2   After the comfort of peeing in the washbasin,
A I/a.3   remember to wipe off the edge. Far more than by the

act, Daisy is disgusted by the yellow spots (really orange: rusted-autumn-leaf orange).

B II/b.2   Can I persuade someone to murder Mr. Valde? Bad idea. In his way I almost like him. But he should suffer. Maybe saw off his toes one by one, one per hour, not counting meal breaks? But messy! Arteries must extend into the toes.

A I/a.3   Daisy said Pater called me three times at the office
(a.1)   during lunch hour (won't the old bugger ever listen?) and never got more than a "big click for his pains." While I was talking to Maganoff the phone occasionally rang and I would rattle the receiver to cut off the call. Maganoff looked perplexed when I did this. Maybe that was what made him think I had "another woman."

B II/b.2   Another invention: tongue picks – i.e., toothpick-like caps fitted to the end of the tongue to clear the interstices in the beloved's teeth while kissing. Unsalable – "unpalatable."

A I–II   Exactly what have I left out today? Reviewing my nineteen categories, I see that three are empty. When I identify one of them as "Correspondence" I want to bludgeon myself for forgetfulness – for downright callousness. Not that Sukik's letter matters that much,

A I/a.2   but it gripped me when I read it on the tram home. He has written to say he no longer plans to move here. He has two uncles on his father's side (actually second cousins once removed); they are twins, aged 87. Sukik has been devoted to them because they are the only relatives he has left. He has always visited them regularly at their house outside the little town where he lives. He writes that their closest friend, two years their junior, had stayed in this house for the past three decades and four months earlier died of a stroke. Why Sukik has gone into these details can be explained by his almost offhand revelation of the friend's sex. He writes that the death required no "divine fortitude" on the twins' part, since the stroke had left their friend in such pitiful condition that the end came as a deliverance – on the day of the death, in fact, they had taken up smoking as a kind of homage, "since she had done so with such pleasure" five years earlier. Nothing except this solitary *she* shows that the friend was a woman. Sukik then tells how all of this concerns him: it is not, as I expected, that he now feels obliged to look after his cousins; they refuse to leave *him* alone. Every evening they come to visit him; on his days off they arrive before lunch. Their purpose is to persecute him. At first Sukik thought they were trying to turn him into a replacement for their lost friend, but hints dropped during their very first visit soon developed into outright accusations: the twins assert that Sukik is responsible for their friend's death. He had neglected her shamefully and done his best to poison her relationship with them and so destroy her well-being. When she was hospitalized, he rarely went to see her, certainly not on that last fatal day when, knowing that his uncles had been detained at home, he alone could have comforted her. ("And on that day," writes Sukik, "I was away on business – hundreds of miles away!") Sukik understandably believes the twins are going mad. Unfortunately they exhibit no overt symptoms of madness. Their admonitions are couched in language that is courteous. When they address the topic with their acquaintances in town, they do so in judicious terms. Sukik feels trapped. He cannot move elsewhere until he has cleared himself of his cousins' insinuations (he has already had problems with his neighbors) and — a much harder task — made sure they are properly cared for. He is therefore withdrawing his plea for my help in finding a place in our town.

(A I/a.2)   In a necessarily short reply I pointed out that I had already advised him not to move here and was glad my advice had proved well founded.

A I, II   The other empty categories are A I/b.1 (culture & entertainment) and B I/a.2 (things heard). I have nothing for them: I haven't had ten minutes to spare for my reading (not even the morning paper because on the tram I talked to Gert), and since I've spent my whole day *listening* to people there was never a chance for *hearing* anything. Anyway it's not this or that category, it's the overall problem I can't master. The more I put in, the more I leave out. I'm glad I got down most of what Maganoff said, but I missed how he looked and moved (and didn't move), and the light outside while he spoke, and the crows in the plane tree. What about my fierce intestinal spasm when he arrived (I thought, Add an asshole lock to your inventions)? What was Mr. Valde wearing (something dismal) or Cherry (something nice)? What does Cherry look like *from one moment to the next*? How can I salvage such realities and write coherent paragraphs? Should I stop writing coherent paragraphs, let incerpting worm into the telling, why not? But that's a delusion — what Sukik's incoherent letter was like. This is why I didn't simply refer to it: I recorded *my* reading of it, something very different from what he wrote. Better go on perfecting my categories. I should do that in any case.

B II/a.1 [WEDNESDAY,] 12:30 A.M.
I dozed for a few minutes and dreamed — not like an ordinary dream; events happened in a penumbra like black metallic dust. About Sukik — revenge for my criticizing his letter? Sukik, the twins, and their friend. I "knew" that one twin had left to visit the friend in the hospital. Sukik was with the other, fucking wildly, the two churning one another in a darkness of cowshed or coal cellar.

A II/b.3 I woke up disagreeably aroused. I felt pressure directly below my Adam's apple. I thought I heard a nightingale outside. Nothing on my desk but paper. Why don't I ever have flowers?

A I/b.2 Something has to be considered, not now.
There's more than writing left undone:

A II/b.2 — exercises (due to late return)
A II/b.1 — accounting (okay — itemized expenses kept)
A II/a.1 — reading (*Young Days*) (see above)
B I/a.2 — developing observational skills. Possible complementary category: developing inner skills — watching & listening to *myself* (or *oneself*? Which is correct here? Not necessarily the same.) Does Maganoff count?

: III :

A II/b.3   — no contribution to the household, nary a dish washed. Yes: Daisy's breakfast.

A I/b.2   These negligences could be avoided by better record keeping. I'm not waiting till tomorrow to make the obvious improvements in my categorizing. "Obviously" there will be more than these few now apparent to me:

A
- I/a.3a = speech
  - .3b = other (e.g., necking)
- I/b.1a = theatrical & all away-from-home events
  - .1b = other
- II/a.1a = books
  - .1b = other
- II/b.2a = medicine (not only medicines)
  - .2b = exercise, diet
- II/b.3a = things not done
  - .3b = other

B
- I/b.1a = Daisy
  - .1b = Gert
- I/b 2a = C.
  - .b = others
- II/b.3a = developing inner skills
  - .3b = other

B II/1.3a "Now apparent to me": a long day, undoubtedly, and that delicious pinot noir. Half the bottle of bubbledom for me myself and I and, with each course, one two three glasses of the red. It adds up. It subtracts. Stop. As of the last glass. Cold duck no, cold turkey yes. Undeniable regret: by breakfasttime I imagine noon and evening moments of surge and ease (I admit this). I won't always be drinking with Maganoff, Colette, and Daisy. I drink with myself anyway, whoever's around, and why not? Keeps the iron out of my rust-prone soul. Let the iron in, and my wits with it. It seems I'll be needing them.

B I/a.1 A last look outside: hazed darkness, two stars in the west, five in the east. Mars? I swim up into the flourishing field of light, thinking of bread and wine, listening to night slugs gnashing their understandable vegetable ways.

WEDNESDAY, 6:30 A.M.

B II/a Across flat wooded ground that reminds me of the walnut plain up north, my younger sister and her brother who looks so much like her come towards me hand in hand, draped in pre-Raphaelite veils that ill conceal aging bodies under their adolescent faces. The faces keep changing, as if into those of cousins I never knew. I try to run away but can't, being ankle-deep in snugly sticky earth. They stop before reaching me and continue to walk in place. Their veils are turning into family skin – I think, Next of skin. They are becoming unattractively naked. They constantly switch features. I start seeing ideas I'm having about them, not

: 113 :

wishing to: I'm convinced these are other people, with only the bodies of sister and brother. As soon as I admit this, the faces come back into focus, the figures move freely once again and come nearer. The couple pick me up as if to bathe me. No words emerge from their lips. My sister lays me down on her brother. I struggle: "Why him?" From a distance a girl's voice says, "He thinks we're different." I feel his skin against mine. Someone is stretching full-length in the earth. There's a quiet pleasure in this. I yield. My sister is gone. Why? I start punching the other face: no response. The person under me is my sister – the person who looks like my sister, I remind myself. In a zombie's voice she says, "Dear sir, this is entirely for your benefit." She dissolves into the soil.

I'm standing on a stepladder in an old wood-paneled, high-ceilinged library. I've taken a book about Florence from the shelf in front of me, something like an 1890s Baedeker. Two older men are chatting at the foot of the ladder, one of them grasping its legs to steady it, leaning against it. The men walk over to a far corner of the room and sit down in leather armchairs in front of an elliptical table. The older of the two is dressed in a dark-red smoking jacket, black silk trousers, and a cream-colored silk shirt with a paisley ascot swelling neatly at its throat; the other wears a gray, almost black single-breasted mohair suit, a mauve and white striped shirt, and a polka-dot tie (pale yellow on dark blue) with a gold pin under its knot. Both sport slippers of cheap checked-gray felt. Their remote features remain as distinct and as foreign as those of celebrities in a newsreel. I can't make sense of what I'm reading about Florence, except I know that the Palazzo Numero Uno does not exist. I do not care about these men since they do not care about me. They talk louder: "You can't get a crêpe suzette to settle down unless you're French." I listen closely. "Are you referring to my sister?" the other man asks — does he mean *my* sister? "I'm talking about *him*," the first answers. The space between me and the others feels infinite, loneliness assaults me, but I don't give in to it. When I next look at them, a woman in male evening attire is standing erect behind one armchair. I long to go over and be taken in her arms. "It's not him," one of the voices declares; then, to the woman, "Madam, this has nothing to do with you." She slaps the speaker hard enough to pitch him sideways out of his chair.

I decide to read about Palazzo Numero Uno. The description abounds in terms like *trabeations* and *architraves*, terms whose meanings I have many times learned and forgotten. In the portal stands an immense and wonderful wrought-iron gate. It is decorated with intertwined snakes, paired wings, fig branches drooping with first fruit, hermetic figures with arms pointing left or right (except for one, at the center of the work, whose arms point both left *and* right; it is adorned with a phallus thick as a fasces, reaching nearly to its chin and girdled from base to tip by two overlapping spiral coils). The guidebook recommends looking through the gate for our first view of the fountain in the courtyard beyond. I get only a glimpse: urns at the corners, at its back the sagging body of a spent young male being lowered to rest by two melancholy, monumental nymphs.

B II/b.3 I woke up telling myself, Now you know why you're alone and why you have to sob, this is what your everlasting neglect and cock-twiddling self-centeredness have got you, not to mention the aggressiveness and unkindness you show right and left, most of all towards those you claim you love. I lay in the dark not daring to sob – what would Nina think? That was the name I used, wanting to sob all the more (little fist-banging sobs against the puny struts of my talk-machine). I almost woke Daisy up (it was 4:30 A.M.) to tell her I knew but would she forgive me anyway? Lying there as still as I could, I became weightlessly light, floating on the soft mattress like an empty eggshell. This disagreeable sensation led me into another dream, but one of the waking kind. I watched myself make it up. A male victim is lying on a bed of massed down pillows thirty-four layers deep. He, too, feels light as an eggshell, barely sensing the billowing silk underneath him. As he waits in complete repose, anticipating he knows not what, a hammock appears, suspended a few yards above him. Loosely strung together out of flax strands, with melon-size apertures, slowly sinking down on him, the hammock contains, nestled in one of its apices, the oiled, honey-colored body of a young woman. Her pouting face is swathed in a mane of black ringlets, her lips and nails are cranberry-red; she wears only a gold chain necklace and a single gold anklet; one leg dangles through an opening in the hammock. As the tips of her toes approach him, the prone male cannot help wriggling in expectation – he sinks a little into the pillows. The woman twists her pelvis slightly; with her turned heel she kicks him brutally in the solar plexus, then from a paper bag at her side sprinkles handfuls of empty peanut shells over him. He has doubled up breathless from the kick; he now turns this way and that to escape the aggravating shells. Within moments he realizes that he must spread out his arms and legs to avoid being engulfed by the pillows. It is too late: down, down. Time passes. The hammock has been

B II/b.1 hoisted out of sight. A canvas sheet is draped over the mound, then roped into place. Not a tremor. – I had a fantasy of playing hide-and-seek where I hid in a trunk in the attic. When I dropped the lid of the trunk, its clasp flipped over and locked. No one came near enough to hear me. Or I hid under my parents' bed and it collapsed on top of me, everyone deserted the house to go on a picnic, and I was left with a crossboard of the box mattress jammed across my throat. Why had these things never happened? I deserved them. How I knew this lay beyond explanation. All my adolescent prayers stank of anxiety, supplication, rejection, dependency, wild hope, boredom, and despair, my bowed head in one hand, the other playing pocket pool.

A II/b.3   I slid out of bed, picked up my robe, and went to
A I/a.2   my desk. After finding Nina's letter to make sure of the address, I wrote her an apology not for my life but for my lifelong unfairness. "How could I forget the time we were together? Those months taught me so

much — *you* taught me. Your freshness and energy have remained to this day as vivid to me as in that season long past when we climbed together beyond the timberline into exotic domains of stone and grass, or pro-

B II/b.1

jected ambitious careers side by side in smoky cafés, or lay in one another's arms in contented exhaustion." And why did I then remember Nina's snoring, which used to rouse me at three in the morning like childhood nightmares? She said I snored, too, and of course

A I/a.2

that may have been true. I put the memory aside and continued my homage — all lies, imploring lies, but they let me pour my dejection and shame, which now

A II/b.2

included my shame at remembering her snores, into this belated tribute. I sealed the letter and put it straight into my briefcase. Daisy would be sick if she

B II/b.1

read it — sick with hilarity. She'd be right to laugh. I can recall scarcely anything about Nina that charmed or interested me. There must have been something. What I best remember is my panic at leaving her, an emotion I have done my best to ignore ever since. I *had* to lie to her, then and now; more generously now, I hope. All this remorse because one day we literally collided in a bookstore — we were milling around looking for course books, bumbling newcomers to the university, to life,

B II/b.3*b*

to expectations of life and love. Why do I have to drag these repulsive feelings through the years? Why did I have to have them in the first place?

B I/b.1*a,b*

In a while I'll make breakfast for Gert as well as Daisy.

B II/b.3*a*

Deciding to stop drinking was smart. Look at this morning's abrupt early waking with its conscience-blistering recollections, and the drained, dizzy feeling

I had for almost a minute when I got out of bed. Since I keep reminding myself to notice things, I might well start "noticing" the state of my health. I stumble from yesterday to tomorrow as though I never had anything worse than neck rash.

A II/b.2a   Here is a first list of signs and warnings gleaned from my sinful body after inspecting it from bottom to top:

- left foot: tendency to cramps in sole
- right foot: sore big toe (inner edge of nail? too-tight shoes?)
- left and right calves: little splotches that look like bruises but are painless and chronic
- left knee: when leg straightened, clicks
- left and right thighs: faint continuous muscular twitching beneath skin (not felt but visible)
- right thigh: spasms in big muscle in back
- left hip: slight soreness when I walk
- penis: urine dark, burns somewhat (*very* somewhat)
- perineum: summer(?) pruritus
- bowels: (viz. yesterday)
- back: "put-out" pain on right side since rotating tires (minor)
- diaphragm: as if blunt bone swallowed and stuck
- right hand: ligaments of 3rd and 4th fingers strained (last week, but how? pulling at something that wouldn't give, but what?)
- left hand: stable Dupuytren nodule (identified by Dr. Max Melhado)
- left elbow: funny-bone twinge when arm extended

— left and right shoulders: quasi-soreness when arms raised above head

— neck: slight crick on left side (from last night's position in bed?)

— mouth: after brushing teeth, chronic but not inevitable bleeding at 2nd left molar

— right cheek: superficial numbness (when did I first "not notice" this?)

— right eyelid: flutter when tired

— head: ache.

B II/b.3b This is a good start. Why do I find writing down these trivialities so comforting?

A II/b.3b It disgusts and depresses me to see everyone wearing summery clothes day after day, as in mid-July. I disgust and depress myself. At least *I* can stop. What do I have that's dark — black? "Black of night and of December" — that would show what a serious citizen I am, mourning my summer pruritus. But my *tux*? Only black jacket in the closet. Would I dare appear in the office with shiny lapels? Daisy and Gert would send for the nutcrackers. Shirt: Paul's penultimate Christmas present, silk, with my initials embroidered in cursive silver where a breast pocket might have been. Black jeans. And black shoes — a hard choice between patent leather, clodhoppers, and sneakers, but was life ever simple?

A I/b.2 I'm avoiding a basic problem whose name is incerpting. Last night (early today) I stuck with it till past 2 A.M. Each addition to the system means more time taken, at the least adding another page to my loose-leaf binder and locating it when needed. While listing my body omens I thought of putting each class of entries directly on a different sheet, but I already have 27 classes, with more to come (so I hope and fear). You or I or we may ask, so what? I'll tell you and us: it would bust up the continuity of my life on paper – i.e., would kill it – and this is the only place I succeed in thinking or at least in sustaining a reactive sequence of words while my body and mind carom (or succumb) off (or to) one thing and another.

Why not index? I thought of it and rejected it outright. Why do I resist it so? Wouldn't it save hours of copying?

Or perhaps writing in different colors. That means pencils. Enough colors available? (Made a note to check.) I could skip from yellow entry to yellow entry and reconstitute, e.g., all B II/b.3bs. Would that be better than a simple marking procedure? The entries are marked *already*.

WEDNESDAY, 10:30 A.M.

A II/b.3b After completing my early pages I had a careful breakfast of yogurt (2), toast, and tea with honey. I shit hardly anything; no blood but foamy mucus and multitudinous farting. My gum felt sorer.

A I/a.3b Making breakfast for the others was like Christmas Eve. I trod barefoot so as not to be heard. I set out Gert's ham, cheese, and bread in three rows of four alternating items, enough to require a serving platter. As it turned out, he wasn't hungry. I didn't mind because I'd enjoyed figuring out the pattern for arranging his food – it seemed capable of infinite

A I/a.3a symmetrical extension. Taking in Daisy's tray, Gert said he'd have a nibble of something with her.

A I/a.1 I phoned Paul. He was having breakfast, too. I asked him what he ate. "Slugs and snails and pollywogs' tails!" he cheerfully answered. I told him that I missed talking to him – that I needed him. "We see each other all the time, and what can you possibly need me for?" I said I was having a confused period and that anyway I felt our friendship deserved more than routine encounters. He chuckled and replied that our friendship didn't depend on anything in particular; as far as he was concerned, it was ineradicable and unspoilable. "I'm glad to hear it. But I do like to talk. Tell me," I added for no special reason, "are you enjoying the sporting life?" A ghostly pause followed, one long enough for me to send jittery feelers into the aural darkness looking for signs of disaster, for which there were no grounds except this horrendous silence, during which I asked myself, What did I say, what did I say? Paul answered in a level, crisper-sounding voice, "Why don't you join us? Games are more fun than pulling weights, or whatever it is you do. We can talk whenever you like."

B I/b.2 This is not true. That was why I called.

A I/b.2 Gert emerged in time for us once again to start off together. A tram showed up promptly. As I was paying
A I/a.3a for my ticket, I glimpsed cold eyes quickly averted: my antagonist of yesterday. When the last passenger had gotten on, I began apologizing. He stared down the road, his whole face clenched. Having spoken my piece,

I went to the seat Gert had saved me. But I could not leave matters there. I had publicly insulted this man, and he had every right to be disgusted with me. I walked back to the front of the bus to tell him so. I explained that when I yelled at him, it was because other circumstances had upset me and led me to behave in a way of which I was thoroughly ashamed. Unfortunately the tram reached its next stop before I finished, and the advent of new riders obliged me to interrupt myself until we were again under way. I then resumed, his obduracy notwithstanding – whenever I spoke, he began whistling "Playmates" (curious choice) through his stained teeth. He did not otherwise respond until, after yet another stop, when I again addressed him, he turned and hissed at me with repellent clarity, "I finally got to see the real you. For me, that's it." Shrugging my shoulders emphatically to signify to the perplexed onlookers the pointlessness of dealing with this bonehead, I returned to my seat. But my gesture did not express what I felt, which was that I was to blame, still to blame. I told Gert this. He shook his head: "Now you've seen the real *him*." "I treated him badly." "Good. That's what it took to flush him out. We need shits like him to show us how not to be." Maganoff *dixit*. For a while I stared out the window. This frostless autumn has tired the summer leaves, the summer leavings: they dry and curl and drop the more conspicuously as the hot light that so densely burdened them thins. Getting off the bus, I went straight to the ticket dispenser to buy a book of one-way tickets (12.00). When I next see that driver I shall

A I/a.3b

B II/b.2
A I/a.3a

B II/b.3b
B I/a.1

hand it to him with a written request to save it for passengers who've forgotten their passes. That should settle his hash.

A I/b.2   I next procured a box of sixty-eight Hermes colored pencils (40.00). I had expressly brought with me
A II/b.3*b* my nine days' output to make my experiment in "color-incerpting" conclusive. I could have saved my money. Many pencils produced handwriting so pale that it was hard to read, even with a familiar text. Worse, among the sixty-eight colors only seven were genuinely distinct; the rest were no more than gradations. To achieve sufficient variety, I would have had to resort to combinations of the basic colors. I calculated that by using pairings of blue, red, orange, green, brown, purple, yellow (closer to a beige), and black, I could dispose of thirty-five markers – that is, blue plus each of the other colors = 7, red plus the other colors except blue = 6, and so forth : $7 + 6 + 5 + 4 + 3 + 2 + 1 = 28$; together with the pencils used separately $(8) = 36$. This might work, but why bother? Was purple plus yellow that much quicker to identify than B II/b.3*b*, when I had the latter already in my head? Although I knew the answer, I conscientiously tried out the pencils.

B II/b.3*b* Allowing for their novelty, the colors were only mar-
A II/b.3*b* ginally quicker to read than my usual tabs, clumsy as they may be. I decided to stick to my present method. I then made another decision: I must drop my bias against indexing. I did so on the spot. It was as if the time spent on the color experiment had exhausted my capacity for resistance. Indexing had become obvious. Once the index is in place, adding a page number to

the appropriate entry at each appearance of a category will give me concise access to the subcontinuities I have so laboriously been reassembling by copying them out. Incerpting has value as a concept, but applying it so literal-mindedly costs time.

B II/b.3b A I/b.2 The relief I then felt swept away all projects but one, that of setting up my index. I glanced at my stack of company work — letters to suppliers, letters to new clients, letters to old clients, sales projections for a lightly glued lined pad with pages punched for loose-leaf binders. I wondered what the fuck I was doing here and also reminded myself that increased efficiency in A II/b.3b the handling of my daily resumés meant increased efficiency at the office. I gleefully opened a ream of fresh paper and began the Index on the top page.

B I/a.3b A I/b.2b About half an hour ago, as I leaned back to rest my eyes for a moment, my office doorway came into view. Paul, Fritz, and Mr. Valde stood there looking at me B I/b.2b with varyingly amiable degrees of wonder. Mr. Valde was wearing trousers of emphatically dismal gabardine (their color somewhere between clinker-black and the unknown vast), a blue-gray hounds-tooth-check sports jacket of (let's say) weathered linoleum, the inevitable white shirt half hidden by a broad brown tie apparently decorated with discarded finger-nails, and coal-colored loafers of genuine imported granite; Fritz a gray-green suit that had been nurtured to floppiness during the many years since its manufacture, a shirt so densely patterned that its motif defied identification, a solid puke tie, and brown wing tips dating from the reign of Franz Josef; Paul a handsome pseudo-mohair blazer (a blue and red foulard in its breast pocket), off-white shirt, white-on-burgundy polka-dot tie loosened under the open collar button, and dark-brown buck shoes. When my eyes met theirs, Paul reminded me in an oddly hurried manner that the morning mail drop was due, and did I have any letters going out? No, I answered, but they'd be ready for the afternoon drop. Mr. Valde asked, "Is that what you're working on now?" He was still smiling. "Mr. Valde," I answered, in a tone of no less smiling reproach, "you can see these aren't letters. But they'll get done, have no fear!" "Might I know exactly *what* it is you're so engrossed in?" "Mr. Val" (same playful tone), "surely my numerous years here entitle me to confidence. I only ask that so long as I get my job done, I be permitted to do it my own way." Mr. Valde nodded. "Of course." The three turned away. I heard them talking, about other matters, some distance down the hall. While answering Mr. V. I had conspicuously placed a company file on top of these very pages; I now addressed its contents with what I intended as conscientious determination. The first item required filling out an order form for fiberboard cut to dimensions suitable for single-tag systems, which meant dimensions changed a millimeter here and two millimeters there, which meant having to recalculate all the specifications (and what would be least inefficient: adapting previous orders filed I wasn't sure when or starting over from scratch — that is, lugging out enough manuals and log tables to design a bridge?). After ten minutes a figure I had not iden-

A I/a.3a

B I/a.2

A II/b.3b

tified vanished from my office door. I set the orders

A I/b.2 aside and went on catching up with my day. I had vir-
A I/a.3b tually done so when my sanctum was once again
invaded, this time by Cherry, nicer of course than Mr.
Valde but no less an interloper. Her attitude didn't
help. She barged over to where I sat and (the first time
we've touched except to shake hands) laid her left
hand on my right cheek exactly where it's so peculiarly

A I/a.3a numb (*hypersensitively* numb, pardon my oxymoron),
and after looking meaningfully into my eyes asked,

A I/a.3b "Everything all right?" I almost asked her if I'd broken
out in bright boils or smelled like a bedpan, but I
merely shrugged my shoulders and (she looked so
prettily well-meaning) fished up a happy-as-a-lark
grin from the junk heap of sociable clichés. It worked;

B I/b.2b at least, she left. She was wearing a startlingly purple
skirt, white blouse, and, on the lapel of the mouse-

B II/b.3b gray jacket she'd draped over her shoulders, a pin
whose entwined silver snakes squirmed like freshly
dug worms. It matters that I note such things.

WEDNESDAY, 1:30 P.M.

A I/a.1 Late-morning phone calls:
— From Colette: she had rung Daisy earlier to thank
her, she wanted to thank me also, she especially wanted
to thank me, etc. She said she'd been so happy to see
me after such a long time (of course, she'd dreamed of
other circumstances. At dinner she'd longed to take off
a shoe and lay one stockinged foot on my cock. So why
hadn't she? She'd had doubts about my self-control).
When would I come and see her? Was something

wrong? she asked. Was something wrong with my health? Didn't I love her anymore? (In fact her question was, Did I not love her anymore? which is something else, though both answers, as far as I know, must be the same.)

B II/b.3b She made me feel the old longing. My life is so busy now.

A I/a.1 She didn't mention Gert. Not a single word.

— From Schacht-Consuelo Floor Furnishings: they were trying to reach Daisy. Did I know where she was? I told them to keep calling her number; she would answer eventually. I asked if everything had gone well last week. Answer: Oh, fine, fine. Question: Was your trip together worthwhile? Reply: Where do you mean? Question: Aren't you collaborating with my wife on that out-of-town project? Answer: That's me. Question: Well, I meant the place where you're installing your carpeting? Answer: Yes. An excellent idea. Question: I gathered it was *your* idea? Answer: An excellent idea. Something to do at various stages, I would say. If you speak to Mrs. — Question: Shall I have her call you? Answer: Please.

— From Pater: Madre Mia is at a bridge lunch. He's tending the oven — autumn pies. He hoped his call was permitted. No, I replied, and what was on his mind? The usual, plus why hadn't I visited, when was I planning to visit. He's started his first Stephen King:

B II/b.3 "Like going to the movies at home." (My neglect of *Young Days!*)

A I/a.3a I went to Cherry's office. She was on her way out. I asked her point blank: Is she the one who's spying on me? She shook her head with a stupid look of resigna-

A II/a.2   tion. She reminded me about her recital. (Where did I
note the date?)

B I/b.1c   Back to my desk. The silence of the offices made me
frantically restless. Silence, and sunlight also, piling up

B I/b.2c   all over the place. I wanted to talk to Paul; he was gone,
like the rest of them. Maybe they're all meeting in the

B II/b.1   park to discuss my case. As I struggled to recall what

B II/b.3b   besides phone calls had happened this morning after
10:30, I dreamed of ripping my window out of the wall.
These surroundings, most of the time as depressingly
present as a red light in a traffic jam, turned remote
and fluid, like draining soapsuds. I was plotting excur-
sions into the other offices to scissor a few work pads

B II/b.3b   when I heard a dry noise above my head, like a cracking in the ceiling boards: I saw myself as if through an
eye in the ceiling, fidgeting and sweating like a
demented inmate, a disgrace. I calmed down.

A I/b.1a   Maganoff appeared, without food, without wine,
and without much time. He had come to say good-bye
and to drop off a copy of a new student magazine. His
role was ending. Someone called Dreba was running
things – I gathered without book-filled pianos or inscribed paper airplanes. Maganoff has no regrets; he
hopes to stay useful a while longer. "I know that all
good things *don't* have to end. But they sometimes do.
I loved every second of it. Gert will always know where
to find me."

A II/b.3b   Lunch (my first drinkless meal): a yogurt, a pear,

B I/b.2a   feeling inexplicably forsaken and old and full of regret
for things I didn't know I'd missed.

I was determined to catch Paul when he came in from lunch. He arrived last, so I caught everyone else, too — an experience or series of experiences that left me irritatingly irritated. Stan (usual slouchy brown summer windbreaker, blue and pink creepy-crawly shirt with *yellow* tie, cordovan moccasins, slacks of glistening blue — who can dream up, who can actually market such material?) barely said hello as he headed for his desk. Tangerine (neat-looking in her short-sleeved print dress and tan medium-heel shoes, but her hair needs washing) utterly misunderstood my own attire: she asked if I was going to a rock concert. Edith (stiffish gray suit, no visible blouse, black high heels): "So *are* the letters ready?" were her only words. Cherry (she was chewing gum, and who's perfect?) wafted me a smile. Louis (decent green suit, white shirt, blue tie, oxfords) looked pleasantly surprised at seeing me (our paths rarely cross) and said, "Seems we wrap up the unfinished business tomorrow" (the pernicious clamp). Fritz, shuttling a toothpick across his little front teeth, peaked his eyebrows in not unamiable greeting. Why did running this gauntlet gripe me so? By the time Paul appeared on Fritz's heels (had they lunched together?), I had forgotten what I wanted from him. He put his arm around my shoulder and shook me gently. "What's up?" "A couple of things. Daisy most of all. She's been acting odd. I can't figure it out." Paul squeezed my shoulder before withdrawing his arm and said bluntly, "I promise you you don't have a thing to worry about. Of course we must get

together," he added. "Next week I'll have plenty of
B II/b.3   time — whenever you like, lunch, drinks after the office.
B I/a.2   Breakfast!" *Not* dinner, however. Back to work — on the
way, Stan's voice on the phone: "But she shouldn't be in
a *ward* for this." Being in plain view, I didn't stop to
hear more.

B I/b.1b   Yesterday I established four hypotheses that would
explain Gert's meeting with C. The first of them, family affection, can now be excluded. I mean excluded as
an explanation, not per se — last night's dinner showed
that it exists in abundance. However, Gert's embarrassment at revealing their last meeting points to
something else, something concealed, and eliminates
not only my first but also my second hypothesis (an
accidental meeting, not likely to occur two days in a
row). The third hypothesis — that Gert was consulting
C. about his "problem" — was undermined by another
incident at dinner. Gert's embarrassment followed his
words "what you said this afternoon"; what C. had
apparently said was (I think I heard right) *"Oy geveh —
whatever that may mean!"* — the punch line to some
story that Daisy and I were not entitled to share. Telling Jewish jokes does not suggest a heart-to-heart talk.

Once again this leaves only the something-else possibility. What wrecks my efforts at thinking clearly
about it is Colette's silence. After all, Gert doesn't
tell me lots of things, and I don't blame him, even if
I'm not monstrously older than she is. But why should
she consistently not confide in me? And yet she acts
perfectly natural about the situation. Yesterday
evening, in the wake of Gert's gaffe, she showed no

trace of nervousness, and I know her too well to be fooled on that score. She does not hide her fondness for Gert or bother to discourage his obvious *infatuation* with her. But infatuation is the wrong word, since it implies another kind of intimacy. That is surely irrelevant? As I ask the question, my heart sinks into a puddle of jittery metallic slime; I hardly know what I mean myself, but given the way I've neglected C., her having an affair with my son would serve me right. Let us climb out of the puddle and collect our thoughts. The phrase suggests picking grapes with boxing gloves. New hypotheses:

1. Their second meeting: Gert consults C. about his problem. Still *possible.* (*Oy geveh!*)

2. "Something else" – I write down the words to expel this all-too-elusive option, which only leads into dark banks of fog.

3. An affair.

4. Gert feels drawn to C., drawn to seeing her (he may have a one-sided infatuation, nothing wrong with that, it might help dispel the effect of Maganoff's remarks – was that yesterday?), and C. has decided to handle it in her own way and not get me "needlessly" involved. Or Gert has made her promise not to tell me, and *of course* she should keep her promise.

B II/b.1 When I consider 3 and 4, I'm reminded of a scene in a postwar avant-garde play. A man is teaching a young woman arithmetic. When he tries to explain subtraction to her, he finds himself getting nowhere. In desperation he asks her if she can visualize the number 4. She says she can. Can she also visualize the number 3? Yes. And can she picture both at the same time – 4 with 3 next to it? She can. Then tell me exactly what you see between them, he asks. She struggles dutifully with the question, finally crying out in belligerent despair: Nothing!

A I/a.1   About to leave the office, I remembered to call Colette. I made clear why once again I couldn't meet her, I had piles of paperwork to get through, afterwards I was going to the opera, the performance started at 6:30, "etc., etc." What I said somehow offended her or at least dampened her warmth (what did I inexplicitly encode in "etc., etc."?). She paused a moment; I could almost hear her collecting herself (but without boxing gloves!). She then said, "Darling, wait till tomorrow – till after tomorrow. I promise you everything will be nicer." I made no comment. What was going through her petite head?

A I/b.2b   I have deliberately written this on company time. A risk, but tonight I'll get home late and I have to make sure I've kept up. What would I do if I fell as little as half a day behind? Easy: a night with no sleep at all could handle the lag. Anyway, absolutely no one noticed.

THURSDAY, ABOUT 3 A.M.

A I/b.2   Going out of the office, I came face to face with Marapliz, comely enough in her long-sleeved, off-the-

A I/a.3b   shoulder dress of loosely fitting material. I was curious to know what it was and asked, "Is that silk, Mrs. Valde?" "Call me Mara, please. Silk crepe. Imported." She never responds otherwise to our respectful "Mrs.

BII/b.3b Valde," hence her less respectful nickname. She had doubtless come to fetch her husband for some lugubrious gathering of littlewigs. I decided next time to try out "Comrade Mara."

AI/b.2 "My" driver was not running the tram home, which was packed. Between the third and fourth stops it slowed down. We inched past an ambulance that had drawn up behind a car diagonally rammed against the curb. The car's back window displayed the snake and staff of the medical profession; its front doors were wide open; the driver lay half supine on his lowered seat-back, jacket and shirt pulled loose, mouth open, cotton wads in his nostrils. One white-jacketed man leaning over him pressed a spread hand against his chest; another was lackadaisically extracting a stretcher from the back of the ambulance. Four people in front of me and at least three behind simultaneously exclaimed, "Physician, heal thyself!" Nervous smiles all around.

AI/a.3a I had no sooner crossed our threshold than Daisy uttered her ritual warning: "You're going to make us late! You know the curtain's at – " "Six-thirty, I do AI/b.3b know, I won't." But I checked the time available with particular care: if I didn't dawdle, enough for an unhurried bath. Lying in the tub, conscientiously soaping myself, I felt my cock stiffening in the pleasurable slippery warmth; and idly taking it in my hand, with no premeditation and scarcely a pause, I began masturbating, something I last did on July 7 seven years ago BII/b.3a in the apartment of a friend away on vacation. I let my AI/b.3b hand do its own thinking, and it managed expertly.

Have I ever experienced such "pure pleasure"? The final spasm came to me directly, without images of any woman, or parts of a woman, or anything else – just it. (I missed seeing the sperm, but sloshing as I was in muddled water, it must have been sudsed away during that last second of clamped-shut sightlessness.)

B II/b.3b   I now have worries about that event. The time spent was tantalizingly short, but could I begin to describe it? What happened during those two minutes? What determines these pages if not the repetition of precisely that question: what happened? Does sex, like drink, annihilate recall? Going blank is what I least need. Having given up drinking, should I give up erotic pleasures as well? (Considered thus, it's much worse *with* a partner.)

B II/b.3a   At the time I felt wonderful. Sitting on the bathroom stool and drying my feet, I noticed my softened bluish cock resting on my scrotum against my left
A I/a.3 thigh. Tears of tenderness came to my eyes, and I spoke
A II/a.2 to it – "My sweet little girl!" – not worrying about
A I/b.2 what I meant. Through the bathroom door I could hear Casadesus playing a B-flat Mozart concerto. Would he have disapproved of my jerking off?

A I/b.2   The opera house has good parking facilities, so we
A I/a.3 took the car. On the way Daisy asked me if something was on my mind. But she'd spoken no more than I had.
A I/b.2 We were inside the theater half an hour before curtain time. I made no comment on this, since Daisy had
A I/a.3 hardly pestered me – her intermittent reminders that
B I/b.1a we mustn't be late were like a melancholy ritual incan-
A I/b.2 tation. We bought a program, identified the quickest

way to our seats, and went to the bar. Daisy drank a B I/a.1 glass of bubbly, and I a virtuous split of sparkling water. I tried not to be disgusted by the dress of other operagoers. Why do people feel obliged on these occasions to make needless points? Forgoing evening clothes, okay (and yet who could have resisted Daisy in her deftly embroidered black jacket, softly frilled off-white blouse, and close-fitting ankle-length black A I/b.2 silk skirt?), but sunflower prints? T-shirts? fluorescent suits? It was I who now urged Daisy to drink up so that we could reach our seats early. Once we were settled, while Daisy rubbernecked languidly, I opened the program and began reading the producer's explanation of his aims. Given what was to follow, this proved a good use of the remaining minutes before the house-lights dimmed.

A I/b.1a Can I provide an accurate rendering of what I saw and heard? I did hear *Die Meistersinger*, but my eyes were open, and the sequence of images and events onstage weirdly modified its familiar sounds. Bye-bye Nuremberg and the Middle Ages, hello Planet Hermes, wherever you are. With the opening chords of the prelude, a movie, projected on a screen lowered in front of the curtain, "redefined" (I quote the program) "certain hermeneutic/epistemological parameters." Thus: Planet Hermes is a tyrannically elitist society where a male oligarchy (the Meistersingers) controls all property, the production of basic goods (food, clothing, shelter), and the bureaucracy that regulates the functioning of society. The masses live in submissive dependency; the only escape from servitude lies in the humiliating and protracted process of apprenticeship. Towards the end of the prelude, the movie showed Walther, an earthling, dispatched by rocket ship to Hermes together with a squad of commandos disguised as ordinary Hermetics; their mission is to bring democracy to the planet. On his arrival, Walther is welcomed by Hans Sachs, a fellow earthling sent on a preparatory mission many years before.

The stage action followed this premise with a certain plausibility. The altar in St. Catherine's church displayed the inner workings of an atom in particolored, shifting lights; on the walls were emblems of the elite's professions (from electronic baking to computerized banking), alternating with symbols of cultural authority (flashing consoles, texts pulsating on backlit screens) and military prowess (space rifles?). A second bridgelike stage was suspended high in the proscenium, and here the hidden significance of events was mimed or otherwise elaborated. The first such visual gloss had us all on the edge of our seats: during the opening chorale, while Eva and Walther gazed at each other across the nave, a perfectly naked couple was spotlighted on the bridge, embracing with an intimacy just short of penetration. (I was aghast to feel Daisy's hand come to rest on my cock and give it a squeeze. I needn't have worried: no one was looking anywhere but up.) I had read that the bridge-stage functioned in the producer's eyes as a "memory/desire continuum." After this example of desire, we were treated to a memory item during David's attempt to teach Walther the rudiments of official poetry. A series of slides

A I/b.2
A I/b.1a

recapitulated David's early life: his purchase by a commission of Meistersingers from an impoverished family; his apprentice's school, where lessons in shoemaking conducted under the lash alternated with brutal military drills.

David and the other apprentices were all now hobbled with real shackles; their "frolic" before the arrival of the Meistersingers raised a chillingly clanky din. Beckmesser, in his role as marker, appeared in a virtual replica of an SS officer's uniform. Most illuminatingly (if such a word applies), during Pogner's declaration of his readiness to bestow his daughter's hand on the winner of the next day's singing contest, an elaborate dumb show overhead related how, after his arrival, Hans Sachs seduced Pogner's wife and himself fathered Eva; he now planned to engineer Walther's victory in the competition so that he could propagate a new race of earthlings on the planet. Meanwhile, on the lower stage, Eva submitted to traditional Hermetic customs: she was led forth by Magdalene, who, after removing the cloak that turned out to be her only clothing, left her on her knees, naked among the Meistersingers. They examined her like a prize sow.

So it went. Beckmesser's marking chalk became an electronic wand that provoked sirenlike screeches on a high-tech blackboard. The cobbler's last used by Sachs was also computerized (and versatile enough to record Walther's dream song on a diskette later on). Because they were subversive, Sachs's soliloquies were sung "inwardly" — i.e., prerecorded for transmission through a hidden loudspeaker. Sachs stopped Eva from eloping because her impatience (renewed copulation on the bridge) endangered her earthling role. That Sachs was her father, unbeknownst to her, gave their teasing duet a special intensity. The night watchman made his rounds at the head of a fiercely armed riot squad. At the end of the act they viciously quelled the sudden pandemonium that was here depicted as a popular uprising, with the downtrodden committing pillage, arson, gang rapes, and summary executions on the property and persons of their masters.

Act 3 (by this time my attentiveness had been seriously undermined by Daisy's dislike of the proceedings): Sachs sees Beckmesser coming and, having written "Prize Song" on a particular diskette, conspicuously leaves it for the town clerk to find. (This is surely an improvement on his usual ambiguous behavior.) The diskette in question also contains a computer virus that will destabilize the central information network on which the elite's control depends. This makes possible an intervention of the earthling shock troops at the start of the final scene. On the banks of the Pegnitz they (nonviolently) disarm the guards and free the shackled revelers from their chains. Walther then teaches them to dance and sing as only free people, at least in the guise of a Wagnerian chorus, can. When the big shots arrive, they are in turn "disarmed" by the gaiety of their liberated people; to the delight of all, they command the troop escorting them to lay down its weapons. However, after Pogner declares Walther a Master, they are all led away, brought before a firing squad on the overhanging bridge, and executed with silent blue flashes, while below Sachs sings his final harangue about the sanctity of German (i.e., "earthling") art. Walther and Eva's marriage epitomizes the alliance of Earth and Hermes: on the upper stage, the glowing letters of *Hermes* fade into those of *New Earth.*

A I/a.3a   During the intermissions, Daisy's irritation with the production had grown increasingly vehement. When I turned to her after the final curtain, she was trembling with fury. "It was horrible. That good-natured, touching story – they've wrecked it for good. They've made me see how hateful it is." I suggested that she blame the producers, not the work. "No, they're only arrogant, arbitrary, and stupid. They're

A I/a.3b not *psychotic*." She refused to applaud. When the director and designers were called onstage, our backwoods respectfulness was rent by a series of falsetto hoots; for all I know, they were uttered by a solitary spectator, but they worked, and brought a smile to Daisy's pursed features.

B II/b.3a,b   My own feelings about the evening remain confused. The production kept me too busy for uncluttered reactions – busy following text and subtext, busy wondering if Eva or anyone else would again take off her clothes. I noticed that when absorbed by the futuristic interpretation of the story, I was less aware of the music and words, except for rare moments such as the Eva-Sachs duet, when I heard them *better.* I also noticed that whenever I recognized the sung words, the interpretation fell apart. How could there be a Nuremberg or a Pegnitz on Hermes? How had these Masters come to hear of Walther von der Vogelweid? Why should they celebrate *Johannistag*? But fundamentally what I felt throughout was that I wanted to learn, to appreciate, to be in touch, and this meant not wanting to doubt. The alternative was to resign myself to uninformed

B II/b.3a provinciality. Paying serious attention to the proceedings made me question my habits, tastes, and attitudes towards the issues and powers that invisibly determine our lives. It gave me a chance to submit.

A I/a.3a Not that I was a model student. Between the acts,
B I/b.1a conversation with Daisy languished. I think she was bemused as much as offended; in any event, she spent most of her time silently sipping her metachampagne. I had no desire to force her silence, because she might well have expressed her dissatisfaction, whereupon I would have had to ask her if she felt like leaving, and she might have said yes. As a result, I overheard more of our ever-changing bar neighbors' conversation than I normally would have. Most of it showed our fellow spectators making a considerable effort to disguise befuddlement and at the same time nudge their interlocutors into saying something that might ease it – if not in explanation, at least in acknowledgment of a confusion like their own. "Yes. Why can't we get a regular conductor like that?" "Mm." A promising pause, but: "And how is it they always find tenors who look the part?" "Maybe.... But did you notice the scar on her right cheek? Haven't they heard about body makeup?" "You're *merciless!*... Interesting, the earthling concept, don't you think?" "The what?" "How

B II/b.3b about another glass?" I shouldn't have cared, but I longed to pour out my little knowledge and make things easier for them. Not one in fifty can have read the libretto.

What most interested me in all this eavesdropping came at the end of the second intermission; it had nothing to do with *Die Meistersinger.* As I was settling our bar bill, a woman passing behind me said matter-of-factly, before dropping out of earshot, "My husband was French." I missed a sizable chunk of the prelude to act 3 speculating with maniacal obstinacy on the potential meaning of this perfectly plain statement. I settled at last on four possibilities (and one improbability) that at last enabled me to feel that the topic had been exhausted and that I could again turn my attention to R.W. and his interpreters, viz.: 1) the woman's husband was a Frenchman from whom she was now separated or divorced; 2) the woman's husband had been a Frenchman but was now dead; 3) the woman's husband was a Frenchman who had adopted a second citizenship – American, for instance (in some countries dual nationality is recognized, and her "was" would not have applied); 4) the woman's husband had adopted French citizenship but when doing so had concealed the fact from his country of origin, let's say Insanistan, so that when he died and his secret came out, he was under Insanistanian law imperatively reclaimed, body, soul, and bank accounts. The unlikely fifth alternative required the woman to have spoken in quite different terms, terms with which the sentence might have been completed thus: "My husband was French . . . but now he's Greek," the word *French* having the meaning assigned to it in the personal ads of specialized magazines, so that the extended sentence would have signified, "My husband used to lick my cunt, but now he fucks me up the ass." This was hardly a remark an operagoer in this backwater would make so audibly, no matter whom she was addressing; nevertheless, the notion stayed with me and livened my cockles sufficiently for me to wish that the naked girl would reappear on the overhanging stage (scar or no scar) and I could fancy performing one or both so-called unnatural acts with her — I wished that Daisy would at least put her hand on my thing again. But when I made a gesture to that effect she huffily pulled away. The action overhead during that meditative prelude must have pushed her impatience beyond recall — I gather (as I said, my thoughts were elsewhere) that it included a gruesome identification of Hans Sachs with John the Baptist, in which he was not only beheaded but castrated, quartered, and fed to small dogs. I may have imagined this (imagined its being done to me?).

Daisy's tribulations had not ended, and mine were about to begin. I was obliviously leading her towards the parking lot (and on to a probable pizza or a bowl of soup, just the two of us, then the drive home for a nightcap — not for me, of course) when she grabbed my coat-sleeve and whispered, "Slow down — that's the Furmints in front of us, you know, the decorator of the place I'm doing the rugs for, in fact just stop and pray they don't see us, because if they want to have supper with us, there's no way I can say no," but as Mr. Furmint turned to open the next glass door for his wife, he did

: 143 :

see us, and they not only invited us for supper but insisted on driving miles from the haunts of comfort, civilization, and hope, to a new restaurant in the suburbs they'd heard about. The place, called Little Bratislava (what do you know), claims to be the only authentic Czechoslovakian restaurant in our region; this may be the best news of the evening.

The restaurant is run by two brothers, Martin and L'udovit Smrek, who have set up shop in a wallpapered garage on the southern fringe of town. It has four tables, capable of seating fourteen at the unlikely most. On arrival I felt inclined to tolerance and sympathy: we were hungry, and an agreeable smell of broth simmering, bread baking, and goulash cooking down consoled me momentarily for the grimness of the setting. A garage it had been, a garage it remained — I sniffed for oil patches in the thinly matted cement. The walls, concealed by paper of a yellow so dismal that in the drooping light from a single ceiling bulb it made my eyes ache, were decorated with colored photographs of landscapes sliced from calendars that dated, to judge by their sturdy romping blondes, from the triumphant years of Nazism. Nothing on the tables but minimal ware and undersized paper napkins — no place mats, no candles, no salt and pepper. No *glasses* — plastic cups instead — and food served in tin containers that we had to empty onto chipped enamel plates.

We spent two hours in Little Bratislava. No later than twenty-five minutes after we sat down, the meal began auspiciously enough with a sizable dome of white bread, hot from the oven, yeasty, crackling-crusted. The bread tasted even better with the thick lentil soup (adorned with slices of disappointingly mild kielbasa) that finally turned up twenty minutes later. That was when we should have left. My goulash (sixty-five minutes after sitting down) was heavy and tame, served with a dollop of coarse-textured, unsalted potato dumpling as well as cooked-to-mush carrots and khaki peas. Daisy's *Jägerschnitzel,* whose *jäger* implied wild mushrooms, was garnished with flat-tasting plain ones. Mrs. Furmint offered me a bite of her stuffed pancake: it combined a crust the color and texture of coal dust with a slushy, underdone interior into which had been poured all the salt so wanting in the other dishes. I pleaded hereditary gout when Mr. Furmint suggested I try his jaternica, a sweating, bulging pork sausage that he assured me was delectable. The desserts brought some relief: apple strudel and what *they* called palacinky (surely its correct name is palascinta?), but once again our pleasure was half wrecked by an exasperating delay. It was towards the end of this final interim that Daisy abruptly demanded, in a voice that probably was heard in Bratislava itself, "Who do I have to fuck to get out of this place?" The remark enchanted me if not Mrs. Furmint. Resuming the conversation unconcernedly, Daisy quaffed, as she'd been doing all evening, another cup of red Yugoslav "riesling." When I joshed her, "Can you remember what you're trying to forget?" she replied convincingly, "It's the only way to get this plonk down." Thanks to the wine, to the relief of having *Die Meistersinger* behind her, or to a desire to please her colleague, she had chattered inexhaustibly throughout the meal. After her recent quirky behavior, this talkativeness reassured me as to her well-being, and at the same time it disturbed me because it sounded slightly skewed — as though she were furiously filling

up conversational space to keep anyone else from saying too much. She spoke about me, my work, Gert, the student movement, about the opera (I was proud of her frankness, whatever the respectful Furmints thought), and each subject disappeared into the grinder of her vivacity until there was nothing left of

it. I still don't understand it. When she listened she again became familiar, her eyes open in almost moist attentiveness, her shoulders sunk into their natural

lovely slope, and my too often unexpressed adoration of her then revived. Without her, we would have all gone stir-crazy in that squalid hole.

Good night, Martin, good night, L'udovit. And good riddance, O Smreks! They had spent two hours endlessly gliding about their claustrophic space, hovering over the two occupied tables with dedicated concern, fiddling with the volume of the one and only tape of Carpathian mountain music, smiling relentlessly,

getting nothing done. Good night, Furmint the De-
signer and Mrs. Furmint. As we got into the car, Daisy scolded me mildly for taking such abrupt leave of the proprietors — they had, after all, done their best. I said she had hit the nail on the thumb. She added that my agreeing so promptly to let the Furmints pay the check

had not reflected my usual tact. But my only regret was at not having been reimbursed for eating such crap.

Throughout, of course, I had had my own consolation for all that misspent time, knowing that I would later confide its details to my secret pages. And what a consolation it is – a sublime revenge (sublime because not harming anyone, and all mine) against fate, against others, against myself!

A I/a.3a   Driving home, I spoke of Paul's aloofness, about my phone conversation with him earlier in the day and his cavalier dismissal of my wish to revive our old intimacy. With a stagy laugh that did nothing to comfort me about either Paul or other misgivings I've been carefully not thinking about, Daisy declared that I was acting silly or jealous or both. Jealous? I exclaimed. Well, not consciously jealous; but I shouldn't be upset by Paul's funny new enthusiasm for Jago, which explained his "aloofness," and it wasn't aloofness at all – he was simply busy keeping his new friend company. What's funny about Paul's liking Jago? I asked. Why, Daisy quickly replied, we've all been seeing each other for years now, and it's strange that they should suddenly get all palsy, as if they'd just met. She giggled on

A I/b.2   until we reached home, at about 12:30.

She was in a happy mood. After downing a hearty glass of white wine (whatever we had open), she plopped straight into bed. She spoke to me with that new-style questioning inflection that always puzzles me but that I dutifully record: "God, how great sheets

A I/a.3a   feel? It's as though a big stone had been taken off my tummy? You wouldn't care to join me, I suppose?" I mumbled regrets, not admitting what I had to do – at

A I/a.3b   this point it can hardly surprise her, and she must have

: 147 :

A II/b.3b   realized I had at least the whole evening to write up. I
B II/b.3a   went to my desk and got started. What luck I'm not
more tired after so little sleep (and not one benny of
late)! Either the prospect of writing supplies the
adrenaline, or the anguish of not writing does, or both.
B II/b.3b   But now I need a break. So: a walk in cool night air
before finishing.

3:45 A.M.
B II/b.3a   I forgot to describe the Furmints. I paid them scant
A I/a.3a   attention — once again Daisy had to scold me for
B I/a.1   resorting to my notebook so often in company. Mr. F.:
suit of light wool crepe, of a vivid but attractive blue,
cut loose around the shoulders, arms, and legs, with
wide patch pockets, chevalier collar, and emphatic
bands along the trouser seams; a ring-necked black
shirt; gray suede boots (no one would guess he's a
designer). Mrs. F.: simple black silk dress, cut straight
to midcalf, and ample, though hardly ample enough;
on the promontory of her left breast, her one piece of
jewelry, a large patchwork-chrome brooch apparently
recovered from a plane wreck; hair bobbed; I missed
her shoes.

Things not done:
A II/b.3a   — exercise (sacrificed for long bath; masturbation
doesn't count)
— accounting (no rush)
— reading (as Little Bratislava reminded me)
— developing observational skills (e.g., what were
the DNA-like mini-clamberers at the midtown
florist's?)

— inner-landscape skills (at least buy a guide to
meditation?)
— other health matters (the thought of taking "my"
medicines nauseates me)
— bringing up Schacht-Consuelo phone call

Things not recorded:
— Gert's clothes, Maganoff's, how the tram drivers
looked

Things to start recording — I'll jot them in my
pocket notebook tomorrow. New subcategories ditto.

A II/b.3*b*   I've completed my index, so boorishly interrupted
this morning. All in all, an interesting, rewarding day,
B II/b.3*b*   except for Paul (and, of course, the Daisy business).

THURSDAY, 7:30 A.M.
A III/a.2   Waking up after six as if startled by thunder: no clouds,
A III/a.1   but to the north a pall of black smoke covering the
horizon. Mystery. To my left, in the backyard, two
unstirring crows. The ones I spotted last week?
B II/a   I'm standing on the banks of the Suez Canal. A
voice emanating from no one visible comments on the
scene, like a voice-over in a movie, but one with which
I converse. For no good reason it admonishes, "It's not
pronounced *suets*, get it right: the sound of the voiced
g, as in *kruzle*." "The *g* in *kruzle*?" "Not *g*, I told you to
get it right (it *had* said *g*), the voiced *z* as in *gruzle*." The
verges of the canal are thick with vegetation, waist-
high grasses in generous bloom. "The flowers provide
fodder for milk that must justly be called divine. And

: 149 :

in time, to complete the picture, they will all be cropped and trodden until there is nothing but desert to see and the waters wash the baby away." I wonder whether this might not symbolize the emigration of the Gypsies; my merely thinking the question evokes a contemptuous snort from my mentor. I find myself in a desert place. The canal is gone. I stand on a sun-drenched flat hilltop from which through the whitening glare I can see other hills nearby. Yard-long narrow bands of shorthaired buff animal hide, with fifteen-inch thongs at either end, are strewn over the rocky ground. "Old-time protection for dry months." I immediately offer the lady a delicacy called "cock-in-buns" that looks like a hot dog. Lady? There is a shaking of heads: no lady. Amid the ruins, on the shaded side of a marble wall, a panel of instruments is embedded in luminous pumice-colored stone. I remind myself to look for opsidian shards in the rubble and say out loud, "I *know* it's not spelled with a *p*, you fucking bedant." The thermometer reads a torrid 35°, the barometer 30.43 millibars and rising, the hygrometer is broken or in any case registers zero percent. I heave a sigh and feel wakefulness returning. In the sunny space in front of me friends start dancing by. Is it time for the beach? I'm barefoot, it will be painful to run across the stubbled wheat. I again start to sigh, and the inhalation sucks ropes of thick woolly dust into my nostrils and mouth. A furious panic of suffocation. Gongs.

A II/b.2   I'm convinced that the systematic recording of body signs yesterday morning did me good. After being

: 150 :

marked down, some of them faded away. My head aches less, and the spasm in the back of my right thigh, the cramps in the sole of my left foot, and the admittedly mild soreness in my back have plumb disappeared as if they'd only been waiting to be acknowledged before taking their leave. Some symptoms are worse: the funny-bone twinge (I couldn't stop "playing" with it), the fluttering eyelid, the stone in my diaphragm, on which I concentrated at length but which refuses to budge. It's status quo for the others. As for fresh arrivals, the news is not good. To tell the truth, I noticed most of these adversities last night and tried hard to pretend they were imaginary:

1. Nose: frequent sensation of being both dry and stuffed

2. Great red spot where my throat turns into my chest (a lousy start to my mirror day)

3. Thick scary pain in middle of chest

4. Sensation of choking or smothering (cf. dream, one time it occurred) (not connected with (3))

5. Sudden sweating, esp. palms (but not *that* especially)

6. Bouts of pins and needles in hands and feet

7. Trembling, upper arms and torso

8. Cold sensation all over (thoughts of death *following*)

9. Recurrent cramps in calves

10. x-rhea —

— Mother of God, what's going wrong with me?

Compiling the list has not brought yesterday's comfort.

A II/a.1d   I've spent my remaining time writing page references in the index, which now seems as inevitable as the crows in the backyard.

To counter the noticeable effect of yesterday's all-black attire, today I've chosen to outsummer the summer-addicts and dress entirely in white — a much less arduous problem, necktie aside: I finessed the tie with a silk dress scarf. I had to burrow for a while to find a white jacket in a long-forgotten carton. Canvas trousers, athletic socks, white polo shirt, sneakers (my one regret, since I had no whitener and no time to bleach, scrub, and sun-dry them).

A II/b.5   Feeling little inclination to make Daisy's breakfast, I didn't make Gert's, either. Bad to turn nice gestures into *rules.*

I caught Dr. Max at home. He said if it was urgent he could see me at the hospital this afternoon at two-thirty. I assume he didn't mean emergency-urgent. Anyway, I accepted.

[THURSDAY,] 1:30 P.M.

A I/b.2e   Breakfast was displeasing. Daisy joined me in the
A I/a.3a   kitchen. I again mentioned Paul's remoteness, hoping that now sober, she might have something intelligent to say about it.

She only repeated last night's familiar refrain about his "wonderful" new friendship with Jago, so "heartwarming" after all these years . . . I shrugged my shoulders. "And," Daisy pursued, "speaking of remoteness, what about your own? You're a lot weirder than Paul. You wouldn't by chance be having an affair?"

I had long prepared myself for the question, planning to react with amiable delight at this evidence that Daisy "still cared for me." But she had caught me napping. Like a silent-movie ham demonstrating hypocritical innocence, I spluttered, shook my head like a wet dog, and raised my hands protestingly. I also shouted, "You're nuts!" "Oh!" Daisy said. For over a week I had been coming home from work later and later – "The only thing that reassures me is that you haven't been concocting 'marvelous' excuses. And what about last night? You were out of the house for almost an hour." I pointed out that she herself went out for nighttime walks. "Not after you've gone to bed. And the other nights you stayed up so late, when I'd fallen asleep? Did you take nice long walks then, too?" I foolishly hesitated before replying. Daisy went on: "Don't tell me: 'I was working on my journal.' Come on!" I was indignant. "What's wrong with working on my journal? You were the one who suggested I start keeping it, remember? At least partly." "I never thought you'd like it more than me." "What's your gripe? That I didn't bring you breakfast in bed?" I don't know what Daisy said next; I wasn't listening: I was reflecting that in this task I've set myself I'm totally alone, and it cannot be otherwise. I have nothing but the vaguest help and support. How can I ever explain to anyone the high principle that governs my commitment – a commitment to the "perfectibility" of my methods? It may now concern only myself, but ultimately it extends far beyond myself because it is the condition of the noblest of all acts, that of rescuing the precarious imprints of reality; and reality is the world's, not mine.

A I/b.2b Gert's arrival restored me to the present. He ate a piece of bread and drank some of Daisy's tea. Why not mine? (Once again I'd stuck to tea, yogurt, and melba toast. Daisy added a soft-boiled egg to her usual fare.) Gert asked me, "What do you know about Ernst Cassirer?" I said I remembered the name as Cassiter. He went off to fetch Cassirer's *Philosophie der symbolischen Formen*, vol. 3. "Right you are," I conceded. "I can't really help — wasn't he a Kantian? But what a subject!

A III/b.1c Doesn't it cover *everything*?" Gert was wearing rather conservative clothes: a black turtleneck shirt, a light-

A I/a.3b weight beige corduroy suit, medium-brown oxfords. I

B II/b.3b.iii thought better of asking him why. By now I'd calmed

A I/a.3a down, but Daisy again riled me by gently and stupidly suggesting that I shave. I retorted that I had been thinking of growing a beard and expected it to give me a more jovial look. Gert chuckled. "Not today it won't." I decided to take the tram by myself.

A III/b.2e Once again the driver was someone else. On Galileo

A III/a.1 Pond were waterfowl I did not recognize, as well as

A III/a.2 ibis, heron, and the ducks. Bad day for the fishies. Two women were chattering behind me: "The gloom of it, Victoria, the gloom!" "And no gold there to console us!" They discussed a brushfire that had started north

B II/b.3a of town during the early hours; this explained the smoke I'd seen earlier. But why so black — a tire dump? Unlikely. Nothing they said cleared that up.

A I/a.3a I got to work on time, too late to continue extend-

A III/b.2d

A I/a.3a

ing my index. Any such hopes vanished when Fritz told me on my way in that a staff meeting had been called for 10:00. In my office I found Cherry waiting for me. She apologized for being there unasked. Busily clasping her handbag with both hands, she was standing as far away from my desk as the small space allowed, making clear, I suppose, that she had not come in to pry. I hypocritically assured her that she should always feel at home here. She announced somewhat stiffly that she had a sensitive matter to discuss. I urged her to speak plainly. She said that Mr. Valde had told her he was worried about me – "extremely worried." Anything in particular? Yes: last night at the opera I'd walked right past him without saying a word. "So that's where they were going, all dressed up! I never would have guessed it." "What do you mean?" "Mr. Valde is a Mozart fan. He hates Wagner." "You mean this production." "He hates *Wagner*. He told me so. He was emphatic about it." "That wasn't my impression at all. He told *me* that Wagner was one of his favorites. I almost started arguing with him – I don't mean about Wagner; about you. Obviously you didn't see him." "Of course I didn't see him. I didn't expect to." Cherry said she had to get to her desk. "I only wanted to make sure you're okay. You are okay, aren't you?" I was get-

A I/a.3b

ting more and more annoyed. I grunted noncommittally, whereupon Cherry put her arms around me and gave me a hug that was more than warm. Her thighs, belly, breasts, cheek pressed against me so tenderly I would have rebuked her if I hadn't seen tears in her eyes when she let go. She walked away blushing. The

BII/b   equinox has cast a peculiar spell within these unhal-
AIII/b.1a   lowed walls. This event naturally roiled my thinking.
             A question came to me: had Daisy accused me of hav-
BII/b.3b.ii ing an affair on the principle that the best defense is
             attack? I then succumbed to a flush of yearning for
             Cherry's rounded ass and full-lipped mouth. I stood
AIII/b.1c   there in an adolescent daze, finally recalling my tem-
AII/b.4   porary but resolute vow of abstinence, realistically
             taken in the wake of masturbational "oblivion." The
             encounter with Cherry only confirmed my decision:
             nowhere near orgasm, and all my conscious powers
             etherized! Until I've learned how to guarantee the
             accuracy of these pages, my one concern must be per-
AIII/b.2b   fecting my procedures. – Paul dropped in, for no par-
BII/b.3b.iii ticular reason. I wondered if he, too, was going to start
             snooping into my life; could he possibly be *the* snoop
AI/a.3a   I'd been warned of? After all the blarney I'd heard from
             Daisy, I felt obliged to ask about his "great new friend-
             ship." He answered quietly, "It's hard to explain. It's
             been like making friends when you're nine years old.
             Everything we do is fun because we're doing it
             together. I'm taking the afternoon off to go *sculling*
AIII/b.2d   with him, can you believe it? And I know it'll be great."
AI/a.3a   Naomi then appeared to tell me that I had a call and
AI/a.1   would I please connect my phone. Paul left. It was
             Maganoff. He was canceling our lunch date because he
             was appearing before a university disciplinary com-
             mittee and had to prepare his so-called defense. "But
             they'll be doing the defending, not me. Backing down's
BII/b.3a   not in my line." What was he talking about? We had
             no date for lunch.

I looked at the work piled in front of me – orders,
letters, and similar boredoms. What would Maganoff
have done with them? Most of it wasn't fit to make
gliders out of. I went to ask the others what the meeting was about. No one knows: the subject is shrouded
in secrecy; no secretaries will be present. Back in my
office, I wondered if this occasion wasn't perfect for a
presentation of my work on split rings. It was ten minutes to ten by now, with no time to get anything else
done. I took the split-ring file from my briefcase and
glanced over its contents. I regretted not having more
time to prepare myself, but the opportunity was too
good to pass up. I made a point of being the first to
arrive in Mr. Valde's office so that I could atone for last
night's gaffe. I plunged right in: "Did you enjoy the
opera, Mr. Valde?" He seemed taken aback by my
forthrightness. "How about you?" Remembering
Cherry's words, I answered, "With a work as great as
that, every version is enthralling." He nodded approv-
ingly. The others came in. Aside from Mr. V., we were
four in all – Fritz, Paul, Stan, and me (why not Louis?).
Mr. Valde called the meeting to order and started talking. Earlier in the week, Paul had come up with an idea
for a brand-new product. (That old buddy sure is
trusting.) We were to clear time during the next fortnight for programming its manufacture and marketing. Meanwhile, we were to tell no one about it. "*No
one*: that means anyone not in this room. Am I understood?" We mumbled grave assent. Paul would give a
full briefing early next week. And that was all. Scarcely
five minutes had passed. I was expecting Mr. Valde to

The margin notes, from top to bottom, read:

A II/b.6
B II/b.3b

A I/a.3a

B II/b.3b

B II/b.3a
A II/b

A I/b.2a

A I/a.3a

A I/b.2b

A I/b.3a

give us time for questions, but the meeting was clearly over: I had to make my pitch while the rest were starting to leave, not a promising situation, and of course I had to talk fast and to the point. I really had no point, except for the magical phrase "split ring," so (after an introductory "Since new ideas are in the air...") I uttered it with a few additional half-sentences on its physical-energy-generating potential and its design potential and its marketing potential. Unfortunately,

A I/b.2b   I was unable to muster any telling details off the cuff, but after some initial gestures of impatience, Mr. V.

B II/b.3b.iii   and the others settled back and listened attentively. This reassured me because what I dreaded most was

A I/a.3a   the barrage of wisecracks that my colleagues can unloose at such times. If I ended a little inconclusively, everyone, I think, appreciated my brevity, and Mr. V. punctiliously thanked me for sharing my speculations.

A I/b.2a   I waited after the others had left because I needed

A I/a.3a   Mr. Valde's permission to go to my doctor's appointment in the afternoon. He accorded it most willingly and added, "If it's at the hospital, you can go with Stan. What do you know, everybody will be out except Fritz and the girls, and it just *happens* to be Friday afternoon!" I pointed out that this was Thursday. "You're right, and since it's Thursday, be *sure* to go to the hospital!" I didn't get the joke and didn't insist (I know I can be as dull as any Thessalonian peasant).

B II/b.3b.ii   I felt glad that I'd at last broached my secret enthusiasm and that the concept *split ring* had lodged, however fleetingly, in other ears. I was so pleased that for the rest of the morning I attended without stint to

: 158 :

A II/b.6   company business. By 1 P.M. I felt I had earned the right
A I/b.2a   to resume my own work. I'd fallen behind in my record-
keeping and devoted myself to that with only one
A I/b.2b   interruption, by Cherry (who else!), who brought me
A I/a.3a   a *donar kebab*, yet another yogurt ("It can't do me any
harm" – "It'll do you good!"), and a half bottle of
wine (I explained that for a while I had renounced
such pleasure; to my surprise, she scolded me: "You
B II/b.3a   should *give* yourself pleasure, it's what you need – why,
it's better for you than yogurt!" Does this confirm the
suspicions inspired by her earlier embrace?) She saw
A I/b.2b   that I was embarassed to eat in front of her and went
A I/b.2a   away. I ate with gusto – the *donar kebab* was surprisingly
good, though I'd like to know its name in plain lan-
A I/b.2b   guage. After that I went back to my *grand oeuvre*, down
to this very page, line, and period. Here's Stan.

8:15 P.M.

A I/b.2a   We left together a little before two. Stan said nothing
on the way to the tram stop, where, even though it was-
n't my usual line, I stayed behind him to make sure our
driver wasn't my antagonist. I'd left the book of tickets
B II/b.3b   for him in yesterday's black jacket, and I wanted to face
A I/a.3a   him with clincher in hand. During the ride, Stan
emerged from his glumness to initiate a short and
startling exchange. He announced that he was going to
visit his daughter; she had been hospitalized after having a miscarriage. I told him I'd heard as much. "You
did? Why didn't you speak to me about it?" "What I
heard was that she was having an abortion, no problem
with that, but you never know – I thought you might

be sensitive on the subject." "I *am* sensitive on the subject. She's not having an abortion, she's had a miscarriage. Who told you it was an abortion?" I claimed not to remember; in truth I didn't remember. Stan pursed his lips irritably. I asked, "Who's the proud father?" "Somebody called Gert. She won't tell us his last name. He's still in school, for God's sake. It doesn't matter who he is. The sooner it's over, the better." He paused. "What's wrong with these kids? It's not like it was in our time, when all that was taboo. I thought they learned what to do by the third grade." I kept my mouth resolutely shut to stifle the question: what was his daughter's given name? The information wasn't forthcoming: Stan, too, had relapsed into silence.

A III/a.1
A I/b.2a   The outlying neighborhood around the hospital had a Sunday-like emptiness, but once through the gates we found ourselves in a crowd. People scurried around like ants on a kicked anthill. The parking lot itself was incessantly crisscrossed by patients, order-
B II/b.3b.iii   lies, nurses, and doctors. I dreaded the moment of passing through the main entrance: I go into hospitals as though they were reverberatory furnaces refracting anxiety, boredom, stale heat, and the unseen, unheard, unavoidable presence of all that smolders beyond — what doctors slyly call "discomfort" and is simply pestering or excruciating pain. Stuck onto the left-hand
A III/a.1   jamb of the door was a massive wad of chewing gum,
B II/a   looking like my anus thirty years from now, but this disgusting, haunting image may have been only a relic
A I/b.2b   of my dream of last night. We proceeded to the central waiting room, which suggested an airport more than

an old-fashioned hospital, and sat down on a long half-upholstered bench perpendicular to the facade and its curtain of sun-filled windows. Across the entire wall opposite us, from the six-meter-high ceiling almost to the floor, a painting in neo-Mexican style depicted a scene inspired by both Lorenzetti's *Buon Governo* and Cranach the Elder's *Fountain of Youth*: on the left, long lines of ailing citizens, mainly glamorized peasants and laborers, converged towards a central point where squads of physicians smilingly wielded the tools of their depressing trade (one brandished a hammer, which seemed apt), while departing to the the right, emerging patients strode along with wounds bandaged, deformities remedied, diseases cured, and missing limbs replaced with brightly functional arti-

A III/a.1

A I/b.2b

facts. Stan got up and started walking restlessly around the waiting room. He came back to point across the

A I/a.3a

crowded space: "There's Paul!" We walked over to

A II/b.2a

where my ever-so-dear friend was sitting. His ears

A III/b.2b

turned bright red when he saw us, though he kept his

A I/a.3a

features resolutely composed. He spread his arms enthusiastically and announced, "I'm here with a friend; it's completely unexpected." He was clearly

A I/a.3a

stalling – why didn't he ask us what *we* were doing here? I inquired if the friend was Jago. "Oh, no." While he was scanning his repertory for next words, my name

A I/a.3b

was announced: "… Dr. Melhado is expecting you, room Forty-three." Paul smiled in relief and raised his hand as if deferring to my need to be on my way.

A I/b.2b

Dr. Max did not receive me alone. He was seconded by Dr. Paula Abramowicz, to whom I'd been sent once

A I/a.3a   during the summer. Dr. Max invited me to describe my problem. I had prepared a detailed exposé, but I had barely finished two preparatory sentences when he told me to undress (did he really say, "Please dis-

A III/a.1   robe"?). I sat on the edge of the examining table to be subjected to the usual palping and probing: pulse rate; blood pressure; auscultation; eyes, ears, nose, mouth,

B II/b.1   and various reflexes checked. Dr. Abramowicz watched the procedure closely; I had not remembered her as

A I/b.2b   being so unsmiling. During the examination the three

A III/a.3   fingers of my right hand again began twitching. (I chided myself for omitting this omen from my morning's catalog.) While sitting on the table, I was allowed

A I/a.3a   to proceed with my list of symptoms. I spoke light-

B II/b.3b.iii   heartedly enough about them. If I'd implied a certain urgency in obtaining this appointment, now that I was here I didn't want them to take me for a panicky hypochondriac incapable of enduring what was only

A I/a.3a   an accumulation of nuisances. So I spoke in a quiet, lighthearted tone, laughing occasionally at the excesses of my account – for instance, why didn't I call palpita-

A III/b.2e   tions plain shivering? The physicians did not smile back or nod sympathetically; instead, once I was

A I/a.3a   finished, semi-friend Max asked a long, detailed series of questions about my diet, exercise, and sleep habits. I was happy to tell them about my giving up wine without coming apart at the seams (laugh), and how I'd discovered that I needed much *less* sleep than Madre Mia would ever have thought. A last, almost casual question concerned the medicines they had prescribed two weeks ago: had I been taking them regularly? I

countered, "I believe you prescribed me *one* medicine?"
"In that case," Dr. Max gravely replied, "have you been

B II/b.3b.iii   taking *it* regularly?" I finally said, "Pretty much," but I
could see that my hesitation amounted to a giveaway,

A I/a.3a   so I told them that I would speak frankly but that in
turn they must accept the significance of a new devel-
opment in my life, one that had nothing to do with
medicine, though I considered it both a symptom and
an agent of ultimate health — that was to say, my journal project. I talked about the project with what I trust
was eloquence and even passion. I described the com-
plexities of the work and the ever-increasing extent to
which I day after day realized that it required, besides
time, exceptional alertness of mind and sensibility,
something that their drugs might well diminish — that
was why I had stopped using them. Furthermore my
"disobedience" had done no harm ("but I realize I
should have consulted you before making such a decision"), and now that I had spoken to them, I felt that
all the little problems that had so upset me this morning could hardly be considered problems at all — I'd
probably made half of them up, there wasn't anything

A I/a.3b   seriously wrong with me at all, and I should honestly
apologize for wasting their time. My two antagonists
at this point exchanged a glance, perhaps of interroga-
tion or confirmation, but of undoubted complicity. So

A III/b.1c   I was moved to turn as if to an imaginary accomplice
and exclaim, "Friend, it looks like we're in trouble" —
of course I meant it as no more than a joke, I was sim-

A I/a.3b   ply lightening the atmosphere a bit. But as noted, those
people are not long on humor. With tightened lips

(how does one accurately describe that facial expression – the lower lip placed over the upper and squeezing it upwards, with a slight clenching of teeth, the whole indicating pseudo-thoughts like, "Just as I feared," "We've got our work cut out for us," and so on?) Dr. Max suggested I return briefly to the waiting room so that he could talk "things" over with Dr. Abramowicz. It would take only a few minutes. They'd have me called the moment they were finished. Thank you, my Hippocratic paragons. I appreciate your confidence, I have confidence in your appreciation. Gazing into their calculated eyes, I tried to extrapolate where I'd gone wrong.

I left and turned back down the depressing bright corridor. I approached a double door on the right that I'd noticed on the way in because a sign over it read Gynecology and Obstetrics and made me think of Stan. From this door Daisy now emerged. The unexpected sight brought tears of joy to my eyes. I guessed at once why she was there – I rushed after her and, catching her arm, immediately asked her, "How's she doing? Did you see Stan?" She stared at me, speechless. She had gone chalk-white. At last, her hand on her bosom, she gasped, "You scared me to death. I thought I'd met your double. What are you doing here?" "Getting checked out by Dr. Max and a strong, silent female called Paula Abramowicz. I don't think you've met her." "Of course I have. I remember her very well." "But how's Leonora? Stan told me about the miscarriage." Daisy regarded me cautiously. "You know it's definite?" "Yes. Why ask me?" "Only to make sure you

: 164 :

knew." She paused and glanced down the corridor to her right. "We were wondering how to break the news. Now everything's fine." She did not sound fine. She started off at her peculiarly fast pace and, when we came into the central waiting room, headed straight for Paul. I couldn't keep up with her. I reached them in time to hear her tell our bewildered friend, "So you see, it's all over, it's definitely a miscarriage." Paul did not reply but reflectively nodded his crapulous head. My name was again being droned over the loudspeaker. I asked, "Want to come along?" and turned my back on them to lead the way at my own lively clip. I had barely walked through the door of room 43 and sat down in front of the desk when Paula Abramowicz at last broke into speech. She hammered her words home with an emphasis made all the more jarring by her earlier silence: "You have only one problem. It has a very simple solution: start taking the tranquilizers we prescribed. If you do that, you'll be fine. If you don't, you won't. We know you're full of wonderful schemes, but they don't matter. Not now they don't. What matters is that you start behaving like a responsible adult. Take the medicine. It won't slow you down. It won't dull your perceptions. We don't want to hamper your activity in any way; we want you to be well. You should know that. If you don't believe it, ask your wife and friends. We'll give you one drug in moderate doses. If the lorazepam doesn't work for you, or if you feel you're reacting badly to it, we're prescribing another drug you can use. But you've got to take one or the other. You need it, period." She pronounced the name of the second drug, but it didn't register – chrono-some-thing. Dr. Max then spoke, in a gentler tone – the car-rot after the stick: "I added something for relief of your intestinal problems. Start taking it when you go

A III/b.2e.i home. Things should settle down in a day or two." I wondered how long Dr. Max had been playing Mr.

A I/a.3a Nice Guy with me. I'd always taken him for the real McCoy. He went on "I've also given you some tablets – I know you like to be told the generic names for these things: it's bromazepam – a mild relaxant. You should

(B II/b.3b.ii) use it if you have trouble sleeping." Trouble? My trou-ble is having no time for it. As if reading my thoughts, Paula Abramowicz struck again. "If you don't get more sleep, you're going to go to pieces. You're doing to yourself what the secret police do to political prison-ers to break down their psychic integrity. Stop it. Today. Do you understand?" That put the tin lid on it. I could have pointed out that she'd lied when she spoke of "one drug," since I'd just been prescribed a second,

A III/a.1 but I realized I'd get nowhere with such a harpy. As she completed her strictures, she glanced over my left shoulder. I turned around quickly, not quickly enough

B II/b.3b.iii to actually see Daisy before she slipped out of the room. Matters became much clearer. Needless to say, I

A I/b.2a concealed my disgust at what had been said. More than disgust: bitterness that they had heard not one

A I/a.3a word of what I had conscientiously told them about my project. I kept my feelings to myself and said they were absolutely right and I would follow their orders religiously. "It's true," I concluded. "I *have* been feeling a mite allotropic these past few days." They looked at one another, then back at me. I explained, "You know, as if I were turning into white powder." Again I laughed when I said this; again they were not amused. Have they never read the *Dictionary of the Sensations "As If"*? — No sign of Daisy in the corridor, none in the big waiting room, none at the front door. Outdoors the sky pulsed in oppressive glare. For the record, uniformed Dr. Abramowicz revealed no attire other than pearl-gray hose, black pumps, a modest necklace of dark stone with a small bracelet to match, and a wedding ring (poor man). Dr. Melhado sported an undeniably beautiful pale-green cotton shirt, a dark-blue tie, and brown gabardine trousers.

A III/b.2c.i/a.1

It wasn't yet four when I left the hospital. Normally (but who wants to be normal?) I could have taken the rest of the day off — nobody expected me back at work — but I returned to the office because there I would be alone and at peace. During my ride I was depressed by the melancholy blaze of the westering sun (I'd sat down on the wrong side of the tram and was bombarded with light and heat). It was a relief to be at last upstairs, away from the street. Mr. Valde saw me come in. "Go all right on death row?" "Not too bad." "How about Stan?" "I lost track of him after we went in. So did Paul," I pointedly added, assuming that he'd told his sculling tale to all concerned. But Mr. Valde showed no surprise. I was then smitten by unexpected and unexpectedly nasty rage and went off to my cubicle without another word. I plugged in my extension and at once called Colette. I didn't know who else to call (Daisy wouldn't be home yet), and I "had to talk to

A I/b.2a
B II/b. 3b.iii

A I/b.2a
A III/a.2

A I/b.2a
A I/a.3a

B II/b.3a

A III/b.2b

A I/a.1
B II/b.3a
B II/b.4

someone" — such are the idiocies we repeat to our-

selves, as if our survival depended on the dregs of each
other's conversations. So I called Colette. From the
outset I could tell that she had "something on her

B II/b.3b.iii

mind" (more dregs), that something had come between us, and like the rest of humanity I cannot resist

A I/a.1

rising to such bait, or is it the pure pleasure of the
hook? So I pursued this estranging something, through
initial coldness, then hypocritical requests to be left in
peace, then denials, at last to a question, in answer to
my own questions, that dispensed with all evasiveness
and quivered with anger or pain or both: "Are you hav-

B II/b.3a,b.ii

ing an affair with someone else?" I'd had no idea she
would say that. I had no desire for her to say anything
like that. She had dumped me onto foreign terrain
leagues away from my own concerns — aside from
which, being asked this question twice on the same day
struck me as a loathsome indignity. Or at least a big
nuisance. What had gotten into womankind of late?
And I didn't know what to say. I had to say something,
since saying nothing was creating a silence that would
only confirm Colette's suspicions, not that she doesn't

A I/a.1
B II/b.3b.ii,iii

deserve a little anguish for getting so neglectful of me,
so I said the obvious: how could she imagine . . . ? I
meant the question as a purely rhetorical prelude to
the reaffirmations of love that I was sure were expected

A I/a.1

of me, but she took it seriously: why, she asked, had I
avoided seeing her alone all week? She had nothing
against family dinners, but did I consider them appropriate for lovers? Why had I hardly spoken to her on

B II/b.1

the phone? Why did I speak to her as I did when I

called her? Listening to her carrying on, I couldn't help remembering my earlier speculations about attack as defense, but unless Colette has managed to conceal a talent for playacting these many years, an increasingly audible threat of tears made such a maneuver now

A I/a.1 unlikely. I interrupted her harangue to tell her she was talking horsefeathers. "You've got the wrong party. Don't you know me by now? You're making it all up. You're overreacting wildly to perfectly ordinary behavior. You've got to understand, this has been a strange week, I've been busy with all kinds of things, I'll tell you all about it when we do meet, and of course the

B II/b.2a sooner the better." "How about right now?" I asked myself whether I was suffering from a persecution

A I/a.1 complex or merely from persecution. I'm afraid the result is the same. "No, *not* right now. Soon, though. Anyway, that's not what *I* wanted to talk about — that's not why I called. Can you please tell me what's going on with Daisy?" The hurt tone at once left Colette's voice, though not, surprisingly, the teariness, but that may have been physical overlap. "Oh, no," she said, "you mustn't worry about Daisy. Daisy's all right, she really is," and many more words to this effect, all of which sounded so asinine that tears or no tears I felt my temper shriveling, and I again interrupted her and said, Yes, yes, I was glad to hear it but (and I used some pretext as forgettable as it is forgotten) I had to bring our conversation to an end right *now*, and did so, re-

A II/b.6 membering to unplug the phone immediately (not only because of her: I keep my phone disconnected as a general policy because *all* personal calls I get are a waste of my time, and most business ones, too).

Cherry of course picked this very moment for a visit; her excuse was saying "good-bye for the day." I got right up and walked her to the main exit. I realized that my testy reaction fell short of reason or rightness, if such things exist, and also that I was prompted by not only impatience but dread of a replay of this morning's languorous hug. I assumed that in front of the staff I'd be safe. But except for us, the whole staff had left. I couldn't push Cherry out the front door; and sure enough, I was engulfed in so melting an embrace — I felt her nipples through my shirt, the succulent fleshiness above her knees, the not-quite-flat belly nudging my pubic bone — that I scrambled through a lifetime's rushes: my first cheek-to-cheek, the first hand on my cock, the first mouth, the thing with Daisy, C.'s moistened eyes, but all namelessly immersed in womanhood-as-Cherry. I didn't know what to say or do, but it didn't matter: Cherry with a parting caress of my unhinged jaw and a musical "Bye-bye" vanished down the stairs, leaving me teetering in the doorway like a mooncalf.

Coming to, I found my earlier suspicion and aversion redoubled. What game was she playing? What was she after? It had to be a game because Cherry was young and touching and scrumptious, while I was old, or at least older, and today feeling decidedly old. Why have I begun feeling so old? At the same time, my nerves were jangling to another tune, and that was my main gripe. She couldn't have known, but she'd switched on high-voltage circuits when what I needed was to quietly put my life in order. "She couldn't have known" – what a laugh! When she left, her eyes were again wet with the look of utter fondness (the most provocative of all) that renounces any thought of sensuality. She knows what she's doing.

A I/b.2d   No one left but me and the cleaning woman (and maybe someone else: I could hear it, but I didn't know who it was and didn't care). She was standing in front of the housekeeping closet, and I'd noticed stacks of

B II/b.3a   the most promising materials on the top shelf. I thought, Whaddya know! My anger didn't lessen, but it shifted into another mode: no longer a dog chasing

B II/b.3b   its tail, but a dog waiting for a fat cat to chase. But I started boiling again when I got back to my outhouse or office. How many years do I have to spend in this ingrown toenail of unfree enterprise? Is this what the

A I/b.2d   stranger of Mantineia told Socrates, that the superior life means the contemplation of pure shit? I went out every five minutes or five seconds to see whether the

A II/a.1d   cleaning woman had left, and in between thanked my prescience in creating these notebooks to reinvent my

A I/b.2c   life in – "reinvent" is premature, but I'll get to it; at

A I/a.3a   least get my hands on the filthy squirmy thing – it's my only hope of peace. After half an hour I heard the phone ring out front. I was by now in a state of self-perpetuating agitation. In a whimsical display of speed the cleaning woman appeared and announced in her

A I/a.1   Ruritanian whine that I had a call. I plugged in and got Daisy. She said she was worried because I wasn't home. I couldn't believe it. "I'm not home because Mrs. Menopause is vacuuming the lint between her toes. If

A I/a.3a there was something wrong, you'd hear from me." I said, "I *know* it's pointless and I can't really tell you B II/b.3b what it's all about, but if I could find a medium-size A I/a.1 pickax I'd clean up this place in no time." I couldn't write anymore. I decided to call C. back. When she answered, I demanded, "What are Daisy and Paul hiding from me? That's what I meant to ask you earlier. So what do you know about that?" C. had apparently returned the gift of speech unopened. I hadn't as much as said hello, but then we do have this ongoing phone conversation day after day, she's used to that, picking up wherever we left off and forging on from one pilfered moment to the next. "Well?" "I don't know," she finally said. "I don't know anything. I'm not sure I A III/b.2a know what you're talking about." She was lying. My A I/a.1 C.! Crotch-deep in dissimulation! So much, I thought, for lovers' trust. In a whisper I said, "Wait," knowing I must exit as fast as I'd arrived, "wait. Mr. Cinderblock is here." "Who?" "Our guide and leader. So long."

A II/b.6   Out again to reconnoiter: still the tortoise with the hair. Why not finish her work and skedaddle? No one's A I/b.2c checking up on *her* (maybe Mr. Valde installed a clock all for her to punch?). From my desk I heard the front B II/b.3b door close. I could hardly believe it. Mentally rubbing B II/b.1 my hands, or rubbing my mental hands (I'll never get A II/b.6 these distinctions!), I walked straight to the housekeeping closet. It was locked. The lock wasn't much, but in my mood I hadn't the patience for fiddling with it, and I started looking around for appropriate implements. Naturally all bona fide tools were stashed inside the selfsame closet. I tried scissors: big ones wouldn't fit under the door, small ones bent. Rulers broke or buckled. I went from desk to desk yanking open drawers, not knowing exactly what to look for and no less determined to find it. Finally I remembered the drafting room beyond Mr. Valde's office, and there I spotted something I thought might work: the blade of a big paper cutter. First I had to find a way to separate it from the board to which it was ever so robustly bolted. No tools for that, either. Holding the blade handle, I pointlessly banged and kicked the board for a while. I must get back early in the morning and straighten up. At last, after wedging the board between two five-decker filing cabinets with the blade side upward, I stood on its edge, grasped the handle with both hands, and by dint of prolonged heaving up and down worked the blade free. Back at the closet, I forced the jagged metal end under the door, which I jimmied astutely until the blade slid in far enough for good leverage. I then raised the left side of the door and eased it off its hinges. One pull opened it wide. The sound of the lock breaking loose may have been the happiest moment I've ever spent within those revoltingly familiar walls. I now realize that in my exultation I forgot all about the unhinged door and didn't put it even approximately back in place — with a little maneuvering I could have reinstalled it almost perfectly — something else to take care of early tomorrow.

At the time such concerns lay light-years away. I had focused on certain items on the closet's laden shelves, amid the dusters, the paper toweling, and the cleaning liquids in their unshapely, half-empty pastel

B II/b.1

B II/b.3b

A II/b.6

bottles: twenty-four packages of toilet paper, with a few odd rolls to spare. Each package contained six rolls. I pulled out the stepladder, climbed up to the shelf, and, happily impatient as I was, eviscerated one package then and there before starting on my way, appropriately, to the toilet. The appropriateness for me had to do with its window. It opened onto the building's dismal and dismally lighted yard, directly above a solitary tree – a very plain plane tree, under-shaded and lopped off and cut back and all the same

B II/b.3a surviving well enough to rise to about fifteen hard-earned feet. If I were a novelist I would use it in an alle-gorical tale of office life: the image of the poor clerk chained for years to his desk yet indomitably preserv-ing his creativity intact. Aside from that, I've always pitied that shitty little tree, and anyone who laid eyes on the gray dusty untended narrow sunless pit it has to live in would feel the same. So! Time for a small homage to our tree, a little dressing up, a little celebra-

B II/b.2 tion. "Tree, accept this acknowledgment from a stead-fast admirer!" I wished I'd practiced beforehand, but

A I/b.2a where can you practice tossing bumwad out a window? My first roll almost missed entirely, the second caught two lower branches instead of the intended crown, and progress came only gradually. Since I had no lack of materials, I didn't much care (I went back and emptied two more packages), and anyway I knew the point was to enjoy myself, which I fucking well did. I noticed by the beginning of package no. 2 that with no apparent breeze the unwinding strands were nevertheless drift-ing conspicuously leftward, so I began throwing higher and farther to the right. I placed the last four rolls

B II/b.3b beautifully, if I say so myself, getting them to criss-

cross neatly as they draped the tree from near to far

A I/b.2c side. I felt better than I had in all my years in that hon-

orable and soul-degrading place of work. The results

fell halfway between a bandaged giant and a monu-

ment to the inventor of fettuccine. I spent an enjoyable

A I/b.2a couple of minutes surveying my handiwork, then

decided it was time to go home.

Having cleared my desk, I was on my way to the

A I/b.2b front door when I heard it open, and there was the

A I/a.3a cleaning woman. "You're back?" I asked. Her arrival

B II/b.3b almost wrecked my good mood: for a moment I was a

little boy who'd been caught putting flies in the raisin

A I/a.3a cake. She respectfully asked if I was all right. "Of

course I'm all right. Can't you see I'm all right?" She

looked at me quizzically, then lowered her eyes. "I was

upstairs, sir. I heard some kind of shouting. I thought

you might have locked yourself in the bathroom."

"Locked myself in the bathroom? I wasn't — oh, yes,

the shouting — *yes*. I understand. But there's no cause

for alarm. And I'm perfectly all right. Let's all go home

now, shall we?" She nodded reluctantly. I should have

A I/b.2a thought twice before accompanying my final shots

with jubilant cries of "Kiss my ass, Mr. V.!" and "Jago,

stick *this* in your bank account!" I never dreamed that

A I/a.3a cunt was still in the building. "How did you get your

A I/b.2c nice white shirt so dirty?" she then asked, and I saw

that a greasy stripe of dirt now ran across my shirt-

front, a little above the waist. I'd inadvertently leaned

A I/a.3a against the bathroom window railing. I answered

debonairly, "It must have happened before you cleaned things up." She did not deign to smile, nor did she question my reply; to my relief, she turned and preceded me out the door to go back upstairs, while I descended to the ground floor and sallied out onto the populous square.

A I/b.2b

Why this nosy, humorless woman didn't give me a new (and perfectly justifiable) fit remains one of the day's mysteries, but she didn't, and I strolled towards the tram stop rejoicing in my bathroom exploit. I paused on my way to allow the cortege of a Jewish wedding to go by. It was the first time I'd seen a rabbi dressed entirely in white, an attire that made him look garish to my uninformed eyes; I wondered if my own clothes were anywhere near as conspicuous, white as they, too, were except for the smudge the household engineer had so considerately pointed out and also some kebab dribble mysteriously speckling the inside length of one trouser leg. The white rabbi (research note: do any Jews appear in the writings of Lewis Carroll?) had an arm draped protectively over the groom's shoulders (I assume it was the groom – who else at a wedding needs protection?).

B II/b.3a
A I/b.2c
B II/b.3b
A I/b.2c
A I/b.2a
A II/a.1a

When the cheerful-looking bunch had passed, I crossed the avenue to my tram. Once again Son of Wooden was not in the driver's seat. This disappointed me because my calm, happy mood would have given my words confidence, even authority. Since it was late, I had not one seat but two to myself, plus an abandoned evening paper, which I skimmed through as we started home. (I'd begun reading when I picked up a

A I/b.2a
A I/b.2c
B II/b.3b
A I/b.2a
A I/b.2c

conversation between two men behind me; their voices suggested middle age, but I was afraid they'd stop talking if I turned round to look: "She's so dumb she thought houseleek was something you eat." "No kidding? Well, I'm so dumb I think I don't know what it is." "Sure you know what it is, but you may not know it's called houseleek. You probably call it hen and chickens." "No, I don't. I call it hens and chickens." "Lots of people call it hens and chickens, but the right name, not that I give a damn, happens to be hen and chickens. It is more logical, when you think about it — one hen, many chickens." "Well, I do know what it is, even if I use the wrong name, and I also know enough

A II/a.1a   not to eat it. Do you have any idea what it tastes like?")
A back page announced, "Rome Turns To Smog." Aside from what they revealed about headline writing, the words shocked me: is Rome *la blanche* that polluted? Maybe it's better I never went. (Or was the authorities' concern national and not local?) The eds were nar-

A III/b.2e   rowly stupid and the op-eds broadly stupid. A condescending reference to young Maganoff riled me, but he
A I/b.2c   has to expect such things and very likely does. Between the last two stops I noticed that the Mielczewskis were having firewood delivered, to the inefficient glory of their oversize fireplace. When will these people learn the meaning of conspicuous consumption? But the
A I/b.2a.i   delivery means that summer fuel prices are still in effect, and we could benefit from that ourselves.

A I/b.2c   From the street I glimpsed Daisy at a window. She quickly stepped away so that I wouldn't think she'd
B II/b.3a   been on the lookout. I would now be subjected to her

: 177 :

usual lecture about my lateness, and I was thinking of
giving her a lecture or two myself, but then I was

A I/b.2a through the door and met nothing but sweetness and
B II/b.3b affection (I thus found myself hopelessly in the wrong,
A III/b.1a not that that lets me or anybody else ever *admit* any-
A I/b.2c thing). Daisy acted more carefree than she had in days,
almost happy. This surprised me even more than her
A III/b.1a warmth (she insisted on staying close to me from the
moment I arrived) – after the hospital such behavior
seemed strange, though I hadn't bothered to think
A I/b.2b through why. Then it became apparent that Daisy had
B II/b.3a something to tell me and didn't much want to, and I
A I/a.3a thought, What else is going on that I don't know
about? But it was only that she was abandoning me this
evening because the architect of the rug building was
in town, and the decorative Furmint had thought that
the three of them should meet for a "semi-working
dinner." "'Semi-working'?" I asked. "Because I made
A III/b.1a them promise to keep it short. When dinner's over,
so's the meeting. I want to be with you." This revelation gave me no insight into Daisy's good humor,
which two days ago would have relieved and delighted
A I/a.3a me; today, however, is two days later. She told me she
had set the table for me, prepared a nice meal, and
opened a good bottle of wine. I reminded her tartly
that I had gone off the sauce. "Listen to the way you're
talking to me," she retorted. "You're wound up like a
A III/a.3 fiddle. You don't have to drink the whole bottle, but a
glass or two won't hurt." This gave me pause. And how
could I explain – how can anyone understand how crucial it is for me to come to these pages with a clear

head? I simply said, "Gert can have some, and you can polish off the rest when you come home so early." Daisy shook her head. "Gert won't be back till late." "Leonora?" "Maybe. I really can't say." (Did that mean "don't know" or "am in no position to divulge"?) Daisy then asked whether a good hot bath wouldn't make me feel better. I *always* have a bath when I come home. I told her as much. "Of course, darling, and especially today. Being in the hospital all afternoon must have been a strain." "I wasn't in the hospital 'all' afternoon, and it wasn't a strain, just a fucking waste of time." I then wondered if Daisy's suggestion could be due to something besides fond concern, so I added, with a phony laugh that to my unbelieving ears threatened to become deafening, "Anyway, it's good advice, and off I go." "I'm going to make a couple of phone calls meanwhile." I headed for the bathroom via the bedroom and a hurried disrobing. Hurried because I *knew* something was going on. Once the bathwater was splashing loudly through the open bathroom door, I tiptoed, tape recorder in hand, to a position out of sight but not out of earshot – I wasn't going to lose a word (transcription follows). Daisy was on the phone, all right, but the couple of calls turned out to be one long one. I was in at the start. "Colette?... It's me. I've been phoning you ever since I got back.... Great news. The doctor says it's nothing, it's all over. I have nothing to worry about.... Relief? It's my birthday, Christmas, and a full moon in springtime. That's the first thing I had to tell you.... Thanks. You've been an angel. The other thing – it's not something I want to *tell* you – I'm

A III/b.1a

A I/a.3a

A I/b.2a

A I/b.2c

a little embarrassed, but you *do* know?... Yes, about Paul.... Oh, thank God! I'm glad I'm not the one to break the news – especially about who it's *with!*... And you're not shocked or upset?... You're *pleased?* It really is for the best, for all of us.... Did Jago tell you?... He didn't? Oh. It doesn't matter.... Then you haven't talked to him about it at all? Well, why should you? You know best! ... No, don't worry about him. I have to make sure he takes his medicines, then he'll calm down.... I know.... Just who did have the bright idea of his keeping a diary?... No. He hasn't let me see it, and I'm not going to pry, there's no reason to. By the way, he knows all about Leonora.... Yes. I ran into him at the hospital and didn't know how to explain it, but I didn't have to after all, he did it all by himself. ... Are you joking? Gert would never talk to me about anything like that until at least three girlfriends later. ... My dear, with you it's obviously another story. You can find out anything you like. I wish I could be an older woman who wasn't his mother – up to a point, needless to say..... Aha! *That's* where he's going to-night. I might have known. And naturally Jago will be

A I/b.2a

out?" I had to rush to the bathroom to turn off the water (I didn't dare leave the tape-recorder behind),

A I/b.2c

but I was back in fifteen seconds max: "It's a *very* nice idea. But when, that's the problem.... That would be okay, except maybe not at dinnertime. I can't leave home two nights in a row – how about earlier? I can arrange it.... Wonderful ... six P.M. And there'll be nobody else around? You're a sweetheart.... Take good care of my baby." Hightailing it to the bathroom, I

plunked into the water in time. Daisy was twinkling
like a cruise ship. "Feeling better?" She bent over the
tub to give me a good-bye kiss, leaning on the rim,
keeping her eyes only a few inches from mine as she
looked into them so candidly, so warmly.... *O Susanna,
Susanna, quanta pena mi costi!* "Through with your phone
calls?" "I was talking to Milena Furmint – I lost their
home address, and I wanted to send her a box of chocolates after last night and also to make sure she doesn't
lose any of that adorable weight." "Talking to Milena
Furmint made you so chipper?" "Oh, when he's not
around, she can be a riot. She told me a hilarious story
about their trip to Budapest last year. Another restaurant story." "I'm all ears." "Not now, darling. I'd love
to but I'll be late as it is. I'll come back quick as I can."
"Don't worry about me. And *enjoy* yourself."

I washed, then lay in the bath – I lay there until the
water got too cold for my eyes-open doze. Madre Mia
could never understand why I did this as a boy. She
would come in and harangue me with warnings that
had no more effect on me than they did on the tub.
(I've always felt like the tub: a glazed, heavy thing. I'm
fascinated by the wrinkles that appear on my fingertips,
something no one has ever explained to me.) Before
getting out I considered shaving, then chose to wait
another day or two and see how my beard grows. I
emerged feeling totally limp. I couldn't allow myself to
remain in this state and immediately got dressed for
my solitary evening (black jeans, a T-shirt, an old blue
cotton jacket). To give myself a simple task I decided
to scrub the sneakers I'd been wearing, but I couldn't

: 181 :

get the stains out, not even with scouring powder and

B II/b.3b a wire brush (car grease?). I felt no less enervated afterwards, but I shouldn't have been surprised: hospitals always have that effect on me. I wandered around. I thought of going through Daisy's desk but recalled her

A III/a.1 overheard remark: if she won't pry, neither will I. And

A I/b.2a I don't have to. I'm not that bereft of mother wit. On the bureau in Gert's room I noticed one unsmoked cigarette, which I picked up and lighted with a readiness that now amazes me. The first cigarette I've

B II/b.3b smoked in fourteen years, and thrilling. My hands tingled, my feet tingled, my arms and legs swelled with forgotten ease; it was as though my whole body were inspired. If anybody had told me I would smoke a cigarette tonight I would have laughed; if I'd thought of it myself I would have been disgusted. That was why the experience was so "clean": it came from nowhere, from chance and impulse. I didn't try to justify it then, and I don't regret it now, not for a second. Such feelings lie beyond regret and anticipation. There was a golden-voiced eagle soaring inside me. (Would an occasional smoke be worth trying? While I'm off drink? Be careful about this.)

A I/b.2a In the kitchen I discovered my "nice meal": on the sideboard a little dish of her anchovies (I suppose because I had once liked them); in the warm oven a boned roast shoulder of lamb stuffed with thyme, savory, and halved lamb kidneys; on top of the stove a skillet full of pan fries to be reheated; on the table a

B II/b.3b string-bean salad, a hunk of ewe cheese, and a bowl of stewed pears. Desirable as these imagined favorites might have looked in the old days, they had now

A I/b.2a become obstacles to be circumvented as best I could. But I had to eat something. I turned on the gas under the pan fries, put the anchovies back in their jar, cut off a piece of the roast and flushed it down the toilet with the string beans and a pear, and chucked a crumbled slice of cheese out the window for the sparrows and crows. I rinsed the appropriate plates, stacked them in the drying rack, and sat down to eat the pan fries out of the pan.

A II/a.2a I unintentionally ate them all – I had turned on the TV, and it kept me there much longer than I'd planned. I tuned in to a period soap opera set in eighteenth-century France. It had little to recommend it, but having missed the beginning, I was seduced by the challenge of reconstructing the plot. I think I got it straight by the end.

The Marquis of Jumièges is the lover of the Countess of Périgord, one of whose friends is the Duchess of Something, betrothed to the Marquis and suspected of perpetuating a liaison with the Prince of Castelnau. One of the latter's intimates is his privy counselor, Judge Mertens, and it is from Judge Mertens that we learn about the Marquis, when he asks the Prince about him and, tacitly, about his lover, the Countess. The Duchess of Something (she's the Duchess of D-something, I believe, but I never caught the full name) also knows the Judge, but we first meet her in other circumstances: she is writing to the Countess about the Marquis, whose health has been causing her alarm. She makes no reference to her supposed lover, the

Prince of Castelnau. Nor does the Prince of Castelnau mention the Duchess when he speaks about the Marquis; for reasons no doubt revealed earlier, he is discussing the forthcoming birth of a child to someone whose name is not specified – all this during his conversation with the Judge (who is trying to maneuver him into talking about the love life of the Countess of Périgord). The Countess of Périgord, meanwhile, is writing a letter of her own to the Prince about his "presumed liaison." Is it with someone unsuspected (we cut briefly to the Judge's grave features – he is, after all, pursuing a similar inquiry) or, as rumor has it, with the Duchess? We then see the Marquis of Jumièges in his study. (The Marquis of Jumièges's face has been sprayed with talc to indicate ill health.) And now the Countess is reading the Duchess's letter, and we conclude with yet another view of the Judge's countenance, solemn and concerned, as he declares, "The only true power, by Jove, lies in rule and law." I then discovered that I had been watching a single installment of a weekly serial, and that I would never learn in what sauce this tripe had been cooked.

A I/b.2a   I called Colette, to see what would happen. Nothing
B II/b.3b   happened. Same story later. For "nobody home" read: nobody picking up.

A I/b.2a   Returning to my desk and a stack of bare pages
B II/b.3b   brought me a happiness that, though expected, did not disappoint. Dare my meek anonymous self suggest that nothing in the world makes me so happy? The word *happy* doesn't solve anything; I'm not letting it suck me into illusions. This happiness is not elation, ecstasy, revelation, or the druggy oblivion that I once

sucked out of cool white wine after a long day. I mean only that I'm suited to my task, and it to me. The key fits the lock. (My journal is the key, and I the lock. It's opened me up.) This most suitable task strikes me as no ordinary one *not* because I perform it well (the common lie) but because it exudes a whiff of the sublime. I say this fully conscious of the tempting rhetorical glamour of the word. I'm not laying claim to the absolute; I won't justify my work with epithets whose covert purpose is to consecrate me as a righteous jerk. I know I'm not Plato, nor even Boethius, not Diderot or Maganoff either. I haven't got profundity or clout, nothing but a devotion to the truth. So is my activity the pursuit of the truth? It's *a* pursuit of the truth, a laborious, pedestrian, accumulative one, and not less than that. Not profundity but extensiveness (I escaped the lure of *scope*): establishing bounds as broad as I can imagine them, extending them day after day, and within them honestly gathering all I find. Surely in times of devastation and human helplessness monks in their depopulated monasteries must have felt the way I do — which makes me think that this task is unquestionably a calling, even if nobody called me, even if, instead of responding to some grandiose inner imperative, I stumbled into it almost on a whim. And what if *calling* is only another fine-sounding word? I say it isn't. If my work were anything less, would I sacrifice so much time to it, not to mention the delicious riesling that two weeks ago used to reward me for these discomforting labors?

A III/a.2   Shit, Daisy's back. She's been showing up at the wrong time all day long.

Keep things chronological, or you will deform them. Trouble didn't trouble you until it came. Put it in its recorded place, wait for it to occur, as it did so explosively a few minutes ago.

Daisy came back, not all that early, but too early. She was only keeping her word, I'm not casting doubt on her intentions, but I wish she'd stayed out until now. Two precious hours have been lost. She hurried right in without even taking off her wrap, so fast that I covered what I'd been writing – a humiliating gesture that she kindly ignored. She was still in a lively mood. She asked me how I felt; I said great. "You don't sound it. Come along and keep me company. I'm going to celebrate with a glass of your vino." I shrugged. "What exactly are you celebrating? Another hilarious evening with the Furmints?" "I can't explain, not tonight. There's too much to tell. Come *on*." I knew better than to resist, and I hoped I'd get back sooner if I played along. "Darling," she said, not glancing back as she fetched bottle and glasses, "tomorrow I want to really celebrate, and with *you*. Let's go out together, okay? Let's pretend we just met." "I thought you were busy tomorrow." I mentally kicked myself when I said this, but Daisy took no notice. "Uh-uh. I'm all yours." "You sure? You sure it's *me* you want to celebrate with?" She laughed. "I see what you mean, but you can take *one* night off, you'll have the whole weekend to catch up. And what's so bad about having fun with me? You're not staying on the wagon all your life, are you?" "I don't think so. Only for a while." "It's been too long already. Baby, you're turning into a monk." I smiled. "Is that so bad?" "Not for monks, I guess. But you never exactly overwhelmed me with your monkishness." She ran her tongue between her teeth as she said this; I repressed a shudder, she was so pretty and sensuous. Daisy had turned away. She began telling me about her evening. She told about it in fastidious, unpersuasive detail. The only solid news was that the talented, affable architect on their job had shown himself to be an unapologetic fascist; for instance, he invariably referred to their contracting agent as "that Jew Peters." How could Daisy possibly not have learned this before? I wasn't really listening. I was wondering how to get back to my desk – I had foreseen what would happen: Daisy declared that there was no question of my not coming to bed with her. She maintained her position so cheerfully that after our years together, my refusing her would have been as insulting to my own nature as it was to hers. I followed her docilely into the bedroom, undressed, and waited for her to finish in the bathroom. While I was brushing my teeth, she shouted something to me; my impulse was to tell her to lower her voice because of Gert, but Gert wasn't asleep, he wasn't in bed, he wasn't home. How late would he succeed in staying "wherever he was"? Daisy again called out, "You won't forget your medicines?" I produced a foam-muffled grunt, hoping it would pass as an answer. It didn't. I took the brush out of my mouth. Others could break their promises; why should I have to? Isn't a plain lie better than a broken promise? If I told her the truth, it would ruin her mood and expose me to a benevolent onslaught that would ruin mine. And it would go on the next morning, and in fact continue for as long as it took her to undo what I'd done – that is, torn up the prescription before I'd left the hospital. I have regretted this myself because of losing Dr. Max's remedy for my entrails, now apparently incapable of producing anything – but that at all hours – except dust kittens soaked in beer foam. I said, "I've taken it." "It or them?" "Them." I looked at my reflected teeth, at the sink, at my brush. Shouldn't stannous fluoride help bleeding gums? Then why isn't it (or why is there none in my toothpaste)? Uneasiness seeped into me, like a foretaste of what was to come, like a half-perceived tremor before an earthquake. I needed something stupid to think about, so I reconsidered the TV program I'd watched earlier with a view to calculating every conceivable episode, previous and forthcoming. But the possibilities were too numerous to handle.

I went to bed in a state of irrational foreboding. On Daisy's bedside table the lamp was on, her book unopened. She nestled against me as I lay down, running a hand smoothly down my sternum. I took her in my arms and rocked her gently – an appeal for passive affection and repose. Daisy responded in kind, briefly, then slid one leg between mine, wiggled an index finger into my mouth, and started licking my left nipple. All too spontaneously, I recoiled. I said apologetically, "I did this dumb thing – it was while the bath was running, I thought there'd be time for my sit-ups, so I rushed through them and something went out in my back. Right now I'm not much use." Daisy gave me a quick popping kiss on the lips. "That's okay, don't you worry about it. But *I* think you're turning into an old monk." She put out her lamp, gave me a good-night hug in the dark, and gathered herself on one side in preparation for sleep. Her remark made me wonder (though I didn't deserve the name of monk) whether going on a retreat might not solve some of my problems: I would have time to analyze the accumulation of recent events and coordinate (at least mentally) my confused and confusing relationships; best of all, I could bring every aspect of my work up to date and supplant daily improvising with a definitive organization of my materials. While waiting for Daisy to fall asleep, I speculated about where I could go on such a retreat. A room rented in some remote part of town? A vision of Little Bratislava came to mind; there must be cheerier places. A farmer's cottage? Except the weather would soon turn cold – I'd spend half the day splitting firewood. Daily recourse to a library? Perhaps. A monastery itself might not be bad, provided one had survived nearby that took in lay escapists (what do you call a person on a retreat?). Over half an hour had passed when Daisy turned on the light and sat up. "What about our finally going on one of those trips you keep talking about? Gert can look after himself for a week or two. There's Rome — you always complain that it's the greatest city in the world and you've never been there." I said I'd heard that it had become dangerously polluted. "That's hard to believe, but if you say so. And Syria? *That* can't be polluted. Not the desert part." I said I'd love to go there, and love to go there with her, but it would be foolish to visit such a place unprepared; I felt I had lots of reading to do first, and she would want to do some reading herself. "Oh, no, it's better when you do it for me. You always get everything so irresistibly mixed up. Well," she sighed, "thank God for Lake John XXIII." She turned out the light and curled up. In the darkness she reminisced about travels of past years: ten clear days in the mountains one October, a week spent at the seashore early one summer (we had not been lovers long, and sand and sun were spice to our desire). At last she fell silent. Another fifteen minutes went by, and I could hear she was not sleeping. I ran no risk of falling asleep myself, and I resolved to wait until it was absolutely safe before making my getaway.

Thus, as I lay in late-night darkness, thinking of nothing, expecting nothing, waiting for the steady breathing that would signal Daisy's slumber, there rose into view, with no other warning than the tremor of anxiety that I had scarcely noticed earlier, the recognition of the somber truth that I had so stubbornly been shirking during the past days — a truth so obvious that ignoring it could only be explained by unconscious terror. And as I slowly followed its ramifications, I saw how harshly it has riddled the multiple facets of my life — the perceptions of what I do (and of what I've done before, in a past I thought finished), the arduous consideration I've given to ordering my hours and days, the attitudes that I have, I thought, so suitably adopted towards the life around and within me. How could I have been so blind to this harsh, dark truth as not to see it earlier? I would have welcomed it earlier, since the truth cannot be denied and knowing it can lead ultimately only to wisdom and happiness, or at least to less folly and less unhappiness. But I had denied it, and now I turned ice-cold, cold in my bones and in every frozen wire of my nerves. I had denied truth, and all my confidence and resolution dissolved straight into despair. I saw no way out of this despair except to sob childishly, like a child over a lost toy; the toy was not my life but was such a manifold part of it that the rest seemed as distant as figures standing on a far-off, sunny beach must to one drowning in an overwhelming swell. I couldn't sob because my least shudder would have alerted Daisy, and of course I could not confide in her and had no hope of being able to invent some convincingly spurious explanation. And in whom of all those I thought close to me could I now in fact confide? I stared hard into the darkness and let the darkness black out the source of my misery, for the while, for the while only, promising whatever Furies lay in wait that once I was alone I would not run away.

She fell asleep a little past midnight, and a few minutes later I slipped out of bed, silently picked up the clothes I'd been wearing, and came here. At first I couldn't face committing what I had understood to paper. I walked barefoot back and forth for a quarter of an hour, only then guying myself into action: what kind of journalist was I who when I made a discovery couldn't bear to write it down? And I realized that I didn't have to to begin with the worst but could delay it until its proper time. So I sat down and began writing what happened after Daisy came home.

That helped. My icy panic has left me. I can face my failure without the breath-clutching dread I felt earlier. What I discovered is this: all the care I have brought to organizing this journal has been misspent; my laborious classifications have proved worthless; my efforts at competence are an illusion. Why? Because I have left out the chief activity of my life and the chief fact of my project: the keeping of this journal. I devote more time, thought, and passion to it than to anything else, but aside from passing references and noting the hour when I start work, what witness have I borne to it? None. In my elaborate system, what place has been set aside for the compilation of these pages? A niche in A II/b.3*b*, among "verifiable events concerning myself alone"! And it's these pages that keep me from having a dead moment in any of my days, keep me alert, quicken my curiosity, rescue me from indifference (and even from needless sleep). A II/b.3*b*! The making of each page, the making itself, deserves to be accorded its supreme place. The transient mundanities it records survive only through their presence here, while the page itself creates its own transcendent life. Due acknowledgment has been denied. Sub-b, sub-c, and whatnot – the mundanities aren't entirely ridiculous, and they must be recognized for their modest material role. But they do not tell the story, not the main story: the main story of the journal is the journal itself.

How can due acknowledgment be given? I'm so stuck in my habits. I imagine duplicating each existing category with its journalistic parallel: the first records an event, while the second records the event of its recording – for every A I/b.2*b*, a J (for Journal): A I/b.2*b* (or it could be in quotation marks, A I/b.2*b* and "A I/b.2*b*"). I know that won't work. Consider this question: how can I include what happens when I write about A I/b.2*b* (what is happening around me, what I may be thinking about, what my body is feeling, what is experienced by whatever one calls the soul – the self? the selves? the shelves?)? If I put a duplicating frame around my old system, then I would have to make a frame for the frame, to include what was happening while I made the frame, and then another frame for that – a discouragingly infinite regression: not only A I/b.2*b* and J: A I/b.2*b* but J: J: A I/b.2*b* and J: J: J: A I/b.2*b* (or A I/b.2*b*, "A I/b.2*b*", "'A I/b.2'''…). I have to invent a better solution. But not now, in this state of shock. Dear journalist, stay boggled. Go back to what you have to do as honest witness to each perished day: recall and review what you have achieved on this particular perishing day. The results will include a strikingly long list of things you haven't done. Achievement as nonachievement: the plain discipline of honesty. You can achieve *that*. It will help you forget Petrarch and whoever else. Perhaps. A few brass thumbtacks for your daily bulletin board:

You didn't:
— exercise (can you in part excuse this irresponsibility since, while you don't want a runaway belly that unhinges your back or arms and legs like sticks, some blame accrues to the laggard cleaning woman who kept you from finishing your business speedily so that you could get home with time to spare?)
— keep up your accounts (you have them in your pocket but resist transferring them to your account book — the reasons may be worth investigating, but by evading a trivial daily effort you are accumulating trouble)
— advance your observational skills (they have regressed because not only have you not worked at them, you've neglected your habitual practices — hardly spontaneous as yet — and one unanswered question proves this: today, what clothes were your colleagues wearing?)
— develop your inner-landscape skills (what *is* your inner landscape? Whatever you mean by it, what you don't know about the sloughs and bird's nests inside you takes priority over being speechless when you face a mushroom)
— pay attention to your health (why are you sweating in the cool of the day? Did you think your digestive system would release you from its spasmodic coils when days ago it sank its claws into

your being? And your doctor, arrogant though he was, offered
you help and you ignored it)
— organize the undesirable facts of your personal life (but the day
isn't over)
— make systematic use of last night's subcategories (given what
you learned in bed, this isn't disastrous, but it shows the costs of
your impatience; the crux is the word *systematic*)
— summarize your phone calls and mail (they were only cited out
of trivial conscientiousness. But shit like that can wait till
Sunday)
— make a note of Daisy's clothes (forget it)
— contribute to household life (when did Gert come in — maybe
he hasn't?), except for eliminating what I didn't eat
— notice "significant accidents" (and one has just come back to
me! And no sooner come than gone, how could it have slipped
my mind so fast — something to do with "deuce"? But merely its
effect again convinced me that this journal is preordained)

Now, this list you have completed may be necessary, but it's not
enough. Ending each day with a catalog of self-reproaches will only
make the catalog longer and longer. Blaming yourself for things not
done will not get things done; it's a recipe for New Year's resolutions.
You have no doubts about the seriousness of this project; so create
for yourself, besides an index of flaws, a compendium of situations in
which they cannot survive. Examples:

"You intend to":
— make discoveries in the domains of:
  books (later: subdomains of poetry, history, art history, psy-
      chology, anthropology, etc., besides works to develop your
      powers of observation)

theater (different periods and cultures)

music (ditto)

movies

— schedule precise times (by the week if not by the day) for reading, watching films, listening to music, doing research

— schedule a time or times every day for the Memorials — yesterday you were always "too busy" for them

— rationalize your budget and make long-term plans for using money

— establish a regimen of exercise and diet (here, as elsewhere, get advice; here in particular, find a new doctor to replace asshole Max)

— explore the spaces you live in; mentally explore what is in them for a day, a season, a year; see how you can contribute more than dishwashing to the well-being of your household (learning to sew? iron? manage plumbing repairs?)

— catalog your clothes, adding a list of your needs *and your desires*

— learn touch-typing to keep your journal more efficiently

— assign space in the journal to Daisy, Gert, Colette, and others who matter

— (cf. Daisy's request) establish travel possibilities and research them (Syria first)

— before each day (and week, month, year, and decade?), list your expectations, hopes, anxieties, wishes, fears and what is it that I crave? what do I worry about? (getting all this done!) (and:)

— invent the Journal of the Journal — henceforth known as J of J — where at last what I'm now doing will find its rightful place in the accounting of my life.

Thus extending my compendium: generation engendering generation. I've already noted enough, and if I don't stop I may never stop!

(*Plus les carences s'installent, plus ça prolifère!*) This elation – what's it like? The moment before the *Idiot*'s epileptic fits; coming up for air; the lights going back on; taking off shoes that are too small; getting out of the army; getting out of a hospital. Doing the J of J – *that's* what the elation's about. This wasn't a disaster after all. I haven't been a blind fool: I've been completing my apprenticeship, and the God of Journals has opened the gate for me to accede to the royal way. The discovery came when it should have; sooner, and it would have passed me by.

I know better than to court beauty in the dead of night. And my head's full of riot. Why has this taken so long? Time for a break – for my evening constitutional.

4 A.M.

For the first half hour, things went well. There was nothing to see and not much to hear. The air was cool, calm, and sweet. Little by little I calmed down as I advanced, staring ever more cautiously ahead as the street became lampless road. Over the top of the neighboring hill it was so black I let my feet search out the paved surface. I felt like a boy out on a dare, going to meet buddies at some forbidden and forbidding place. I didn't think much about anything, preoccupied as I was with trying to walk fast in spite of the darkness and guess at what I couldn't see on either side of that familiar road. Later I thought more, and wished I could stop thinking. This followed an indisposition or spell of some kind, something unheralded and unnameable – would it have helped to have a word for it, if one exists? In a twinkling it was revealed to me that I was going to die then and there. The revelation left no room for doubt. My heart began beating against my chest so hard I involuntarily cried out. I knew I could not survive without help, but because I couldn't stop gasping for breath, my scream was pathetically weak. I turned and started running home. Or thought I did: in fact, I tumbled across the roadside ditch and crashed headfirst into a rough hedge beyond it. I dove right into the hedge and stayed there. Trying to thrash myself free only entangled me deeper in the dense mesh of angular branches. I knew my time had come. I lay there half suspended, calling out in a panicky, strangled voice. Abandoning the struggle helped; though my terror continued, it gradually became intermittent and not constant, with intervals of relative and wholly disagreeable calm. This calm, which finally predominated, was an amalgam of sadness, coldness, and resigned apprehension; I yielded to its gloom. I began sobbing quietly, almost soothingly – the relief of hopelessness preferred to boiling uncertainty. Unwilled thoughts then came, cool black thoughts in cool black night. I won't try to bring them back. They all led to one question and its answer: what is the point of life, if it has one? It has no point, except that when two or three are gathered together (or two or three million), claims are made to an answer, as if the sharing of names mattered.

By bending and unbending my legs I found I could pull myself towards the ditch. I moved cautiously, as though the hedge's twigs might reinject me with the venom of malaise. In ten seconds I had freed myself. When I got up, I almost toppled back, I was so nauseatingly dizzy – even in sunlight I would have seen black. I stood swaying in the ditch, my clothes reeking of privet (at least it wasn't hawthorn). Stepping onto the road, I was about to turn left when I abruptly wondered about my direction. I tried to recall my earlier movements. I had assumed that when I started running I'd made too short a turn to the right, so that turning left and back onto the road would point me home. But if I'd turned left into the ditch instead, heading left now would put the town at my back. And how could I be sure I'd made too short a turn? It would have been easy in the darkness to turn too *far* and go off the other side of the road. Remembering which way I'd turned wasn't enough, since turning right would have led me off to the right side if I'd made a short turn and to the left if I'd made a long turn, and turning left would have led me left turning short and right turning long – four possibilities, not two. I didn't know what to do. Leaving things to chance seemed crazy in my condition. Except, I noticed, my condition had now dissolved into concern for this urgent practical problem. So I decided to go ahead and take a chance. There were worse things than seeing the dawn halfway to Lake John XXIII. I turned left after all. In a moment the faint, welcome glow over our town appeared; after that, I saw a street lamp beyond the top of the hill where my own street ended.

O Colette, Colette, why now? Couldn't you wait to let me go? That's the worst of it. Why was that necessary? It was not necessary. Leaving me no chance to influence the march of our affairs (but not our affair, which it was *not* – "affairs" itself is an ignoble term). Without as much as a word to warn me; to warm me. You will say it is no longer my business. All right. Nothing is my business (except what I'm now doing). When I called tonight I wasn't surprised to get no answer. To hear you not answer. We'll leave it at "that." I can't face this right now, but I'm getting prepared, opening the door a crack, getting ready to walk through it into another hedge. But not yet, because I have other things to do. Inner and outer demons may gather (yet like my discovery tonight – was it really only tonight? – a demon may turn into a half-divine daimon), but I have basic chores to do (those funny relics of my before-tonight life – but I will come to it).

Rule for right now: no chore will be listed until it's done.

4:55 A.M.
All recent subcategories have been added to my index (up to tonight's dislocation of my house of cards). Why bother with them? Answer:

why waste them? They may be dumped next week, or not, but they will have been recorded. In any self-respecting account of the J they deserve at least a mention. Not until the J of J takes shape can I be sure they won't be used. (Should I restructure them?)

5 A.M.

I sketched all new subcategories into my old "journal tree" – my basic tool for finding sense beyond ordinary events. It's too early to establish a new organigram – that must wait until the J of J problem is solved. (Should I start now and draw a line down the middle of the page?)

(I hesitate to write this next chore down – but the significance of the J of J is that the Journal is not only fact but act. Do it. There is nothing to regret about the skepticism you feel, and that you'll go on feeling.)

5:25 A.M.

Gert and C., original hypotheses:

they met out of family affection

they met accidentally

they met to talk about Gert's problem (at last we know what that is)

they met for some other reason

Hearing Daisy on the phone to Colette makes this easy.

Why Daisy and Paul were at the hospital together, résumé of hypotheses:

because of Leonora (if so, unforgivable: they told me nothing)

because I was seeing Dr. Max (so much for professional secrecy)

because of business of their own

. . . .?

. . . .?

and in the Gynecology & Obstetrics department?

I am Bishop Berkeley. Nothing guarantees that phenomena are real because perceived. In other words, I may be nuts.

I conclude that the hypothetical method does not yield satisfactory insight into my problems. This last sentence should be revised to emphasize expressive understatement. But I don't feel inclined to hone my prose right now. I don't feel like taking *any* next steps, although one presses me forward. And I know what to do. But first I'm going to stare at the dawn, my first in a sunth of moondays. Gert tells me that these days Venus is leading the way.

6:30 A.M.

Twilight had begun as I walked back up the hill. The land to the east is flat, with a little roll here and there. At a quarter to six the light started getting much stronger. Past the edge of the town I gazed into what is still predominantly country. At first, with light swelling behind it, it all looked the same, like a wilderness where everything except the sky was dark if not without color – not only black but gray, brown, cinnamon. The southeastern sky was gray, too, like embers blanketed in ash. The embers were heaving upward, but the landscape remained murky; it might have been an American desert, all rocks and billows of sand. I suppose dawn is always like being at the beginning of things. When the sun peeped up, places became clearer and the air itself seemed to clear – miles away I could see vines glinting in tilted vineyards. Another sunny day for the harvesters – a little hot, but better than wet bluster and mud.

Here a passion that had stirred me intermittently through the preceding hours reached its culmination. Standing at the top of the hill, quite alone, opposite an eastern sky majestically filling with light, I felt that I had at last been consecrated in the sacerdotal lay office to which I had elected myself. The sunrise's authoritative, unforeseeable perfection confirmed me in my pursuit of the absolute and in my refusal of compromises that no one would condemn except the imperturbable sun and my perturbable self. How could I otherwise resist the trivial sufficiencies of an ordinary "diarist" (the word revolts me; I've never asked myself why)? I haven't got Plutarch's philosophy or Rousseau's wily gift of confession. I can only enviously admire, and never emulate. What else could sustain me but a sense of dedication *to* and almost *by* a pure idea? My work is not for "the world" (by that I mean *anybody* else) or for me (I hardly have time to read what I've written). It's for "It." "Its" fugitive name does not matter. I've called it truth, and before that reality; since it is never to be completely attained, it may be beyond naming altogether.

No sense pretending it's still Thursday. I won't sleep (I'd never recover – it would be like going to a hospital to get healthy: sleep, our daily hospital). What I'm going to do now is make up a new category. Nothing exalted like the J of J; something down-to-earth. I thought of it while I was on the hill: the Category of Personal Snoopery. I like the name, crude though it may be. Too bad. I would never have thought it up on my own. Others are strictly responsible. One might say I have no choice.

Next I'll take an early tram into town. After breakfast I may go sit in the park to meditate on *the* problem. Before confronting it directly, I must think it through calmly, thoroughly.

8:30 A.M.

I had to avoid waking Daisy at all costs. She would realize at once that I'd not slept with her – and why hadn't I, and where had I been, and so forth. So I ran water softly in the washbasin for a silent if slightly drippy washup (Memorial: a sponge on the edge of my grandfather's bathtub); when I tiptoed into the bedroom to retrieve a much-needed change of clothes, my anxiety grew so violent that I withdrew empty-handed. This meant putting yesterday's clothes back on. My jacket and trousers had inevitably suffered in the battle with the hedge, but the rents were not conspicuous, and I promptly set to work on the smudges with a clothes brush and a cloth dipped and redipped in warm water. (A few bloodstains on the collar and shoulders – the result of inconsequential scrapes to my head – were indelible.) When I was fully dressed, I took a look at myself and decided that for my own peace of mind I should stay clear of mirrors, though plainly it was knowing where all the blemishes were that made me so aware of them, and they might well escape the notice of a neutral eye. I packed all my materials in my briefcase for my forthcoming speculations.

The seven-fifteen tram was as full as my regular one, with blue-collar and not office workers. I'd forgotten all about "my" driver, but there he was. I was unprepared for him. However, in place of his usual belligerence he stared at me with an air of sympathetic consternation, speaking in tones of such unmistakable gentleness that if I'd had any presence of mind I would have hit him. He asked, "Sure you're all right?" I was so flabbergasted I only muttered, "Yes, thank you," before heading aft. I forgot to use the ticket punch, and he forgot to remind me. Luckily there was a window seat at the back. Only swans on the pond today. I noticed wild teasel at the edge of a field of rich plowed earth.

Many places were open for breakfast. I chose one that I knew well (that knew *me* well), near the tram stop, with mediocre coffee but a lively atmosphere, cops and tram drivers stopping in for a quick cup and a pastry. Downtown was already full of people. The veg and fruit shop next to the café was getting ready to open; a young woman came out with a flat crate of green apples to put on display outside. Across the sidewalk a handsome, full-bosomed lady fed crumbs to sparrows hopping appreciatively round her feet. I had time to spare, so I sat at a table; the waitresses are all the same anyway. Mine was no stranger. She took not only my order but my jacket, insisting it would greatly benefit from the equipment backstage. I sat there in an agreeable daze, imbibing five coffees and nibbling what passes in these parts for a croissant. In time, my insides started up their circus of gurgles and spasms. I went to the men's room with little hope of relief; I managed to shoot a little methane out my asshole. Looking at myself in the mirror over the washbasin, I saw that my shirt had kept the imprint of the window ledge in the office bathroom where I'd had such fun yesterday afternoon. I must remember to keep it covered. When the waitress brought my jacket back, she remarked to me cheerfully that in case I needed a barber, the one around the corner opened early. I thanked her and explained that at this stage, growing a beard had inevitably unattractive results. Two secretaries sat down at the next table. On this warm day, they were drinking hot chocolate and eating slabs of cake the size of cobblestones (white, brown). I missed their conversation except for the following: "Her husband wasn't gay, not until now. Then out of the blue he had an affair with a guy. The wife was no problem, but the husband's lover had a friend, and *he* was a problem. He knew something was going on, but nobody cued him in, and he decided the lover was having an affair with his wife, can you believe it?" I paid my check and left (9.00 with tip). On my way here I passed the waitress's barber shop. Through the open door I saw a man being shampooed. His head was encased in a bush of hair so tough that even when washed it didn't wilt. A cloud of foam expanded above his temples, and through it the barber's fingers were inching their delicious way across the immobile skull.

I would have arrived at work in time to write these pages twice over, but I'd barely gotten through the front door when there was a call for me on the switchboard, and thinking that it must be Daisy and that I'd have to deal with her sooner or later, I said I'd take it in my office, whither I then scurried. Plugging in my phone, I found myself ear to ear with Colette. I bluntly asked how she'd known I was here. "Darling, you always come in early – to do your own work, at least that's what you told me. I only wanted to say hello." I refused to indulge her with expressions of contempt for this hypocritical remark. After realizing that I was not about to break the silence, Colette went on with all-too-casual cheer, "Anyway, *I'm* fine." Another long pause. I asked, "Is that all you're supposed to say to me?" Colette laughed as though I were a petulant child. (I may have sounded like one, but I had my excuses.) She said, "I spoke to Paul a half hour ago. I think you're being a little obsessive about him and Daisy. Why shouldn't they spend time together, go places together? *They're* old friends, too. Why should it be Daisy he's having an affair with?" The idiot didn't realize what she'd given away. "So he's having an affair. You know that." "I didn't say so. No one can *ever* be sure about affairs! But it's – " "Possible? Probable? Highly probable? Inevitable?" "God, you're so touchy. I should have said *if* he's having an affair. Look, darling, why don't you come and visit today? I'd love to see you. I'm *longing* to see you. Can't you take the afternoon off?" "I called you last night over and over. You never answered." "Beloved, what's wrong? Is it me or you? Listen to me: I'll be here all afternoon, with nothing to do that you wouldn't like. Okay?" "Oh, yes, that's wonderful." "Whatever you're doing to yourself, stop it and come and see me." And take my medicines, like a nice boy. The failure of imagination among those "concerned" for my well-being would give me sleepless nights if I didn't have them already. But in time it will become plain that I act not out of selfishness but out of *care*.

I barely had time to write this down before the others began arriving.

I had a special reason for finishing up fast. Yesterday I forgot to record what people here were wearing, and I intended to catch them on their way in to remedy this insane oversight. So I dashed out onto the landing like a novice pollster and stopped each comrade-in-drudgery before he or she disappeared into the customary grind or ersatz thereof. After quickly noting what they had on today, I quizzed them about their Thursday attire. Several arrived together, so that one or two got by me and had to be pursued inside. Most responded willingly, others less so (one implied I was demented), but I stuck to my guns. Cherry, of course, cooperated. Fritz and Louis unfortunately weren't sure what they'd worn. Stan said he had other matters to worry about, and if I could spend half the afternoon with him and not notice what clothes he had on, I didn't deserve to be told (later, visualizing him on the tram and at the hospital, I salvaged everything but his socks). I encountered Naomi back out on the landing; to her precise answer she added a terse "Speaking of pants, XYZ!" – I zipped up my fly, probably open since breakfast. Edith, before replying, asked me, "Didn't you go home at all last night?" Paul knew what he'd worn yesterday because he had the same clothes on today. This double information lessened the repugnance I felt in looking at him.

Back at my desk, I immediately mislaid the data I'd just assembled. They're sure to turn up in the mass of stuff I'm taking home this afternoon. For a while there were comings and goings in the corridor outside my door (it has the bathroom at its far end). I stepped out to see what was going on. Around one corner I came unobserved on Fritz and Paul intently engaged in a conversation too low to overhear. They were standing by the housekeeping closet, on whose shelves the fractured door revealed several big paper packages ripped open. I slipped away unnoticed, irritated at my carelessness. Now, I thought, get conspicuously to work, and I did. I took off my jacket, opened up the filing cabinet, piled every workable surface with papers, and set-tled down to create a durable flurry. My activity didn't prevent me from sensing that passersby were slowing down at my door as though sneaking a look inside. If people care to turn a lighthearted prank into a significant event (significant of what, exactly?), there's nothing I can do about it. I enjoyed myself; why don't they? I wish Maganoff were coming today. He'd approve; he might add my "technique" to his debonair arsenal of subversion. With this thought in mind, I crumpled up a discarded sheet of paper, and when I next heard steps coming my way I turned and with nice anticipation hurled it at the open door. Naomi, who was on her way in, fielded the paper ball with one hand and brightly (if less than wittily) remarked, "I can always get a job as a wastebasket. A gentleman's here to see you." "What's he want?" "He didn't say. It's personal business." "Send him on in." She paused. "The normal thing would be for you to meet him out front. Here's his card." I read: C. B. Gotthardt, Matrix Publications. There followed a partner's name and a list of a dozen magazines, most of which I'd never heard of. "Okay?" Naomi was turning to leave. "Don't forget your jacket."

I followed her without complaint. C. B. Gotthardt was using up company time, not mine. From my desk to Naomi's takes less than half a minute: yet in that span I not only grasped why my visitor had come to see me but foresaw in detail the interview I would have with him. He will be in his late thirties, I thought – short, plumpish, his wiry dark hair thinning, with a smiling air of frankness that I will rec-ognize as a tool of the trade. In my office he will say that he has heard of my journal (he of course says "diary") and would like to see it. I manifest shock and anger: how has he learned of my work? how could he imagine that I would publish an intimate account of myself ("like being scheduled for a public colonoscopy")? He claims that he doesn't want to pressure me, then embarks on a eulogy of my project.

He supports anyone's providing so meticulous a record of our time as mine, whether or not he ever reads a word of it himself; he considers me the antithesis of all those who hurry through life as if their only purpose were to get where they are going without noticing where they are; he envies me my living each day and saving it to live again. Touched, I show him a few pages. He nods his head with pleasure as he reads and stops to ask about my marginal notations. I explain my classification system, and he recommends using a computer – his company can supply one. He also suggests that I add references to contemporary events to my account to expand its admirable specificity and make clear to my readers where and when each entry takes place. I object: *I* know where and when they all take place, and following his advice would mean wasting scarce time. He again mentions my readers; I protest that I have no need of them; he insists that it is a question not of needing them but of deserving the world's recognition. I retort, "'What porridge had John Keats?'"

C. B. Gotthardt held out his hand as I approached, rapidly scanning me from head to toe. After introducing himself, he explained that I had been referred to him to discuss the possibility of our taking out advertising in his company's publications. I started to explain that we rarely advertise and that such matters are no concern of mine, but the day is short enough as it is, so I waved him over to Naomi and went back to my desk. He was unpleasant-looking.

Enough about C. B. Gotthardt, though his was, for once, an intrusion that I didn't resent. In my fantasy he taught me something I needed to know: others will someday read these pages. Even if those "others" are only me, at some future time an act of reading will take place where words on the page must be more than shorthand for a recent, accessible past. I must therefore judge what I write more severely. Up to now I've been critical only of the mechanics of classification, and given last night's discovery, there must be no relaxation on that score. But I should also start reviewing my "results." The project has to work as a narrative, one unknown to me and materialized in whatever way it is that sentences work. As I mulled this over, I realized that the first step has to be rereading what I've written – everything I've written – and more than once. My heart sank at the prospect; where can I find the time? As it is I spend every spare moment merely keeping up with my life (for the moment not an eventful one). How can I start rereading without falling hopelessly out of touch? – And then . . .

"And then a wonderful thing happened." There was a knock at my door, a most gentle knock; and since the knocker was none other than Mr. Bossman himself, who can barge in anytime he likes, including when the door is shut which it never is, this knock unmistakably betokened a consideration and discretion I have not credited him with in earlier reports. When I turned towards him, he smilingly asked how things were going. "Pretty busy." I smiled back, pointing to the files, letters, and miscellaneous junk papers with which my furniture was bedecked. "If it goes on like this, I'll need a bigger office." "Yes, yes," he replied – a little nervously, I thought. After some chitchat about the scarcity of space, he wondered, using the same mild tone, if I could allow him a few minutes of my time. Perplexed, I hurriedly assented. He suggested that we would be more comfortable in his office. As I got up, I couldn't help remarking, "That's for sure." I waited for him to lead the way, but he ushered me out ahead of him, and we walked down the corridor side by side. I noticed that he kept his head turned away from me, I assumed because of my scruffy appearance, which I hastened to explain. I told him the truth, though not about the time of my bout with the hedge: I claimed that it had happened on my way to work. I had gone after a rare mushroom I had spotted in the shrubbery near my tram stop. (I even improvised a name for it – what is rarer than a nonexistent

mushroom? — *Russula pompeïana*, vulgarly known as Venus's dimple.)
While I spoke, Mr. V. moved to my right side, and when I was
through, he said wryly, "You're quite mistaken. Your appearance has
nothing to do with it. I can't straighten my head because I've got a
stiff neck. You don't happen to know a cure?" True enough, he kept
his bent face screwed in my direction. I recommended a hot soak,
adding silently, Works best when entire head is submerged.

When we reached his office, Mr. V. closed the door and motioned
me to an armchair before retreating behind his desk. Another smile,
and he said, "I won't waste time dressing up what I have to say. It
would be an insult to your intelligence, for which I have the highest
respect. Your contributions to this outfit over the years have been
consistently good, and perhaps they would continue to be so in the
future. Lately, though, you haven't been functioning at your usual
level. You haven't done anything disastrously 'wrong' — it's more a
general impression. I think you're overworked. No crime in that; it's
happened to me. But I don't see any use in your staying in your job if
it's wearing you out. I think the best thing for you to do is get out of
here, at least for a while. Take a nice long rest. Think things over.
After that, if you're still interested in working here, come back and
we'll talk about it. Okay?"

I had seen unmistakable if well-controlled apprehension in Mr.
V.'s gaze, and it added to my pleasure when I replied, yielding
unabashedly to my contentment, "Mr. V.! I never imagined you in the
role of ministering angel, but that's how I feel about you now. It's a
wonderful offer. I'm so far behind in so many things, and this will
give me a chance to catch up. Including the split-ring business — I
sure messed that up yesterday, it would have been better if I'd kept my
mouth shut. But I'll get it into shape and it'll make sense to you next
time." "No, no," said Mr. V., "don't worry about anything like that.
While you're away, enjoy yourself. Forget this place completely." I

had no intention of working on split rings, I don't care how interesting they are — my rule now is company work on the company's time — but my heart sang at the prospect of unhurriedly concocting the J of J, of developing a new system, also — and this had dismayed me twenty minutes earlier! — of rereading and editing what I've written. I jumped up from my seat so enthusiastically that I had a kind of blackout and half fell on top of Mr. V., who kept me upright with a laugh that was almost grandpaternal. We were both laughing as we left his office. Mr. V. then stopped and looked at me seriously: "One last thing. I haven't told anyone here about this. I'm going to say that you asked for indefinite leave — if that's acceptable to you?" Of course it was acceptable. Mr. Valde took me back to my desk. His parting words were, "Leave any stuff you want here." It will not be missed.

The anticipation of unlimited time so elated me that I became almost fond of this life and its creatures. Unlimited time: is that enough to allow for a complementary project? I now admitted to myself a closeted vision, that of writing a novel — a novel about someone whose passion is keeping a journal. . . . Until now this idea had struck me as arrogant — how could my present task be worthy of fiction? But if a midget could be a heroine, why not midget me? For the moment, this remained a secondary wish: I had a more urgent problem to solve, and I would have been eager to try doing so if my will hadn't been paralyzed by the knowledge that I could start this afternoon. I didn't have to wait even that long — nothing prevented me from getting right out of there — but I was full of gratitude and planned to complete my morning with an exemplary performance: I would handle all the unfinished business on my desk. I knew, however, that I first had to give vent to my dizzying happiness and talk to somebody. When Mr. V. brought me back to my office, I found a message from Daisy — "Call if you can. Worried not seeing you" — and I asked Naomi to phone her and say there was nothing to worry about. I wondered whether I should call her now myself, and if not, who else. I had no sooner connected my line than the phone rang. It was Nina — Nina, whom I hadn't spoken to in years. I felt that this sudden reemergence was yet another "inspiring coincidence," and forgoing all circumspection, I told her my extraordinary news forthwith. She was hopeless. She didn't bother to try to absorb what I was telling her. In tones of unshakable impatience she repeated, "That sounds very nice," or "I'm happy for you," and other bromides *ejusdem farinae.* At last she frankly interrupted me: "Look, I'm phoning to tell *you* something." "My God, what's wrong?" I asked, alarmed that some catastrophe had prompted her to call — a mortal illness, a crippling accident. "Nothing's wrong. That's the main thing I have to say. I got your letter yesterday, and you should forget that whole business. It's ancient history. You have no cause for remorse. You didn't do anything reprehensible. It happens all the time, it's one of life's routine irritations. In the long run everything worked out perfectly. I've had a marvelous life. I'm *having* a marvelous life." I was disgusted. Under no circumstances was she going to listen to me. So I told her that while I appreciated her concern for my feelings, this was a busy morning, I looked forward to hearing from her in the near future, talk to you later, good-bye. — A forlorn asshole. She couldn't grasp the simplest thing I said, or what I wrote her, either. Unfortunately I couldn't recall exactly what I *had* written. I should have kept a copy of the letter. I should have copied the letter into my journal and not mailed it at all. At least then it would be in sympathetic hands. And I wouldn't regret writing it, as I now do. As I recall, it did me good at the time.

I sensibly prevented my burgeoning irritation from turning into a choleric frenzy. First of all, Mr. V.'s intervention clearly mattered more than insults from Nina; and to make assurance double sure which is the correct wording of that battered phrase and, as well, to acknowledge my good fortune by finishing the work I was still being paid for, I at once made myself busy. I wrote five letters. I made two phone calls I'd been postponing for days; it turned out that someone else had already initiated a discussion, but I was able to insist on a full review of details (they concerned markups on a range of spring binders we've started producing; this is no place to summarize that grotesque data). Before I knew it, lunchtime had arrived.

I soldiered on while my colleagues trooped out like schoolboys starting recess. Someone stopped at my door. I pointedly did not turn around. Cherry has no place in my immediate happiness. She might not have reacted as expected, but I doubt it. She's too full of sweetness and "understanding" (for which read: pity — as though I were a chewed-up cat), not to mention her role of cockteaser. I could escape the pity by relating the morning's events, but she might well have rewarded me with one of her Velcro hugs, again turning me into a thirteen-year-old hole-poker and drenching my new horizons in Vaseline. So I scribbled away until her outward-bound footsteps faded.

I then took a break. The lunchers had all gone. I looked out my door and into neighboring cubicles before padding down to the bathroom to take a last look at my handiwork. It hadn't been touched: the delicate paper had suffered only from exposure (does dew fall in town yards?). I had nothing to be ashamed of. Even tattered, the complex design eloquently revealed the simple concept behind it. A trickle in the washbasin reminded me that I'd neglected to piss for a couple of hours. I enjoyed it, enjoyed seeing myself in the mirror less. My eyes were so red that when I shut them I expected my lids to explode with green. I splashed coldish water on my face. Wiping it dry, I felt that if my fatigue surfaced for three seconds I would sink to the ground in a heap. I went back to start work on the Great Problem.

It was hard. My few notes opened doors onto nothing. I lacked conceptual agility – how could I grasp the problem from inside the system it had demolished? I had to invent a new approach and context. And I wasn't up to that. I mustn't risk falling out of one of those opening doors into total discouragement. So I looked for something easier to do, something else connected with my beloved project. Among my notes I found a jotting about my plan for a category of snoopery. This seemed more manageable than unprepared speculation: I need only assemble, classify, and collate available facts of a particular kind. (There was also room for speculation here, but who needs to extrapolate complicated theories of behavior? With these people, the crudest theory of behavior will do.)

(Editorial note: work begun at 2:20 P.M., written directly in journal.)

I know I could classify this material by situations rather than by persons, as I'm about to. That must come later.

To put it more bluntly: it's hard enough to think of these actions as the work of individuals. Admitting that they're collaborations is, for now, painful. I'm frightened enough. Yet truth is best. I've avoided facing it long enough.

LAST WEEK: DAISY

Wednesday. After a phone call, she decides to leave on an overnight business trip.

Friday. She discourages gestures of desire; she does not ask what I have done while she was away; she never reports on her "trip." Something has happened. She cries for no reason. She behaves strangely – late at night she insists that we go for a walk, then deliberately leaves me behind.

Saturday. Another very long walk alone. Pale on her return, she refuses to talk. She has not told me Paul has been asked to dinner on Sunday. While I work, she slips out again for a long time.

Sunday. She suggests that we drive out to the lake. Paul has lunch with us; she seems happier. She drives Paul back to town.

LAST WEEK: PAUL
Tuesday. He arrives late at work (something he never does) in a lively, enthusiastic mood.

Wednesday. He takes the afternoon off "to go to the dentist and see his old friend Jacob Barrett," unknown to me, who knows of all his friends.

Thursday. He is busy for lunch; he does not say with whom.

Friday. I notice that his discretion about his private life, which I have never failed to respect, has this week become obsessive. Colette tells me she is meeting him for coffee. He never mentions it.

(Saturday. Even Gert wonders what he is up to.)

Sunday. At lunch he laughs excessively over Daisy's account of her business trip. At dinner I ask him what he knows about Gert's problem; he does not answer.

LAST WEEK: COLETTE
Thursday. She mysteriously advises me to "be good" to Daisy.

Friday. She gives a patently false reason for having coffee with Paul.

Saturday. When I learn that she is home alone, instead of suggesting a visit, she asks me to call back later. When I do, she tells me not to come. Someone unidentified is with her.

Sunday. She does not appear at the lakeside lunch or tell me she will again be alone.

LAST WEEK: GERT
Thursday. He reproaches me bitterly for being inaccessible.

Friday. Claiming to have been with Paul and Jago, he does not reveal where he has spent the evening.

Saturday. Late in the afternoon he comes home in high spirits, again with no explanation.

Sunday. He gets up uncomplainingly at 8 A.M. and thanks me for reminding him why (a date with Paul and Jago). According to them, he joins them for only an hour, and his thoughts are elsewhere. He misses the lakeside lunch. At the end of the afternoon he seems transfigured — affectionate, helpful. He says nothing about his day.

LAST WEEK: JAGO
Sunday. Like Paul, he laughs too much over Daisy's business trip.

THIS WEEK: DAISY
Monday. She looks haggard. Tears (of shame?) come to her eyes when I tell her she is beautiful.

Tuesday. She regrets my coming home for dinner. She wants to talk without me to Colette, about Paul.

Wednesday. Daisy's rug manufacturers know nothing about her trip out of town. At supper with Mr. Furmint, her colleague, she eliminates any opportunity to refer to her trip. On the drive home, she speaks with transparent hypocrisy about Paul's coolness.

Thursday. Attack as the best defense: she suggests I am having an affair.

In the hospital, I find her in the gynecological section. She lets me think she has been visiting Leonora and hurries ahead to warn Paul. I then discover that she has been conniving with my doctors to mesmerize me with tranquilizers.

During a telephone conversation with Colette, she reveals that she has seen a doctor at the hospital; he has given her good news. This news must concern her, since she does not refer to Leonora. She has made sure that I am not present when she mentions it. The reason for this becomes clear when she speaks about an affair with Paul that Colette may or may not know about, an affair about which Daisy is "ecstatic."

During this conversation:

— she confirms that she is in league with my doctors
— she thanks Colette for providing a meeting-place late on Friday afternoon
— she wishes Colette well in her relationship with "my baby."

Afterward she lies to me about who was on the phone.

Returning from her "semi-working dinner," she has a glass of wine "to celebrate" and refuses to say what she is celebrating.

THIS WEEK: PAUL

Monday. Disregarding my feelings, he announces that he may get a job someplace else. At the staff meeting, he engages in a private discussion with Mr. Valde during my split-ring presentation.

Tuesday. He ridicules my request to see him more often. When questioned about the "sporting life," he shows by his coolness that he takes this as a reference to his affair.

Wednesday. He will not talk about Daisy. He responds to my enthusiasm for our old intimacy with trivial proposals.

Thursday. He tells me he is going sculling that afternoon; I find him at the hospital. Mortified, he claims to have come with "a friend." He has accompanied Daisy to the gynecologist.

(Paula Abramowicz's admonition to "ask my friends" about my treatment must refer to him; this means he is abetting Daisy and the doctors in their plans.)

(Daisy's phone call to Colette only confirms Paul's intimacy with her.)

THIS WEEK: COLETTE
Monday. She makes no mention of seeing Gert.

Tuesday. She confesses that she "sees Gert all the time."

Thursday. Like Daisy earlier, she viciously accuses me of having an affair with someone else (is this a concerted decision — to defend herself and Daisy *both*?). She lies to me and denies knowing anything about Daisy and Paul.

From Daisy's phone call I learn that she knows *all* about Daisy and Paul and that she approves — an attitude made understandable when Daisy expresses affectionate "jealousy" of her relationship with

Gert. She lends Daisy her place for a tryst on Friday afternoon.

In the evening she deliberately lets the phone ring unanswered (Jago is out).

Friday. She calls me before hours at the office. While trying to reassure me, she blurts out the fact of Paul's affair. She tries to undo the damage by urging me to visit her.

THIS WEEK: GERT
Monday. He has lunch with Jago – Colette tells me this, so I know they have met. Later I trick him into admitting that he has seen Colette. He comments unguardedly, "I really love her."

Tuesday. He monopolizes the dinner table in courting Colette. He lets slip that he has seen her earlier in the day; this visibly upsets him.

Wednesday. He declines to eat the breakfast I prepare for him.

Thursday. Fastidiously dressed, he is obviously meeting someone special, who is never named.

THIS WEEK: JAGO
Monday. He finds Paul a job elsewhere, away from my scrutiny (and love).

Thursday. Daisy's call to Colette suggests he has been told about her affair, presumably to provide alibis.

THIS WEEK: MR. VALDE
Thursday. His lack of surprise at Paul's presence at the hospital surprised *me*.

I am too grateful to suspect him.

Who can she be working for?

> Paul: her crude attempts to seduce me would distract me from other fun and games.
>
> Mr. Valde: her frequent visits strongly imply that she is his "eyes."

And who else, and what else? No one else matters, and these are all joined against me: Daisy with Paul, Colette with Gert, Daisy and Paul with Colette and Gert, with Jago picking up the tab, and here I sit holding the steering wheel that long ago came off in my hands.

I've started feeling dizzy — because my eyes are so tired? I'll sneak out now (why say good-bye?) and go spend some time in the park.

4 P.M.

I'm sitting on a bench, pencil in hand, open notebook on lap. On my way here I stopped to buy tapes for my tape recorder. I thought the park would be a good place to try dictating a journal entry — I've wondered whether speaking, even into a machine, couldn't by its spontaneity tap ideas or ways of expressing myself that the self-consciousness of writing scares off. I also thought it might furnish an approach to the J of J quandary: surely the recording machine would record the recorder as well as what *he* was recording. I went to the shop where I'd bought it, a place run by nice people called Belit, who, whenever Gert's not available, always patiently explain how things work. Pleasant Hungarian music — a zither and what other familiar instrument? — issued softly from a tuner-amplifier-speaker system on display. I was lucky I couldn't sit down in that comfy atmosphere, or I might be there now. I bought only one pack of five cassettes. My briefcase is already stuffed to the limit — I stocked up at the office on paper clips, erasers, rubber bands, and other sundries.

I took the nearest park entrance to come here. It wasn't the way I used to go when I met Colette. A distant life. Illusions cannot give durable comfort. It was bound to come to the same nasty end. I passed the big statue of Mars and his doxy — *ed io nuovo Vulcan del secolo!* Beyond it, down a lane running obliquely left, I arrived at the quarter-moon-shaped pool where I now sit. Across the little pool from my bench stands a smaller and more attractive sculpture, a dolphin carved out of some elemental eruptive rock, perhaps basalt. Behind it extends a broad grassless bed adorned with unexpected plants such as cultivated specularia, monkshood, and what looks like wild lady's slipper (could it have been found growing here and then propagated?). Before sitting down I stood by the pool and saw my reflected face deformed by the water. There are few people around. It was the seclusion of the spot that led me here: it seemed a favorable place for dictation. A crowd might in fact be better. In the silence, each of us here is too conscious of the others. I'm resorting to my customary tools.

I'm too sad for conceptual acrobatics. The autumn light is of a frailty that enforces melancholy; the veiled sky is of a blue so discreet it seems the reflection of a sky gone elsewhere, and "we who are here have all been left behind." My attention has been switching between an intensely passive awareness of things I can see (the black statue, a red child, a tea-colored dog) and memories lying in shadow at the edge of an inner room. I should coerce those memories and others after them, bring them into view. It has been another of my plans, and I can manage that.

I look around. Where can my first Memorial rise into the light of day? Immediately, by the pool, I see Gert (age three?) sailing his first toy boat. He wears dark-gray short pants, a big-collared blue shirt under a light cardigan whose color I can't specify, and brown sandals over mid-season white socks. There is little wind; he sees the problem and thinks to solve it by blowing hard and long into the sails. It "works," who knows how. He looks pleased but not surprised as jib and mainsail gently fill and propel his foot-long craft towards the middle of the pond. It was not this pond; was it in this park? I have enough sense to say nothing and rejoice. He takes me by the hand and leads me to the far side.

Jago appears. A six-year-old boy has been dribbling an undersize soccer ball down a thither path. In autumn about ten years ago, on the muddy terrain of a village fifteen miles away, Jago took part in a soccer match with his club's team. Why had I gone with him, by myself? He played center-half spectacularly, turning into an incidental forward when he zipped up unexpectedly to penetrate the defense and make accurate passes and sharp goal shots. On one occasion he positioned himself expertly fifteen feet out from the goal line and took a shoulder-high pass that was too far in front of him for the head shot he was looking for. Charging, he slipped, skidded on his back across the slick, soaked terrain, and banged headfirst into the goalpost. It knocked him out. He stayed knocked out. He was taken off the field on a stretcher. An ambulance was called. I accompanied him, stupefied by my uselessness. Sitting next to him in the ambulance, I desperately repeated a few hopeful words. Through the rear window I watched the dirt road turn to tar; telephone poles appeared in rhythmic recession; crows dotted sunny gray fields. I bent closer to him, imploring him to move or speak. His hands were pale and strangely unsoiled. Under his torn orange jersey his stalwart trunk was a startlingly feminine white, but his mottled legs were stockinged in fine mud-caked hair. I held back tears, renewing my appeals in quieter tones. I had never before observed his features, which had always been swamped by his general robustness. His eyes were set neither close nor wide apart; their lids were delicately veined. His nose had a slight Roman hook and was of a remarkable slenderness. How could I have thought this man coarse? His lips were full and now limp and pallid. His chin was faintly cleft, as if in apology for its strength. The ear into which I spoke surprised me most – it was small and perfect like an Egyptian stone fragment. I whispered, "Jago, it's me." "I know it's you, dear friend," he said matter-of-factly. "I haven't worried a second because you're here. Stupid thing to do, looking back for the fucking ball." He squeezed my knee weakly before going under again.

How could I have forgotten? How much else have I forgotten? I wonder where Jago and Paul go sculling together – river or lake? Lake, most likely. A seizure of jealousy doesn't last. Why does my disgust with all of them grow milder when I write my thoughts down as they occur? Two men on a lake with a green shore, reeds and fields of cattails, some poplars and aspens unyellowing in this benign fall, greenness in stillness, silvered where the breeze ruffles them. The seasonal birds: barnacle geese, bobbing mallards, ibis, greater and lesser quasi-resident herons. When the breeze passes, the sun scatters across the water an angelic largesse. I remember this. I never went sculling, but when we were students Paul and I spent occasional afternoons rowing on the vast lake south of town. One day in early October a wind came up from the north when we were a quarter of a mile offshore. One moment was calm, the next an episode from the *Odyssey*. Paul tried heading back, bow into the waves, but he quickly shipped oars and let the wind push us where it would. He told me to sit on the bottom of the rowboat and start bailing. With what? With one of my shoes. He sat facing me, doing the same with a bait can some angler had left behind. We sat together amidships, between the rower's bench and the stern, his knees clamping mine. While we bailed, he began singing, leaning forward so I could hear him against the storm. The song was long and obscene. It concerned a brother and sister who at an early age began fornicating in all possible ways. As soon as they could, they begat children, two sets of mixed twins in rapid succession, and when the children reached a satisfactory age, the parents included them in their sport. The parents each had four usable attributes; in the family of six, twenty-four became available, and the possibilities, which Paul recapitulated, multiplied accordingly. Eventually the two daughters each bore two more sets of twins, who at approximate maturity joined in the family romps. The number of attributes was now fifty-six, but Paul had scarcely begun enumerating the consequences when the buffeting wind spun us into the lea of a point on the far shore. Paul broke off. We finished bailing in silence. Paul began shaking violently. I asked if he'd caught a chill. No, he answered, he had never been so terrified in his life. I had been so absorbed by the mathematical progression of combinations that, soaked and queasy though I was, I hadn't for a moment imagined we were in danger. Paul huddled in the stern, and I rowed the few remaining yards to shore. Once we had landed, Paul again became his confident self. He called the house in town where we all had our rooms. Daisy and Paul's girlfriend came to pick us up, and we repaired to a country restaurant for a festive evening.

I have been sitting on this bench too long. A numbness has possessed me. Not exact. A certain "I" has been possessed by a faintness, a faintingness. Numbness has taken hold of the me sitting here, which is, if not me, at least recognizable as part of what I am or was. I'm not here or anywhere else, apparently. While these sentences were being inscribed, another sensation began waving its pustular arms: dread of going out of control, also a conviction that all I can do is watch myself go out of control. That was why Daisy and Dr. Maxhole, or he and Daisy, first advised me to keep a journal, last July. They were concerned for my stability. Can't a man feel sad? Fifteen minutes have gone by since I finished writing about Paul.

Walking down a lane curving through the trees on my left, I found an ice cream vendor. I thought a little glucose might help. I bought a cup of strawberry because I don't much like it and so would eat it slower. Among the flavors painted on the cart I read "Cyprians." I asked what that meant. The vendor reached down into her murky misting hoard to bring forth a cone whose vanilla sphere was topped with a cherry.

The ice cream I swallowed produced nothing but familiar tinglings in my extremities and then a lump moving inconclusively upward from my diaphragm into my esophagus. Having sat down to consume my cup, I got up and started walking again to stop this lump from choking me. I walked through a thick wood. Branches of old horse chestnuts spread out over a path strewn with their brown, prickled, cracking fruit. Light pierced the shade with unbearable reminders of how inescapable it all is. Farther on I came to the grassy expanse where I'm sitting, in mottled, warm darkness, under the skirt of a linden tree.

When she stood in front of me (could I find that end of the park from here?), Colette sometimes melted into the light and dying leaves. She herself became a pattern of shade, with only eyes and teeth like sparks or icicles among muted colors. Then we would be elsewhere, in a residual primordial world of our own, and we spoke as if we would stay there forever, as if she would never go away. But she went away, sliding her tongue against mine to get me back to the place where things had happened and might happen again, with a well-defined rift between.

Did I ever come here with Daisy? That is, without Gert? I've always done everything with her. It's uncannily still today. But when I lean my head against this linden, I feel the trunk sway slightly. This does not matter. I can't remember. I expect Daisy to appear now and take me home.

She won't. I cannot write about them any longer because I've lost them. How has this come to be? Who's the scriptwriter for this part of my life, because I need to have a serious talk with him. All I know how to do is mentally fiddle with other people's wishes so that before everything falls apart I can piece it together. So that afterward I can say I knew all about it, and you can't fool me. Like someone who gloats over dice coming up boxcars when a five and a seven would turn the trick. You can't fool me, but I'm a dumbbell. What's better, eating quahogs with Walt Whitman on a Long Island beach or listening to Goethe discourse on specularia while trapped in a fly or flying in a trap as we circumspectly circumvent the Hörselberg? Goethe'd take the quahogs anyday. You forgot. Look at what you've turned into: a bearded androgynous sanctimonious self-mutilated self-paid whore. You can list your heinous errors with pathetic expertise, pitifully accepting your pitiful state, Lazarus swaddled and twitching and no way left to chuck off all that picturesque filth and stand up as your naked nonself, naked as you emerged from your birth or your bath. You feel like crying? You're not worth crying over.

After writing this, I walked over to look at a little chrysanthemum garden. This initiative, taken perfunctorily, greatly improved my disposition. As I gazed down at the prodigious variety of blossoms, I had an erection. I wasn't thinking of anything erotic, only staring pensively at the chrysanthemums. My cock became and stayed startlingly hard. The unforeseen event had immediate significance for me. Earlier, while clearing out my desk, I had glanced through the student magazine Maganoff had left and skimmed a few items before throwing it away. In one poem (entitled "A Turd for Count Rasumovsky") I had noticed the line "Erections surprise us in gardens." It caught my eye because on the tram coming into town I'd conscientiously read a few pages of *Young Days in Bratislava*, and I remembered a passage that I now copy out: "I sometimes used to go walking in the lower part of the garden, where no one could see me, my sex in glorious erection under my schoolboy smock, caressing it, endlessly, with no further end in view." As if to drive the point home, another passage in the student magazine read: "The man who's the newspaper man is standing in the garden. His part is huge and extended." These literary coincidences had astonished me because I'd never imagined a connection between gardens and sexual excitement; I couldn't begin to understand it. I still don't understand it, and now the same thing has happened to me. This is a portent of redeeming clarity. It signifies that only through my Journal can such things ever be manifested. (Isn't this a *first instance* of the momentous J of J taking form?) So my work has not been wasted. Nor has my life been wasted. Whatever is lost, I have this. It's incontrovertible, and enough.

I bummed a cigarette from a neighboring smoker. He gave it to me with the prompt pity reserved for the downcast.

It's almost 5:30 — time for Colette's. It will be the worst labor of this day, but there is no escaping it. I must assume my role of witness. After Daisy said on the phone, "Nobody else around," I tried hard to believe she meant Colette and herself, but considering what had gone before, this is impossible. If Daisy and Paul meet there, it will mean the end of my life as I think of it — but I'd rather know. I shall write it all down here.

11:45 P.M.

The nurse was surprised to find me so alert when I woke up. She called the intern, who told me I needed another intravenous sedative. I readily assented, provided I could first write a few pages in my journal. He said that could wait till morning — the sooner I was asleep, the better. Hiding my despair, I made my voice as reasonable as I could: "Things just happened that I ought to get down right away. By tomorrow they'll be over the horizon."

I dreaded the prospect of six more drugged hours. When I saw I could not sway this single-minded young man, I must have looked somewhat frantically around for my briefcase, in a way that suggested violent intentions. The nurse, who had already wheeled in a double-decker rolling table, its top stacked with syringes, cotton, alcohol, and vials of lethe, now fetched two hairy-armed orderlies. It seemed that if necessary, the sedative would be administered by force.

The intern said, "It's not up to me, you must understand that. I'm following instructions." Dr. Max came in.

I refused to look at him. I felt a hand on my shoulder and heard him ask what was the matter. A glance informed me that if he was my enemy, he avoided acting like one. I said all I wanted was some time to write: "I've got to catch up on what's happened." Dr. Max patiently replied, "What you've got to do is stop keeping that diary." He paused. "Will you promise to do that if I let you write now?" I began experiencing some kind of "inhuman" grief. "You mean for good?" He laughed. "No, *not* for good. A couple of weeks. Whatever it takes."

A couple of weeks was the same as for good. I didn't know I was crying until the nurse handed me a Kleenex. I realized that I was spoiling my chances. I accepted. "Give him his notebook and pen." "Pencil. Please." "How much time do you need – twenty minutes?" I didn't bat an eyelash. "How about forty? So much has happened." "You're an old hand at it. Half an hour, and not a minute more." The nurse checked her watch and smiled. I started writing before he was out the door.

From the park I walked to Colette's. My old secret key, that love relic, let me into the shadowy garden. I quickly found a hiding place with a view of the gate and the front steps and settled down there, briefcase and all, crouching amid myrtle and the dark, flat fronds of two large hinoki cypresses. Out of the garden's sheltering greenery, doves fluttered away to neighboring trees. My watch read 5:50. I waited.

A minute before the hour, someone stopped in front of the gate.

With a pang of regret – regret at being there – I looked to see who: Daisy or Paul? Through the lower bars I recognized Gert's familiar sneakers and felt gloomy relief. I was to be spared nothing. I would contemplate the whole panoply of betrayal. So be it. Colette came down the front steps and went to the gate. I made myself watch.

Colette greeted my son cheerfully enough, to judge by her wave and the amiable sound of her words. They kissed each other lightly on either cheek – and that was all. Gert may have reached for an ampler hug, but Colette only laughed as she pushed him away. They spoke by the gate for a minute or two. Gert seemed eager to talk. The only words of his I heard were "broken off"; he repeated them. Colette kept shaking her head, once tapping her wristwatch to emphasize her point. Then, as she turned away, I heard her say, "Later, *maybe*, if you really feel like waiting." Gert nodded. Colette led him to the little summer house at the bottom of the garden. My despair flooded back.

Colette was returning when a second visitor arrived. Daisy was let in. The women embraced like giggling schoolgirls. Then Daisy stepped back, an almost frightened look on her face. She clasped her hands tightly as she spoke. I caught the word *disappeared*. They went inside. I decided to shift to another vantage point. If the women settled down in the sitting room, nothing would be gained; but they might prefer the kitchen, on which I could eavesdrop from outside unobserved. There was no sign of Gert (the near windows of the summer house were shuttered). Before I could move, footsteps again approached the gate. I thought, Paul, at last. But two pairs of male feet appeared. The gate was unlocked from the outside.

Paul entered, followed by Jago, who pocketed his keys and closed the gate. Paul at once turned towards his friend, who laid a cautionary hand on his shoulder, took a few steps forward, and attentively surveyed the garden and the house. Sure that no one was in sight, he beckoned Paul to a spot away from the gate, and there the two men embraced. An electric iciness ran through me that I could not put down to shock, or shame, or any reasonable cause. Faced with a nuclear breakdown of my expectations, I realized nothing, made no deductions, drew no conclusions. I had not known that men kissed like that – Rhett and Scarlett! I was moved. If I mention shame, it's not only because I had turned into a Peeping Tom but also because in my whole lifetime I had been too perverted, even though I was a man, to think that men could share such ardor. I wished they would stop.

They did, but not by choice. Because an old, thick-branched apple tree stood between them and the summer house, Gert, coming out for a look, did not see them. He had apparently decided to leave (his mother's presence meant a long wait and possible embarrassment). The sound of his footsteps separated Paul and Jago. With the feigned aplomb of those found out, they walked with preposterous deliberation towards the house. Gert came face to face with them. Mortified at being discovered, he managed an extraterrestrial laugh but no words. The men began uttering rhetorical cries of pleasure, slapping him gaily on the back and talking to him with a kind of sporting brashness that made me briefly feel like the only sane person present. I wished that the scene, where no one was sure what the others knew, would continue long enough to entangle them all in its farce.

This was not to be. Colette and Daisy appeared on the steps. They kissed the two men in turn, Daisy with that slightly outrageous zest that never fails to charm its recipient. She treated Jago as warmly as Paul. I looked for a way to sneak closer and hear what they were saying; but in less than a minute Colette had taken Gert by the arm and led him away, straight towards my hiding place. I could not take the risk of being caught. My only hope was that she might then turn right into the gloom of the garden, but she didn't. It was unreasonable to imagine that, on a path passing not four feet from where I shrank, they would not see me, and when they were a few yards away I chose to reveal myself. I jumped to my feet – jumped, not stood – the change of posture was violent. Bottomless nausea clutched me as my trunk and head were drained of blood – of life, I then fancied, while vignettes of death and paralytic old age flashed past and I toppled like a drunk into a huge old-rose shrub. It was last night's hedge all over again, except that now I had fainted as utterly as any heroine of melodrama.

I came back to my senses after a time I could not determine: five seconds, five minutes, fifty minutes? (Minutes, not seconds, because an ambulance presently drove up.) I experienced a sensation, unfamiliar but not disturbing, of absolute emptiness – an emptiness bathed in light. My body was fingered by uncanny, sweet uneasiness, as though a delicious secret were being disclosed. The late light of day above the breathless trees looked like a dusk not of evening but of dawn. I gazed at the sky, with a star or two. I was here, I had never been anywhere else, but I had no idea where "here" was, or why I had come here. I saw drops of blood on my hands – and so there were drops of blood on my hands. The "I" who could recollect was absent: I had been reduced to the things I saw. I saw the sweet faces around me, filling up with joy at the sight of a countenance that must have reflected (however faintly) this soft exaltation.

The medical men came. I wondered briefly why none of us felt surprise at their taking charge of me. They set me on a cot in the back of the ambulance and politely asked if they might give me an injection.

As I was writing this page, the joy of that blessed moment returned, in spite of gusts of unconsciousness from the tranquilizers, against which I have struggled rather well. Of course, recording these events has given me supplementary strength and happiness – and they've let me write for an hour!

SATURDAY

The following day, the patient kept his word, making no apparent attempt to write or read in his diary. The bundle of loose used sheets and fresh pads of same format lay, with a few soft pencils and an eraser, untouched in a drawer of his night table. In front of his doctor or his visitors, he once or twice opened the drawer and pointed to its contents with signs indicating that not a page had been disturbed, or would be. Otherwise he never looked at them.

From the time he woke up on the morning after his arrival, he renounced the use of the spoken as well as the written word. (That this was his choice is beyond dispute: he never exhibited symptoms of any physical or mental impairment of his powers of speech.) Judging from his demeanor, his lapse into silence was not meant as a protest. The patient greeted all comers with affable smiles and listened to them as attentively as his sedated condition allowed, reacting with frequent nods and other gestures that indicated not only a normal but a good-natured disposition. But he would not be persuaded to add to these responses so much as a spoken yes or no. His doctor and the rest of the hospital personnel jointly decided that it was best to respect his choice, whatever its cause, and they encouraged his family to follow their example.

Whether the patient's silence was, as seems likely, a consequence of his having to abandon his diary, it complicated the task of his wife, son, brother- and sister-in-law, and best friend in giving him the reassurances of affection and loyalty that they felt he needed — mistrust had plainly fueled the eccentric behavior that had culminated in his spying on them in the garden the previous evening. After an early visit, Dr. Melhado, to whom they transmitted accounts of their own interviews, urged them to persevere in their efforts and, especially, to review recent events that might have provoked misunderstandings, some of them undoubtedly still lodged in the patient's imagination.

Daisy, who with Gert was the first to pay a visit, had another kind of difficulty to face. She had lied to her husband at some length, and while she may have had good reasons for doing so, she found it unduly painful to admit and explain her subterfuge to someone who would not speak a word in reply. She limited herself on this first occasion to saying that she had been through a harrowing time during the past weeks, promising to reveal every detail later on, and adding that it was because of this that she had turned to Paul for help and made him swear to keep her difficulties a secret.

Although he had not an inkling of the patient's suspicions, Gert did more to allay them. He hoped to please his father by talking about events that he had hitherto kept to himself, explaining, for instance, that when faced with the disturbing problem of Leonora's pregnancy, he had been too embarrassed to ask his parents for advice and had instead consulted his aunt. Colette had "saved his life" with her readiness to listen to him day after day and, on occasion, to intervene.

In the afternoon Paul and Jago visited the patient together. After ascertaining that he had witnessed their embrace in the garden, Paul talked only about his unexpected but requited passion for Jago, which he could not explain (Jago diagnosed it as "delayed prepubescence"). Just as Daisy had relied on him, it was she in whom he had confided in this disconcertingly new situation. He confessed how hard he had found it to tell the patient what had happened and pointed out that increasing indications of suspicion on the patient's part had further discouraged him. Jago confirmed this, citing as example the hurt reaction to Paul's prospect for a better job — a possibility that had meanwhile collapsed "like an old puffball."

After the patient took a long nap, during which a female colleague from work silently appeared and departed, the night orderly arrived. He seems to have inspired immediate confidence: the patient agreed to be shaved.

Daisy and Colette came in after the patient's supper. They had clearly consulted one another, and no doubt Gert as well – Colette told of his visiting her a week before and then bringing Leonora to meet her the following day, when everyone else was at the lake. Colette said no more that evening, only reminding Daisy of the book my mother had sent – *Tales from All Our Lands*, a childhood favorite. The patient sat up expectantly. Daisy offered to read aloud to him. Shaking his head, he dismissed several titles before approving "Hans and Lady Pamela." Daisy then fussed over him at some length, retucking his sheets, fluffing his pillow, and straightening the articles on his night table, until, after silently manifesting his growing impatience, he stated with abrupt injunctive forcefulness, "Once upon a time, a little boy lived in a village on the banks of a wide river..." Although these were the only words he spoke, they boded well for the future.

"Once upon a time, a little boy lived in a village on the banks of a wide river. His name was Hans. He lived by the riverbank in a white cottage with a woman called Maria. He had always thought Maria was his mother – he called her 'mother' and she allowed him to do so, because she loved him as much as any mother ever loved her son. Then, one terrible day, when Hans was nine years old.."

SUNDAY

When Dr. Melhado stopped in early the next morning, the patient again declined to speak. The doctor, pleased by the report of his "lapse," made no reference to it in front of him, only thanked him for setting his diary aside and promised that his medication would be reduced as quickly as his recovery permitted.

Later Jago paid a brief visit, this time with Colette; before leaving, presumably at her own request, she spent a few minutes alone with the patient. She recapitulated her account of the previous weekend, at greater length. Saturday afternoon: listening to Gert (then wallowing in confusion over Leonora's pregnancy and comforted only by her offer to receive the young woman). Sunday morning: waiting for Jago to come home from volleyball (the Lake John excursion had been a last-minute decision). Sunday afternoon: talking to Gert and Leonora, with whose plight she sympathized and whom she found bereft of all recognizable attractions ("she even *looks* like a rabbit") – an opinion that, though unexpressed, may not have gone unnoticed by the patient's son. She told the patient that she loved him.

He did not see Daisy until midafternoon. She had prepared herself to tell him what she had done. She began by confessing her elaborate lie about the business trip: her night away had been spent in this very hospital. Two months before, she explained, the results of her routine Pap test had been abnormal. Such results are classified on a scale of "1" through "5," in ascending order of gravity; hers were "3." Daisy reminded the patient that July had been no time to break such news to him, while afterward she had been reluctant to jeopardize his recovery from his recent breakdown. Six weeks later the results of another test were again "3," but this second "3" was far more preoccupying because it signified that her cells were undergoing further change. A colposcopy and a punch biopsy were immediately scheduled. Normally she would have undergone the examination as an outpatient, but she entered the hospital at the urging of her gynecologist. (Daisy kept silent about her own motive for this, which was to conceal what was happening from her household.) Upon her discharge the next day she was instructed to return a week later for the results, a time passed in ill-concealed worry; it was at the end of this week that the patient's path had crossed hers in the hospital corridor.

Seeing that the patient was becoming agitated, Daisy at once announced that the biopsy had revealed no abnormal cells ("*That's* what I was celebrating"). She spoke briefly of Paul's help during the previous fortnight: he had brought her twice to and from the hospital and kept her company, there and elsewhere, throughout her ordeal.

When Gert arrived, he tiptoed to his sleeping father's bedside, but the childhood scent of a rose-laden branch the boy was carrying woke the patient immediately. The branch, Gert explained, had been cut from the bush into which the patient had fallen two days earlier. He had also brought him a box of chocolates from Wollkowsky's.

Gert talked about Leonora's pregnancy. He felt regret at not having confided in his father, which Colette had encouraged him to do, certain (at least before meeting Leonora) that if the child was born, his parents would offer to take care of it. He had then been too unsure of anything – most of all the reality of what was happening to him – to appreciate her advice. He was happy that the entire episode was finished – not only the windfall miscarriage but his intimacy with Leonora. Last night she had said that he might not have been the father after all; more likely it was Maganoff. He was not angry, only relieved to be through with her. Seeing her with Colette had disillusioned him. He hoped that her father, the neighborhood butcher, would not come after him.

The patient's last visitor was Paul, who addressed his old friend with great warmth. He filled out Daisy's medical history. The ambivalent results of the July test had convinced her from the outset that she had cancer and that it would kill her. Being told that a negative biopsy would at most reveal a precancerous condition did nothing to weaken her conviction. Paul explained that she hadn't said anything to the patient because she had counted on keeping her problem a secret as a way of holding her terror in check. Meanwhile she confided in Paul, since he was not prey to a husband's vulnerability.

Paul concluded his visit by describing the start of his new relation with Jago: last summer they had been swimming at a lake, they were momentarily alone and out of sight, and the unthinkable had suddenly occurred. Neither had ever had a homosexual encounter. Paul at least had his bachelor's past to help him; as a confirmed monogamist, Jago refused to believe what was happening to them. But, Paul said, he "submitted graciously to his fate."

By day's end it seemed that the patient's visitors had succeeded in lessening and perhaps even dispelling the suspicions that had so troubled him. Unfortunately, in the moments after Paul's departure, from the corridor a woman's voice much like Daisy's was heard asking the question "How much does he really know?" Whoever spoke them and with whatever intent, these words were audible to the patient. Soon afterward the night orderly discovered him in tears.

A sympathy had sprung up between this orderly and the patient the day before, when the latter had consented to be shaved. The orderly had witnessed the effect of Daisy's reading to the patient the previous evening, and he asked the patient if he wanted to hear a story now. The patient declined the first subjects proposed: the impoverished artist who inherits a rich man's finery; the worker's son who becomes a world-class violinist only to ruin his career by gambling; the abandoned little girl who every night sneaks into the houses of the wealthy. My hesitation in rejecting the last subject led the orderly to think that another children's story might be acceptable. He suggested the tale of "Michael the Orphan," and to this I agreed.

What then took place marked an evolution in the patient's condition, to what effect it is too early to say; the professional consensus is optimistic. It is true that dialogue, in the strict sense, did not occur, and that this night's event could conceivably be discounted as an extended repetition of my interjection of Saturday; on the other hand, the length and consistency of the utterance seem to indicate a difference in more than degree. Only time can determine whether it was a step towards the resumption of normal life, a parenthetical aberration in an essentially static condition, or a spectacular demonstration of the power of involuntary memory, where the orderly's narrative provided the cues for the patient's associative or antonymic interventions:

"Once upon a time and a very good time, monkey chew tobacco and spit white lime, once upon a time there was a young boy named Michael. He wasn't really an orphan, but he might as well have been, because he hardly saw his parents at all. His father had a job on the night shift, and his mother was so tired when she came home from work that she fell asleep as soon as she'd heated up Michael's supper. They may have loved Michael, but it was hard to tell, because they never had time to talk or play with him. He certainly loved them, and he could not understand why they never had time for him or for each other. When he was still a little boy he realized he was a burden to them. Without me, he thought, they might be happy. So one winter day when he was nine years old, he took his clothes and his few possessions and ran away. He did this very cleverly. He had observed how to hide on an express train that would take him so far off that his father and mother would never guess where he was. He had coached himself in telling different kinds of lies. For instance, he would tell a sentimental lady that he had left home because his parents were cruel; to a working man, he would only say that he was traveling to his grandparents'.

"Michael did not have to tell many lies, because after getting off the express train far from his home town, he met — "

" — a street musician — "

" — who agreed to take him on as his helper. This man had sometimes had trouble with the police, and since Michael was a boy who was nice-looking, well mannered, and full of ingenuity — "

" — by claiming him as his son — "

" — he hoped to win sympathy and respectability by having him at his side. For several years — "

" – Hans and Sipario, as the musicians were called – "

" – *worked their way* – "

" – as singing beggars – "

" – *from town to town. Michael learned to* – "

" – sing Sipario's songs and play a number of instruments: the tambourine, the glockenspiel, then the castanets, and finally the harmonica."

"*Later he took lessons* – "

" – on the violin from another itinerant musician – "

" – *who traveled with them for several months. This other man also had a young boy in tow* – "

" – called Ali – "

" – *and when he* – "

" – separated from Sipario – "

" – *and Michael, all agreed that* – "

" – Ali should become a member of Sipario's troupe."

"*This made Michael* – "

" – happy – "

" – *because he* – "

" – and Ali had become the best of friends."

"*One day* – "

" – Sipario, Ali, and Hans were approaching a town along the towpath of a canal. They stopped at one of its locks: in the bight of water upstream, where boats moored overnight after the lock had closed, lay a beautifully equipped houseboat. Sipario recognized it at once, and so did Hans: it was Lady Pamela's. They asked the lockkeeper if he had noticed its passengers. He said that an elegant lady had come ashore, together with a blond girl in a wheelchair leading a white Labrador retriever, and a florid man in his thirties whom he heard addressed as 'Mr. Davison' and who, in spite of his fine clothes, had a devious air. The captain and his mate had secured the boat after the others departed. The lady had told him that her party would return in a few days, after proceeding by carriage through the nearby town to the neighboring village of Fahl, where they hoped to enjoy the lake and the surrounding mountains.

"Sipario, Ali, and Hans continued on their way. At the town the two boys left Sipario, who had volunteered to ply his trade without them for a day or two, and walked the few remaining miles to Fahl. Early the next morning they began their search for Lady Pamela and her group. They had no success. There were too many foreigners vacationing in the region for either Lady Pamela's name or Hans's descriptions to be of any use.

"Around noon the boys took time out to earn their lunch. A few minutes later, in front of a high stone wall abutting the village square, Ali was singing and Hans rattling his castanets when Ali suddenly cried out, 'There's Alice!' Above the balustrade that topped the wall Hans spied a familiar blond head. The boys ran to the end of the wall and up a steep lane that lay at right angles to it. They came to a small gate that opened onto the private park of which the balustrade over-looking the square formed one side. 'Wait here,' Ali said, and he went off to explore. After a few minutes, he returned in a state of great excitement, preceded by Bob, the white Labrador. 'We are saved, and your happiness is assured. Davison has been shown up for the scoundrel he is, and you have been identified as Lady Pamela's long-lost son. Follow me!'

"Ali led Hans along a path that wound through beeches, firs, and lofty cedars of Lebanon, past flowerless hydrangeas and lilacs, onto the broad flagged terrace of a spacious two-story house. There, amid giant terra cotta pots of geraniums in many-colored bloom, Lady Pamela was taking tea. With her sat a woman whose back was turned to the approaching boys, but Hans had no need to see her face. It was his beloved Maria. He called out her name. At the sound the two women rose with cries of wonder and, their hands outstretched, hurried towards him. He felt a momentary pang at the choice he would have to make of embracing one before the other, but his anxiety was needless, because it was together that the two happy women buried him in their devoted arms."

Harry Mathews is the author of numerous novels and collections of short fiction, among them *The Conversions, Tlooth, The Sinking of the Odradek Stadium, Country Cooking and Other Stories, Cigarettes,* and *Singular Pleasures.* He is also the author of volumes of poetry, books of nonfiction, and *The Orchard* (a reminiscence of his friendship with the French novelist Georges Perec) and translationor of works by Perec, Raymond Roussel, Georges Bataille, and others.

Harry Mathews was born in New York in 1930 and educated at Princeton and Harvard.

DALKEY ARCHIVE PAPERBACKS

DALKEY ARCHIVE PAPERBACKS

Dalkey Archive Press, ISU Box 4241, Normal, IL 61790–4241
fax (309) 438–7422
Visit our website at www.cas.ilstu.edu/english/dalkey/dalkey.html